HART
of
MADNESS

A NOVEL

LYNNE KENNEDY

Copyright© 2018 Lynne Kennedy
All rights reserved.

ISBN: 978-1-79287-520-5 (print)
ISBN: 978-1-54393-550-9 (ebook)

No part of this book may be reproduced, scanned, or distributed in any printed or electronic form without permission.

Also by Lynne Kennedy

DEADLY PROVENANCE

TIME EXPOSURE

THE TRIANGLE MURDERS

TIME LAPSE

PURE LIES

Historical mysteries solved by modern technology.

5-Stars for *Time Lapse*: "... a gripping tale of history meshed with the present day in jagged, frightening ways."

Praise for *Time Exposure*: "Lynne Kennedy collides past and present with the force of a train wreck. A must read for civil war buffs."

5-Stars for *Deadly Provenance*: "Maggie Thornhill ranks up there with Michael Connelly's Harry Bosch or David Baldacci's Sean King. She is brainy and tenacious with a very human side."

5-Stars for *Pure Lies*: "... a finely crafted mix of classical murder mystery, high thriller and majestic historical fiction."

5-Stars for *The Triangle Murders*: "Like landing at D-Day, this author recreates a murder at the tragic 1911 fire at the Triangle Shirtwaist Factory (a turning point in NYC history) with such detail and terror that you feel like you're watching it."

"Science has not yet taught us if madness is or is not the sublimity of the intelligence."

Edgar Allan Poe

Hart Island
New York City
1902

Prologue

March 15, 1902

Her hand touched cold wet stone. She recoiled. By now her body temperature had dropped, and shivering was all that kept her blood from freezing. Still, she reached out again and groped in the dark for the slimy wall. Another nail broken. Nothing left but nubs.

One bare foot touched down on the first uneven step. Another footfall, and another, the biting cold worked its way to her heart. She tread lightly, lest she slip. Far below stretched the tunnels beneath the asylum. Tunnels that would lead to her freedom.

She stumbled, gasped, and righted herself. The lightheadedness never left now. Her last meal, when did she last have food? What did it matter? Soon she would be free, back in the real world.

Finally, she reached the bottom. Darkness forbade her running, although she desperately wanted to. She scrabbled the damp walls with two hands and placed one foot in front of the other, stubbing her toes often on the lumpy floor stones. She'd become accustomed to the fetid smell. It wasn't much different from her cell, actually. Simply add a few dead rats to the putrid mix.

She kept moving, praying for that tiny glimmer of light that Bridget had promised. And Liam. Could she trust them? Would there be a boat waiting on the shore, one to carry her off the island? And what then? Bridget's assurance of escape did not include a final destination.

Now was not the time to reconsider. No choice but to move forward.

The tunnel veered left and she could hear water drip. It seeped down the walls and dribbled from the ragged underground ceiling, which created puddles along the stone floor. Something poked her ankle and she screamed, swirled in a frenzy, and covered her mouth with both hands. Sound carried in the yawning cavern.

She slogged faster now through the passageway that seemed to have no end.

"Please, please, please, God," she whispered.

What was that? She stopped suddenly. A voice? Her hammering heart would not quiet enough for her to listen. No, nothing. She kept going.

Her foot caught a loose stone and she stumbled. Before she could catch herself, she ended up sprawled on the wet ground, face down. She lay there a moment, sobbing, exhausted, and out of breath. With a groan, she spurred herself up, felt a twinge of pain in her wrists. God, were they broken?

She inhaled a breath of foul air, which forced her to her knees, shivering out of control. Through sheer will, she rose to her feet again, her knees and palms scraped and bleeding. Pain screamed from every joint. She begged her lungs to accept every foul breath.

This is what it's like to be old, she realized. Something she would never be if she remained down here. The thought propelled her to move, one foot, then another, forward, until she regained her stride. She trudged like a walking corpse.

Thoughts flashed and bounced in her head. How did she come to be here? Locked up like a crazy woman. How long had it been? A month? Two? Time had lost its meaning. Her family, how could they have subjected her to this horror? Wait, no, they were gone. Dead, dead. They weren't to blame. But a flicker of a memory stabbed at her brain. She tried to force it to surface, knew it was important, but the treatments had robbed her...

She clutched her head and stifled a scream. Don't think about it. Not now.

Look forward, not backward, she berated herself, fearful her resolve would falter. The future, that's where she headed. Once she was free, out of this chasm of hell, her old self would return. Her competent, self-reliant, keen self. Not this mad woman who had been locked away. The truth would be revealed. She would right the wrongs.

A foghorn sounded from afar, giving her strength a boost.

She spied it then. A tiny pinprick of light in the distance. It seemed to grow and shimmer, then recede and darken. It sparked and sizzled. Her feet stumbled toward it, gaining speed, strength. The light grew until it seemed the sun itself had rolled into the maw of the abyss.

Wait. That was not sunlight. It was that awful yellowish, crackling light called electricity. Too late. Her feet kept their momentum and she found herself in an artificially lit cave at the end of the tunnel. There was no blue sky. No ocean breezes, no rescue boat. No daylight, in fact.

And she was no longer alone.

She stood trembling in her sopping, filthy dress. Water streamed from her hair and into her eyes as she whirled about in a desperate circle. Tears welled and she choked down a bitter cry.

Four men in white lab coats stood in front of her.

"Hello, Ruby," one said. "We were worried about you."

New York City
2016

Chapter 1

May 12, 2016

The call came at 7:30 a.m. It wasn't his cell phone that woke him. Rather his cacophonous parrot squawking from the kitchen.

"Awright, Dexter, I hear you." Frank Mead swung his legs around to sit on the edge of the bed and grabbed his cell. "Mead."

The voice of his sergeant, Will Jefferies, was expected but not welcome. It meant another murder in this grand city. His grand city.

"Shit. Ten minutes."

Frank hustled into the kitchen and yanked off the pillowcase covering the cage of the blue and yellow macaw. "Morning to you, too."

Dexter awwwped in reply.

"Yeah, yeah. Keep your shirt on."

Wings flapped.

In his briefs and tee shirt, his grayish blond hair punked out in all directions, Frank looked a bit less than the illustrious homicide lieutenant of the NYPD. He reached under the kitchen cabinet and brought out bird seed, filled Dexter's cup and gave him fresh water.

Then he stood a moment staring at his friend. A rescue bird, who, in fact, had rescued him. Frank sighed and hurried to get ready for the day.

Frank found Will Jefferies waiting for him on the street in an unmarked Ford Fusion Hybrid.

"Morning." Will handed his boss a Venti Starbucks and rolled the quiet vehicle down Prince Street.

Frank noted Will, as usual, wore a pressed suit and shirt, striped tie. In contrast, Frank's sport jacket was rumpled and his shirt would be embarrassed to accept a tie. He popped the lid flap on the coffee. "What have we got?"

"Don't freak. It's an older woman and she lives a coupla blocks from your mom."

Frank squinted through the windshield. A recent conversation with his mother brought an uneasy prickle down his back.

"Something ring a bell?" Will asked.

"What do we know?"

"A neighbor of the vic came to pick her up for yoga class."

"Yoga?"

"Yeah, you know...down dog, up cat, that kind of—"

"What's the vic's name?"

Will brought the car up short near several police cars, lights flashing, and a CSI van. The street was blocked off with yellow tape, and several officers kept bystanders away. He whipped out his pocket notebook and flipped through. "Her name was Sophie Hunt."

Frank let out the air he was coveting. "Fuck." He jumped out of the car and pushed through the throng of cops to get to the scene. That uneasy prickle had become an unbearable itch.

Will followed at his heels. "What? You know her? Your mom knows her? What?"

Frank didn't respond, but with trepidation, he approached the first-floor apartment of a three-story. He walked through the door into a bright, airy, recently remodeled apartment to a tableau of chaos. Furniture tipped and upended, books and papers strewn around the room, drawers yanked out of desks, and wall hangings crooked on the newly painted walls.

"Whoa," Will said. "Ya think someone was looking for something? What the hell?"

Heart beating with fury, Frank stormed to the bedroom. He stopped upon entry and stared at the scene. That cold familiar feeling of grief punched him in the gut. He hated this part of his job. Lives wasted, not just the victim's but all those the victim touched. Like his mother. Shit. "Sophie was mom's best friend."

Will shook his head. "I figured something like that. Jesus."

Frank plodded closer to Sophie. She was lying on her side on the bed, dressed, eyes closed. She looked like a rag doll with limbs askew. A woman in a blue paper jumpsuit hovered over the body, checking temp and rigor signs.

He looked at the M-E, Serena Oliver, whom he'd worked with for five years. Had she always had that much gray in her hair? She was still tiny, with latte colored skin. And a delight to work with. Efficient, smart, always right, yes always. *Not like me.*

"Frank?" Serena said. "You're white as chalk."

He clamped his jaw.

"You knew her?"

He nodded.

"Sorry."

"What can you tell me?"

"T-O-D between ten last night and two this morning. Signs of struggle. There are marks on her arms and wrists as if someone grabbed her. Small caliber bullet to the heart..." she trailed off, thinking, "...close range. Might've gone off in the struggle. I'll call you later today...make sure I get to this one."

He nodded again, felt like a bobble head, a bobble head in shock.

Will strode up. "Robbery gone bad, maybe. Hard to know if anything is missing. Maybe her family, or friends, well—"

"Yeah, I'll talk to my mother. If anyone will know, she will."

"Close, huh?"

"They went to high school together, so, what, sixty years?"

"Jeez. Sorry."

Frank moved to the window, looked out onto Essex Street. Old neighborhood in the process of gentrifying. Still just red and brown brick, a few blooming oaks, their leaves wilting in the heat, and trash cans. *Today must be trash day.* He wondered absently if Sophie had put her trash out before... What the fuck was he thinking? Trash? He spun around and headed to the front door.

"Talk to the neighbors, check the phones, any CCTV cameras around? Right, cameras, what is this, London? And don't forget to-"

"Yeah, Frank, I know, I know. I'll take care of it." Will followed him to the street. "Go see your mother." Will handed him the car keys.

"Nah. I'll walk."

※

63 Orchard Street was a three-block walk from Sophie Hunt's apartment on Essex Street. Frank knew the Lower East Side intimately, having grown up there. He'd left for Washington D.C. in 2000, after his wife died, but returned in 2010 to become the chief homicide detective for Manhattan's 6th Precinct.

At first, moving back struck him as a failure, laid like a rock in his stomach. Now, he was glad to be home. He'd somehow managed to rebuild a relationship with his daughter, Amanda, and strengthened his bond with Lizzie, his feisty, cop-loving mother over the last few years. All was good. Except for the fact that there was no woman in his life. Still, he had Dexter. Yup, all was good.

The day confirmed it. Blue sky, sunshine, low humidity. Easy to love New York on a day like this. The other bright spot for Frank appeared in the latest Times article he read—about crime across the country. New York City did not even make the top 25 of cities with high murder rates. *Yahoo.* Not a bad recommendation for his own work in resolving homicide cases.

He walked south on Essex Street and turned right onto Rivington for two blocks. At Orchard, he turned left and came to his mother's building.

Reluctant to relay the news about Sophie to Lizzie, Frank shoved his hands in his pockets, inhaled the sun-sweetened air, and stared at his mother's home. The building, more than a century old, five-story gritty brick tenement, sorely needed renovation. Three storefronts: a tiny dress shop at the first level and two below ground; a dry cleaner and a shoe repair inhabited the street spaces. Above, ten units complete with eight sets of tenants. Some families, some couples. The Lower East Side had developed a caché since the Tenement Museum had opened down the street.

He looked around at similar buildings. Quintessential tenements built in the latter part of the nineteenth and early part of the twentieth century. Prior to central heating, these places froze tenants in the winter and roasted them in the summer. Before electricity, darkness pervaded the interiors, particularly the hallways where no windows lit the space. Running water was always cold and sometimes had to be obtained from an outdoor pump. Water closets were situated on each floor, not in each flat. His mind floated back in time to the former Mead ancestors who had occupied the tenement.

Quit postponing the inevitable. He walked to the front door. Lizzie's apartment took up two units on the first floor, and over the years, large mullioned windows replaced grim interior walls. The place was light and welcoming.

So was his mother until she gleaned his expression. "Frank. It's early, what—?"

"You gonna invite me in?"

She stepped back and he walked through the door.

"What's wrong, Frank. I know that look. Someone died. Who? Who died?" The color had blanched from her face.

He closed the door and led her into the living room. "Sit."

"I don't want to sit."

"Sit, Ma."

She opened her mouth, closed it, and then sank down on a dark brown velvety sofa. "You're scaring me, Frank."

He sat next to her, watched her smooth her blouse and slacks. Always a lady. Steel-gray hair neatly coiffed, chiseled high cheekbones, soft blue eyes that now reflected dread.

Both turned to each other.

"It's Sophie, isn't it? Sophie is dead."

"What are you now, a psychic?"

"I'm right, aren't I?"

He tightened his lips and looked at her. "How did you know?"

For a long moment, Lizzie didn't answer, didn't move, hardly blinked. Then: "I knew she was in trouble." It came out a whisper.

"What kind of trouble?"

Lizzie touched her forehead as if trying to release the words from her brain. "She was murdered, wasn't she? Oh God, why didn't I do something?" She struggled up from the couch and waved her arms. "I could've done something, Frank. She didn't have to die. If you had known. If I had gone to you—"

"Ma, slow down, take it easy." He stood and put his arms around her.

She pushed away. "It's my fault."

"Come on, Ma..." Frank dropped his arms and watched helplessly as she paced the room. He waited, knowing full well she wouldn't calm down until she was ready. "How 'bout I make us some tea?"

"Tea?"

"Yeah. They always do that in British movies, right?" He tried a smile. "I can handle making tea."

Lizzie pulled a tissue from her pocket and blew her nose then collapsed on the couch. "First tell me. How was she killed?"

"Ma, that's not important—"

"You let me decide what's important. Now tell me, Frank, please, how was she killed?"

"She was shot."

"Where?"

"In her bedroom."

"Not where in the house. Where was she shot?"

"Ma?"

"In the head?"

"In the heart. I doubt she felt a thing."

"Oh, good God have mercy."

"I'm sorry, Mom." He realized he hadn't called her Mom since he was a kid. He sat with her on the couch again. "I know she was a good friend."

"The best." She turned to him. "You know we were friends for a long time. Went to school together. She always helped me out in math. I was never very good at fractions, but Sophie Hunt, well, she was a genius at numbers." Her eyes leaked tears. "And I know you're going to catch the son-of-a-bitch who did this."

He shrugged. "I'll need your help."

"Me? What can I do?"

"Start with Hunt. That was her maiden name, right?"

"So?" She sniffled.

"Why didn't she change her name to O'Connor when she married Aidan?"

"She was ahead of her time. A staunch feminist. She was born a Hunt and wanted to keep that name."

"And her daughters?"

"They go by O'Connor. There was just so much *feminist* Aidan could stand."

Frank nodded. "How long has he been gone?"

Lizzie bit her bottom lip. "Years. Now they're together again."

They looked at each other, the sudden silence between them like a wispy fog. Frank thought about life after death, Aidan and Sophie together again for eternity. What if they hated each other? Would that be hell?

"Ma, you don't know they're together, for sure."

"Maybe not," Lizzie blurted out. "But I do know you need to act fast before the case goes cold."

"You watch too much TV."

"Hey, I was a cop's wife, a cop's daughter-in-law, and I'm a cop's mother, what do you expect?"

He took her hand. "There's something I need you to do."

She looked at him like he'd grown a second nose.

"Her apartment was ransacked. The killer was looking for something."

Lizzie brought a hand to her mouth. "Oh God."

"Do you know what it was?"

"Sophie trusted me not to say anything to anybody."

"Say what?"

"But I can tell you, Frank. I'm sure she won't mind... now..." Lizzie dabbed her eyes with the tissue. "Now that she's gone. But I should have told you sooner."

"What do you know about her murder?"

"I know what Sophie's killer was looking for."

Chapter 2

Before Frank could breathe, Lizzie began to explain. "For the last couple months, Sophie didn't seem herself. She was nervous, would jump at the slightest noise, didn't want to go anywhere...like out to coffee or Katz's like we used to." She looked at Frank and his *I'm-listening* stare. "She aged, too. I mean she was seventy-five, but always looked younger. Had gobs of energy. Recently, though, she seemed worn out."

Frank waited for her to wipe tears from her cheeks.

"I kept asking her, what's wrong, Soph, but she just shrugged and said she hadn't been sleeping good. That in itself was a red flag, you know? She was lucky that way, always slept like a rock."

Frank leaned back on the sofa, wishing he had another Venti coffee.

"One day, about three weeks ago, she got a visit from her cousin's wife, Madelyn. Madelyn Hunt. Nice woman. I met her a few times. A little younger than us, maybe mid-sixties?"

"Okay."

"Madelyn brought an old suitcase with her, gave it to Sophie. Said it contained Ruby Hunt's belongings, Sophie's great-aunt. The suitcase had been stored in their attic and forgotten. On a cleaning binge, Madelyn decided to go through it and realized it was something Sophie should have." Lizzie stopped, rubbed her arms as if chilly.

"What did Sophie say was in the suitcase?"

"I'm getting to it." Lizzie sucked in a deep breath. "There were the ordinary things you'd expect. Remember it dated back over a century or so. Some jewelry, nothing fancy or expensive. There were photographs of her family. Ruby's father, Jonas, her mother, Laura, and brother, Patrick. And some old clothes, worn and fragile."

"Ma, I've got a murder to solve." He tapped the face of his old Timex.

"Yeah, I'm coming to it." She leaned back into the corner of the sofa as if weary. "There were newspaper clippings...about a horrendous crime... multiple murders. In early January of 1902, Jonas, Laura, and Patrick were brutally murdered." Lizzie paused to catch a ragged breath. "Ruby was arrested for the crime. She was only nineteen."

Frank's neck hairs bristled. "She killed her entire family?"

"That's what the newspaper said. I don't know what kind of evidence they had back then, forensics and such, but there never was a trial."

"What happened to her?"

Rather than a prolonged trial, her uncle, Thomas, her father's brother, had her committed to an asylum. For life."

Frank leaned forward, elbows on his knees and struggled with how any of this was relevant to his murder investigation. "Was there anything else in Ruby's suitcase?"

"Letters from Ruby to Uncle Thomas, begging to be released, claiming her innocence, insisting she was not mad."

"So Ruby saved the newspaper clippings and letters to Uncle Thomas in the suitcase."

"According to Sophie."

"Makes me wonder how Ruby did that." Frank rubbed a hand down his face as if that would make everything clear. "Ruby couldn't have put them there if she was taken away after the murders."

"In the suitcase, there's a letter from a nurse at the asylum, Bridget Monaghan. She'd made a file on the case because she believed Ruby was innocent. Maybe she was trying to help prove it, I don't know."

"What's all this got to do with Sophie's murder? Everyone who surrounded Ruby is long dead and gone."

"Keep your shirt on," Lizzie said. "Bridget also believed that Ruby was murdered in the asylum. Poisoned."

Frank's eyebrows ratcheted up a notch and he let out a breath he didn't realize he was holding. "Why would anyone murder Sophie for a suitcase full of old news?"

"Maybe for the photographs."

"Photographs? Of what?"

"The staff at the asylum. Why those were in there, who knows." She shrugged. "But Bridget must have taken them and placed them there for a reason."

"I can't ask her. She'd be about 140 years old today."

Lizzie sighed. "If Sophie had anything of value, I'd have known. It's that suitcase, Frank."

"Why?"

"You're the detective. Figure it out."

"But why kill her?" he said. "If they got the suitcase, were they afraid she knew too much about what was in it? Needed to silence her?"

Lizzie folded her hands under her chin. "Frank. They didn't get the suitcase."

He narrowed his eyes. "And how do you know that?"

His mother got up and went to a hall closet where she pulled out a small, scratched-up brown leather valise. "Because I've got it."

"Holy shit, Ma."

She handed it to him.

He stared at a beat-up valise that was no doubt pricey in its day. A smell of must, dust and long-ago memories assailed him. He took the bag from her and felt surprise at its light weight.

"Why do you have it?"

"Sophie didn't want to keep it. Bad family vibes. She gave it to me to..." She stopped.

"To what?"

"I was hoping you could look into the old murders."

"The Hunt family murders? In 1902?" Frank whistled.

"I know, Frank." Lizzie shed quiet tears. "Damn, I can't believe she's dead. And I had the suitcase the whole time."

Frank felt the hairs on the back of his neck stand at attention. He did not want to worry her, but he knew her life would be in danger if the killer found out she had the suitcase. He touched her arm. "I'm sorry about Sophie, Ma, but I don't handle cold cases. In this case, ice cold."

She reached in her pocket for another tissue. "But what if the two cases are connected? That suitcase could be the key to Sophie's murder. It must be, don't you think?"

They lapsed into silence.

"Frank. There's something in that suitcase someone would kill for. The photos? They must have some meaning we don't understand."

Frank laid the suitcase on the coffee table. He ran his fingers over the dents and dings but did not open it.

"It's all there. I didn't remove anything."

"Where did Ruby Hunt wind up? What asylum?"

"This is bizarre, Frank. There's been a lot of news coverage these days about this humungous potter's field off the coast of the Bronx. An activist group is trying to get permits for folks who claim they have family members buried there. Buried without identification, notification, nothing."

He stared at her. "Hart Island?"

"Yeah, you know about it."

"I have my sources."

"As I understand it, in the early days of Hart Island, there were buildings, you know, facilities to house all sorts."

"All sorts?"

"It was a prison then a reformatory, who knows what else? That's where Ruby wound up."

"A reformatory?"

"The Women's Lunatic Asylum on Hart Island."

Frank stared into space. All this had a familiar ring. And then it came to him. "Amanda," he said. "She's working on a story about Hart Island, even interviewed that group you mentioned. Somehow they have to prove their family members are buried on the Island."

"Maybe Amanda can help. If Ruby died at the asylum, wouldn't her body be buried in that potter's field?" She patted her eyes with the tissue. "Couldn't they find out if she ...how she died?"

"Even if she was buried there, finding her would be a difficult if not impossible matter. Over a million-people are buried on Hart Island."

"Oh my God, how awful. Are any of them identifiable?"

"That's a question for Amanda," he said. "But assuming we can locate the grave, the body may be so disintegrated that forensic analysis would be impossible."

"But if she'd been poisoned?"

"She'd be dead about what, more than a hundred and ten years?"

"I guess."

"In the ground, possibly without a coffin—"

"What? Why without a coffin?"

"A shroud is cheaper."

Lizzie scrunched up her face and looked about to burst into tears.

Frank touched her hand. "Look, Ma, I'm just guessing at all this. Forensics may be possible, depending upon the conditions under which she was buried. They dug up King Richard the Third, after five hundred years under a parking lot in England, somewhere, and they were able to DNA match him to a purported descendent. So, with science, anything's possible." He drew in a deep breath. "But this isn't my job, Ma. I can't open an investigation into—"

Lizzie scrabbled up from the couch. "I need some coffee." She scurried to the kitchen.

He smirked, knew he was in trouble. She'd never let this go.

Frank leaned his head back on the couch and wondered how he always landed cases that took him back in time. Maggie Thornhill's face came to mind, and he smiled, wishing that the relationship they'd had for a very short time could have been more lasting. No sense dreaming of what coulda, shoulda been. Still, she would love this little mystery. In fact, she may be able to lend a hand. There were photographs in the suitcase. Photographs and Maggie Thornhill were synonymous with solving historical mysteries. The thought brightened his mood.

He caught himself up short. What the hell was he thinking? He was getting way ahead of himself here. The mystery he had to solve was Sophie Hunt's death. Not her Great-Aunt Ruby's murder case.

But even now, in his gut, he couldn't separate the two.

Chapter 3

The doorbell rang.

Frank looked at Lizzie. "That's probably Will, checking up on me."

"I called Amanda when I made coffee. Thought she could help." Lizzie shrugged a shoulder. "Besides, I like having her around."

Frank smiled and opened the door.

"Hey, Dad." Amanda leaned in to give him a kiss on the cheek.

"Hiya, gorgeous."

Amanda wrinkled her nose in disapproval.

Smarts were always more important to Amanda than good looks. Still, every time Frank saw his daughter, a new sense of pride filled him. Not only was she pretty, with long strawberry blond hair and hazel eyes, but she was smart. Super smart. Her job was proof of that. Amanda was a freelance reporter for the Times and had landed several top stories, mostly human interest. The current one was on Hart Island.

Amanda burst into the room like loosed sunshine, set her carryall on the floor, and embraced Lizzie. "Hi, grandma."

They made small talk as Lizzie brought out cups. He could hear, and smell, the coffee percolating in the kitchen. Just the scent of caffeine gave him a jolt.

He worried about his mother, though, who just passed the five-year all-clear-of-cancer mark. This investigation would take a lot out of her.

The doorbell rang again.

"It's a regular Grand Central Station," Lizzie said but smiled.

"Must be Will," Frank said. "He always knows where I am." He opened the door and Will Jefferies entered with a large grease-stained bag.

"Oh yay," Amanda said. "Are those what I think they are?"

"What else is so greasy?" Will grinned. "Kaplan's doughnuts."

Lizzie grabbed the bag and headed into the kitchen, reappearing later with a platter of chocolate, glazed, and sprinkled doughnuts. Then she brought out the coffee pot and filled four large mugs with coffee. "So eat, and let's go to work."

Frank brought Will and Amanda up to date.

"You think the killer was after the suitcase?" Will said. "Jeez, that's a stretch. Those murders were over a hundred years ago."

"Dad always says there's no such thing as coincidence, right?" Amanda gave Frank a wicked smile.

Once again, he was astonished that this young woman was his daughter. It seemed she had grown up double-time in the years since his return to the city. He felt a now-familiar swelling in his chest. This one did not require a Tums.

"First," Frank said, "since we have an expert in Amanda, let's talk about Hart Island for a few minutes. Ruby wound up there."

"You're doing a story, right?" Will asked Amanda and took a large bite of a sprinkled doughnut.

She nodded, chewed her glazed doughnut then set it down. "You know that Hart Island is a huge potter's field."

"How huge is huge?" Will asked.

"Over a million bodies. It's run by the Department of Corrections in New York City. So, in actuality, it's the largest public cemetery in the country."

"I've heard it's difficult to gain access."

"The security is tight but loosening up a bit," Amanda said. "Today, if people can prove they have a relative buried there, they can arrange a visit. The only way to get there is by ferry from City Island, and armed guards watch visitors closely when they arrive. Otherwise the island is off limits. For a long time, even the Times couldn't get approval to go. Now occasionally they can get special permission from the Department of Corrections through the Freedom of Information Act." She popped the last bite of doughnut. "In fact, Nina Bernstein, a Times reporter and friend of mine did a story on this gal, Melinda Hunt...no relation to Ruby Hunt by the way...who heads up the Hart Island Project. She's trying to get permission for families to visit loved ones they believed are buried there.

"That's how Amanda got to go, right, honey?" Lizzie said.

"Yeah, I lucked out. Got to take photos too, which is not usually allowed."

"What's the big deal about a cemetery?" Will asked.

"It's not a cemetery the way we know it," Lizzie said. "There aren't a bunch of gravestones that say 'dearly beloved' and all that."

"No?"

Amanda jumped in. "Traditional graves are about three feet by seven feet plots for a single body. At Hart, the plots are trenches, 70-feet long with coffins buried three-deep."

"Gives me the creeps," Will said. "Who buries all those bodies?"

"Inmates from Rikers Island. They're paid fifty cents an hour and are ferried back and forth twice a week to bury the pine coffins."

Will loosened his tie and unbuttoned his top button. "So, who *is* buried there? Indigents?"

"Lately," Amanda said, "bodies that were never claimed at the morgue and now belong to the city. Bodies that have been donated to science. There are lots of stillborn babies, homeless people, and those whose families couldn't afford a proper burial."

The room fell quiet, each thinking of the sad plight of these people.

"Are many bodies actually identified?" Frank said. "I imagine it's hard to track down someone in such a huge mass graveyard."

"Only about forty bodies are claimed each year."

Silence again.

"Show them some of the photos," Lizzie said.

"Oh, right." Amanda searched through her carryall and brought out a sheaf of papers and photocopies of the photographs she'd taken. "Over the years since the 1860s, there were a number of structures on the island. There was an administration building, which housed records from the different facilities."

"Still there?" Frank asked.

"Yup. The place is a mess, all kinds of files and old, yellowed papers strewn about the entire room. File cabinets still full of records, too. Here are some of the photos I took."

She passed around the images. "That one is the reformatory for boys."
Frank looked at the dilapidated red brick building.

"It's amazing how fast a building goes to seed when it's abandoned," Will said.

"After the 1920s," Amanda said, "Hart Island was an overflow facility for prison overcrowding, and during World War II it was used as a disciplinary camp for some 2,000 Navy and Coast Guard troops. It also served as a prison for the German

U-2 crew captured off the coast of Long Island."

"Busy little place." Will took a photo from Amanda's pile. "What's this building?"

"That was called the Pavilion. It was built in 1885 and served as a women's lunatic asylum. Overflow patients from the asylum on Roosevelt Island, formerly called Blackwell's Island, were its initial occupants."

"Why does Blackwell's Island sound familiar?" Frank asked.

"Do you know the name Nellie Bly?"

"She was a reporter, right?" Frank said.

Amanda smiled. "Nellie was the first woman investigative reporter of her time, the late 1880s. Nellie wanted to do a story about women who were locked up in asylums to prove that many were not crazy but still couldn't get released."

"Didn't she write a book, something about a madhouse?" Frank said.

"She did," Amanda said. "*Ten Days in a Madhouse*. She worked a deal with her publisher, Joseph Pulitzer, to get herself committed to a lunatic asylum. It would be her boss' job to make sure she got out."

"Before she really went mad," Lizzie said.

"Exactly. She was finally released after ten days. She then told the story of the horrible treatment she received there, from the doctors, the attendants, lawyers, social workers. The more she tried to prove she was not insane, the more they believed she was."

"My God," Lizzie said. "Could this have happened to Ruby Hunt?"

Frank took the photo of the Pavilion and gazed at it. "It looks pretty grim now, but when it was new, it could have been rather stately." The photo showed the southern entrance to the Pavilion--a red brick building with a tower in the center of two wings. A large double door with a keystone arch over it seemed forbidding.

"Abandon hope, ye who enter here..."

"Wait, it doesn't say that, does it?" Will said.

"What do you think?"

Will grinned at him.

"What? I love Dante's Inferno."

"Can you just imagine that door slamming closed behind you?" Amanda said. "Here are some interior shots."

"Looks like a giant cafeteria, maybe?" Will said.

Frank said, "Amanda, let me see that photo of the records room again."

She handed it to him.

"You really meant it when you said the files were all still there."

Will took the photograph from him. It showed file folders and papers strewn over the floor, the desks, clearly covered with dust. "More in the cabinets, you say, Amanda?"

She nodded.

"How the hell could they just leave them? What about confidentiality?"

"In 1900, Will?" Frank said. "You're kidding, right?"

Amanda chimed in, "Besides, the persons in those files were long dead. Nobody cared. Sadly."

After a few moments of silent reflection, Lizzie said, "Is it possible Ruby Hunt's files are in there?"

They looked from one to the other.

And can we get our hands on them? Frank mused.

Chapter 4

Frank stood and stretched. "Well, this case isn't going to get solved with us sitting around eating doughnuts."

The rest of them stood.

Lizzie said, "I know you'll find out who killed Sophie, Frank. I just know it."

Frank smiled. "Glad you have such confidence in me."

"We'll get him, Mrs. Mead," Will assured her.

"Lizzie. Don't call me Mrs. Mead. Makes me sound like an old lady."

Frank kissed his mom's cheek. "I'll call you later, Ma."

"Give my love to that dang bird."

"How is Dex?" Amanda asked.

"Ornery as ever. Too late for him to change into a mellow dove, you know."

Amanda smiled. "Let's talk more about this case later." She retrieved all her photos and stacked them neatly before placing them in her carry all. "Maybe I can get permission to go back to Hart Island to comb through those records."

"You also have to comb through Sophie's suitcase," Lizzie said. "Find out why someone would kill her for it."

"Right," Frank said. "We'll take it down to the station, log it in as evidence."

Will picked up the old satchel and headed toward the door. "What a hell of a thing to die for."

By nine o'clock that night, Frank had the M.E. report on Sophie Hunt. No surprises. There was a struggle, with a burglar, perhaps, during which the vic had sustained bruising on her arms and wrists. Gun missing from the scene. A bullet had nicked the heart enough to cause massive internal bleeding. Ballistics confirmed: .22 caliber, no exotic weapon. Frank half-expected to read that it was an Iver-Johnson revolver from 1900. No such luck.

He decided to check the suitcase out of Evidence so he could go through it at home without interruptions. Before he left, he'd made a call to ensure that a patrol officer would keep an eye on his mother's place through the night and the next day in case the killer came looking for the suitcase.

All in order.

After a quick frozen dinner, Frank managed to get Dexter fed and watered. He'd had a heart to heart conversation with the bird and really believed Dexter understood. Truth be told, Dex simply lacked company, but the thought of getting a second squawky parrot gave Frank the jitters. Maybe a dog. How did dogs and parrots get along?

Fuck it, you're delusional, Frank.

He knew he should get some shut-eye, but no shock, he wasn't the least bit sleepy. He donned sweats, turned on Pandora to the T-Bone Burnett station, and settled on the couch to open the suitcase. Dexter stood on the couch arm near him, excited to see what was inside the battered valise.

Frank flicked open the snaps and a sour smell wafted out.

Dexter gave out a loud, "Aawwwp."

"Phew. My sentiments exactly. You'd think the stink wouldn't be this bad since Evidence already opened it." He began lifting out the objects, one by one.

First, he pulled out a yellowed woman's blouse, might have been expensive, silk possibly. One arm had a long thin slice down it. A knife slice or just accidental? Then a black wool skirt with a few moth holes. Were moths responsible for the tears? Or simply age? Both petite sizes. Ruby must have been tiny.

Next came a pair of shoes. Small, size five. Woman's version of wingtips maybe. He held the dry, cracked leather in his hand and felt an overwhelming sadness. He remembered visiting the Holocaust Memorial Museum in Washington and seeing the piles upon piles of shoes from the Jewish camp inmates. This gave him a similar feeling of melancholy.

Then came underclothes. A thin slip with several rents, a bra that looked like it fit a teenager...but she was a teenager. Nineteen. And a pair of knickers.

Frank set the clothes aside, dug deeper. He found a small red velvet sack with a gold pull-string.

Dexter flapped his wings and hopped from the arm to the cushions to get a closer look.

Frank pulled open the drawstrings and gently dumped the contents onto the couch cushion: a pair of silver earrings, a thin gold bracelet, and a gold locket. He pried open the locket but it was devoid of photos. His gaze held the locket. Would they allow jewelry at the asylum? Probably took them from her when she arrived.

He next found a packet of photographs. He moved the suitcase and spread the photos out on the coffee table. Three photos from the turn of the 20th century, he guessed, showed a family: father, mother, brother and sister, dressed and coifed from the early 1900s. Was that Ruby? He stared down at the young woman. Beautiful. Dark wavy hair styled like the women in Downton Abbey. Large, expressive eyes, possibly hazel or green since they didn't appear dark. High, aristocratic cheekbones, and a strong mouth—not pouty like Angelina Jolie, but no-nonsense lips. If this was Ruby, and it must be, she definitely carried the family genes.

Also in the packet were several photos taken in front of a brick building. That's the Pavilion on Hart Island. This must be the asylum. In front of that large forbidding entryway stood several nurses in white uniforms, two men in suits, perhaps doctors, and three women, possibly patients?

How did Ruby get these?

He leaned back on the sofa and rubbed his face with his hands. His mind flashed to the photograph of the Pavilion building that Amanda had shot. He could almost see the women inside those bleak walls.

Under the photographs was a long-yellowed envelope.

He picked it up, its flap unsealed after all this time. He carefully removed the paper within. Several newspaper clippings fell out as well.

To Whom It May Concern Regarding the Case of Miss Ruby Hunt:

I don't know if this letter will ever be found or get into the right hands, but I must lay down the truth on paper in order to make peace with my maker.

I have been a caretaker at the Women's Lunatic Asylum on Blackwell's Island, later Hart Island, for ten years. There have been many questionable cases of women committed for no good reason, but the case of Ruby Hunt was a true heartbreaker.

Ruby was committed on January 10, 1902, because she had presumably killed her family. There was no trial as it was quickly determined she belonged in an asylum. Along with two psychiatrists and Ruby's uncle, Thomas, a judge condemned her to Hart Island. No one stood up for her. If you read the news clippings, everyone believed she was insane.

I say, unequivocally, nonsense! She was committed by an uncle who wanted her out of the way. The question is why? Perhaps so he could inherit the estate, perhaps he hated her, although why anyone would hate such a sweet young woman as Ruby, I cannot fathom. Perhaps, some other sinister motive? I have met Thomas Hunt on several occasions when upon his visit, he deigned to care about his niece. I found him to be unsolicitous, uncaring, even cold. He made the pretense to help her, but he did no such thing. Thinking of him now still gives me the willies.

He had an unusually amiable relationship with the Superintendent here, Doctor Franz Uber, and when he was to visit, I was "commanded" to ready Ruby for that visit. I was to clean her up proper-like, wash her hair, and give her extra portions so she didn't appear starving, as, indeed, she was.

I do not have proof of any wrongdoing, I regret to admit, but I know it is so in my bones. Ruby Hunt was not insane. She did not commit these horrible crimes. She was locked up to get her out of the way.

I have attached the clippings about the murders in this envelope for whomever reads this. As much as I tried to help Ruby, it was futile. If I were caught doing anything kind for the girl, I would have lost my position and Ruby would have lost the only friend she had, excepting, of course, the young detective who was trying to solve the case. He believed her innocent as well.

Near the end of her stay, she started feeling sick to her stomach, vomiting, retching, loss of appetite, worse and worse on each new day. Although she was sent to the infirmary, doctors were not able to help her. Three months later, on April 10, 1902, she died. I believe she was poisoned.

Whosoever reads this letter, I beg of you, please investigate. Read her own words of her living hell. Vindicate Miss Ruby in the eyes of the Almighty.

Bridget Monaghan, April 13, 1902

Read her own words? What words? Frank blew out a breath between his teeth. He put the letter and newspaper clippings back in the envelope. The depressing words and images made him exhausted. He closed his eyes, started to drift off.

A noise woke him. He sat up and blinked. *Scritch, scritch.* Dexter was ripping the lining of the suitcase lid with his beak.

"Hey, what're you doing? That's evidence."

But Dexter had torn a section of the old, dusty fabric. Frank could see something behind it. He pushed Dexter out of the way and gently pulled the fabric off. A small, thin booklet fell out. Here were Ruby's words.

He gently opened the journal that had been hidden in the lining and scanned a few words on each page.

"Holy shit, Dexter. You found Ruby Hunt's diary."

Dexter made a tiny sound in affirmation.

No way could he sleep now. His mind raced from one thought to another. How did Ruby manage to keep a diary in an asylum? Even the pencil or pen would've been verboten. Bridget, of course. She was her ally. And what about this young detective? What did he learn?

He hopped up off the couch with new energy and started brewing coffee in the kitchen. He opened cabinets while the coffee brewed and found an old package of Oreos. Frank took a bite, realized it was stale, but decided it would do for now. He brought the coffee and Oreos back to the living room.

After chomping down three cookies and drinking half the mug of coffee, he pushed the food aside. Wouldn't do to get the pages mucked up. Then he leaned back on the couch and began to read, wishing the light were better in his apartment.

January 18

There is a constant humming inside my head, a whirring, confounding dissonance that will not subside. I am awake, yet I am not. It is as if I am in a dream, a nightmare, that surely must fade soon. And yet, if I wake, it will be to confirm the horrible truth. My family is dead, murdered where we live, and I, who cannot recall one substantive fact of this horror, am alive. Why, was I, too, not murdered? Why have I no memory of that night? A night that forever changed my life?

In my mind, there is only red, the color red, vivid, frightening...on me, around me. I see it, dream it every night. There's a smell of molten metal, like jewelry melting in a flame. And the feeling of loss, terrible loss that causes a pit in my stomach, a pit that has no bottom.

Frank squinted at the pale shaky writing. He felt nausea rise from his gut to his throat and reached for his packet of Tums. But this was not reflux. This was the unbridled feeling of injustice that often got to him on certain cases.

He turned back to her words. The date tells him she's been in the asylum close to three weeks.

January 30

>   *My hand trembles as I write – from cold and nerves and fear. I must scribble quickly as I do not want to get my only friend in trouble. Bridget has been able to secret my little diary and stub of a pencil in her apron should another attendant come along. I want to remember everything in this wretched place. I know someday I will get out and my words will help future patients, no, inmates, for this is truly a prison.*

Frank used his magnifying glass to make out the next words.

>   *Today I received the water cure. At four in the morning I was packed in a wet sheet, forced to remain in it for three hours, then unwrapped and immersed in a freezing cold plunge bath. I have not stopped shivering since...*

He set the diary down, unable to continue reading. His emotions needed a break and he forced his logical brain into action. Think. The murders occurred on January 3rd. This was now less than a month later and Ruby had been arrested, evaluated and committed. So fast, too fast. How can that be? Were people not innocent until proven guilty back then?

Frank exhaled deeply. He had a lot to learn about the law at the turn of the 20th century.

New York City
1902

Chapter 5

January 3, 1902

Ruby swung her purse over her shoulder, its strap made of tiny gold chains. She clutched the chain tightly, remembering her mother's warnings that any ne'er do well could snatch it off her in a heartbeat. That was New York. Her city. She loved it.

She approached her apartment building, turned to say a silent goodbye to her favorite place on earth, Central Park, and headed in. Surprisingly, Henry, the daytime doorman was nowhere to be seen. She ambled across the wide expanse of black and white marble toward the modern lift on the right.

Once again, surprise. Jeremiah, the elevator man was not in his customary place. Ruby crumpled up her face. Well, of course, there must be an emergency in the building. Perhaps old Mr. Coburn had a stroke or something.

She stepped into the Otis lift. Jeremiah had explained it was the first of the direct-plunge elevators of its kind, made for high-rise buildings. She found these *avant-garde* inventions fascinating. Ruby slid the gate closed. She pushed the control lever on the wall away from her. Straight to the top. It was a slow ride to the 12th floor.

The lift opened directly into her parents' home. She stepped out, closed and locked the gate behind her. Jeremiah would just have to walk the twelve flights to come and get his elevator.

She hung her purse on a nearby coat rack, took off her wool coat and new Gage hat, all the rage in *The Delineator*, and did the same. She stopped in front of the full-length hall mirror in the entryway and ran fingers through her shiny, dark-haired bob. A prickle ran down her back and she turned to see if someone was behind her. If so, they were invisible. A vampire, like Count Dracula, the Bram Stoker novel she'd just read. She let out a nervous giggle.

Goosebumps tickled her arms. She tiptoed through the shiny marble hallway. The usual sounds she heard upon entering were absent. No music from the latest model Columbia graphophone that Patrick had gotten for Christmas, on which he played, ad nauseum, his newest record disc of the William Tell Overture. No visitors waiting to see her father to beg for his assistance in some business venture or other. No smells coming from the kitchen even though it was close to dinner time. No footsteps, voices, shouts, or laughter which usually assailed her every homecoming. Only dead silence.

Did she forget something? Was the family out and she was to meet them but it slipped her mind? Very little slipped her mind, so no, that was not it. Something was wrong.

Ruby opened her mouth to call out then stopped herself. Instead, she stealthily crossed the hall into the great parlor. The fireplace blazed with new logs. Teacups, containing only a small amount of liquid, sat on the dining room table with uneaten pastries beside them. She moved closer, looked around the room. She picked up a teacup and touched the liquid with her pinky. Still warm. What had interrupted the drinker?

She clenched her fists and moved slowly toward the kitchen at the back of the apartment. The doors were closed. She held her breath as she pushed one swinging door open. A pot was boiling furiously on the gas range. Her eyes darted to every corner of the room. She ran to turn off the burner.

By now, Ruby's whole body quivered with foreboding. Should she use the telephone? No. Maybe everyone is upstairs...doing what? Her brother, mother and father? Mother refused to have servants on weekends, believing they needed to tend to their own families.

Ruby moistened her lips and pushed out of the kitchen, heading directly to the wide carpeted steps that led to the bedrooms upstairs in this two-story apartment. At the top, she drew in a breath and listened. Not a sound. Uneasiness crawled over her skin.

As she moved toward her mother's bedroom, she could detect a change in the atmosphere. A dampness, like fog, settled on her. Then she noticed an odd smell. Metallic, tinny, slightly sour like milk gone bad. She pushed open the door.

A tiny whimper escaped her lips. On the bed, her mother was sprawled on her back, her eyes wide. She was dressed in day dress, with an ankle-length skirt of wool and a matching jacket with wide collar. Her blouse was once white but now discolored in the most garish red, the same which soaked the bedclothes beneath her. Blood. So much blood.

"Mother," Ruby screamed. She ran and pulled her mother up by her shoulders, shaking her, crying, then holding her and sobbing into her neck. "Mother, no, no, please. Get up, wake up. It will be all right, it will be..." Her voice faded into hoarseness.

After a moment, she gently laid her mother back down and went off in search of her father and brother. Ruby gazed down at her hands, now covered in her mother's blood, and the shakes began. Still she hurried to her father's room.

A new horror awaited. This time both her father and brother lay on the floor in pools of their own blood, each pool intermingling with the other.

She fell to her knees and rolled her father over first. His eyes were glazed, and blood stained his neck and shoulders. Ruby turned to her brother, Patrick, whom she loved dearly, so close in age were they. She could see the thin line of red on his neck, a lake of blood beneath him. So much blood it did not seem possible a human could carry so much in his body. She felt something in her hand and gazed down. A straight razor fell out.

This could not be happening. She must be sleeping... dreaming. That's it, a dream...and she would wake and all would be as before. Ruby pinched her arms, once, twice, harder. Nooooooo. She was awake and this was real. A nightmare, but real.

Her mind shut down as if a switch was pulled. The shaking suddenly ceased and a calmness descended over her.

The foremost thought in her head was that she hadn't said goodbye. Not to her mother. Her father. Not to her brother. Why didn't she say goodbye? It was not fair.

"Patrick," she whispered. "I'm so sorry, so...sorry. If I knew you were leaving, I, I would have bid you adieu, my sweet boy."

Ruby lay down next to him, swept his sandy blond hair off his forehead. She hugged him to her. Tight. Tighter.

"We'll say goodbye now, dear brother. We'll say goodbye."

One Week Later

Rain sheeted down onto an already muddy track. If the temperature dropped a few degrees, it would change to sleet or snow. The horses slogged through the muck, their hooves spewing up clumps of dirt that splattered against the sides of the vehicle. Ruby didn't notice.

She stared, numb and dazed, out the barred window of the paddy wagon. The last seven days had been the longest in her short nineteen years of life. She imagined she was dead along with her father, mother, and dear brother. The police had thought so as well.

They'd burst into the penthouse, led by her Uncle Thomas, her father's brother, and their shouts rocked the brain in her skull.

Then someone screamed, "She's alive, this one, she's alive." She heard someone vomiting nearby, but her body would not move. Her eyes were opened and she could not see. The world blurred before her like gazing through a glass bowl. A red bowl, dipped in viscous red fluid.

Hands lifted her from the floor and her tight grip on Patrick was shaken free. Someone carried her down the stairs, but her body just went limp in his arms, her eyes unseeing.

The same arms carried her into the elevator and down to the lobby. At least she thought so. She fell into unconsciousness and the next sights were of a hospital room.

A few words broke into her stupor. "Not injured...covered in someone else's blood...lucky she was not killed..."

She remained in the bed only a few days, though doctors realized she had no injuries. The blood that covered her belonged to others.

Questions started then. Relentless, brutal, unforgiving.

Where had she been? What had she seen? Why was she not attacked? Why was she covered in so much blood? Why did no one see her enter the building?

Ruby tried to explain, but her words tangled up in her throat and she gave up. Her Uncle Thomas attempted to get at the truth but his harsh questioning brought her to tears.

Night and day, the police, her uncle, the doctors, social workers, tried to pry the truth from her. Finally, after sitting on a hard chair, in a cold, dimly lit interrogation room at the police station, and having no food or drink for at least six hours, Ruby Hunt leaped up and screamed. "My family is dead, murdered. Why are you torturing me so?"

Still the interrogatory went on. Ceaseless questions for which she had the same answers. Over and over.

Why was there a straight razor in her hand? Where did she get the chloral hydrate to drug the tea? How much money would she inherit?

Ruby had never felt so helpless in her life. So alone. Why did her uncle not come to her aid?

When she dropped her head to the table, the police captain—did she warrant such a high-level police officer?—decided to allow her to return to her cell.

"Perhaps a few hours' sleep, Miss, and you'll tell us the truth."

She was escorted to a dank, dirty cell, peeling paint on the wall, a cot with a filthy mattress and a pail in the corner. The heavy smell of urine and worse threatened to gag her. Ruby groaned but fell onto the bed and immediately dropped into unconsciousness.

In the middle of a deep, horrid nightmare of blood and coffins, Ruby was shaken awake by the cell matron, a large buxom woman with thin tight lips and a furrowed brow.

"All right, now, get yerself up."

Ruby blinked, coughed and rubbed her eyes.

"Come on now, we can't wait fer you forever."

Ruby swung her legs over the edge of the bed, pushed herself up and fell back. "I have to...uh, I need..."

"Pail's over there," the woman said.

"No, I cannot use that. I must have a privy. I, please—"

"Miss High and Mighty are we, then? The pail is there for you to use. If not, you can hold yer water."

Ruby toyed with another objection, but she had to go badly, so she stumbled to the pail, pulled down her underpants and urinated. "Paper?"

The matron laughed.

Ruby pulled her panties up, and gulped down a cry. Why were they treating her like a criminal?

"Let's go, then." The matron grabbed her by the elbow and led her out of the cell and back to the interrogation room.

Ruby brightened when she entered. "Uncle Thomas, thank God. Please, you must help me get out of here."

Thomas Hunt, tall, lean and stern, always cut a fashionable figure. Ruby could tell what time of day it was by what he wore. Now he wore a knee-length topcoat of the finest camel hair, trousers with cuffs and creases both front and back and a stiff-collared shirt with tie. It must be midday, a workday.

"I am here to help you, Ruby. I brought with me two doctors, most prominent in their field."

"Doctors? I don't need doctors."

"Ahh, but you do, my dear."

"I don't understand. What are you doing about...what is the police doing about my family. They were murdered, Uncle, horribly murdered, in our home."

"Exactly."

The two stood looking at one another. She could see no mercy in his eyes. Only icy resolve and something she realized she'd seen before. Cruelty. Still, he was her blood, her only remaining family.

Ruby opened her mouth to argue that they were wasting time with her, that they should be pursuing the killers, when a thought struck her mute like a bolt from the sky. He was not here to help her. He did not believe she was innocent.

"You see, my dear niece." He stared down at her from his six-foot-two height. "There is no evidence that anyone was in the house. Nothing stolen, nothing out of place, no sign of anyone who had entered the suite." He turned his back to her and spoke. "No sign of anyone...but you."

"That can't be. Surely, Uncle, you don't think I killed them? I loved them. They were my only...no, no. This is mad, completely insane."

He faced her again, this time resting his hands on her shoulders. "That's what these doctors are here to determine...whether or not you are completely and utterly insane."

Chapter 6

January 10, 1902

A living tomb. Little had she imagined only one week ago, that she would be brought to this place...this chasm of hell, this abode of evil so far from the reality she knew.

The attendant, a heavyset man with a thin mustache, pulled her out of the wagon in a non-too-gentle fashion. She tripped, nearly fell to her knees, but he caught her by the arm, wrenching it hard.

"Oy, now. Mind yer step, missy."

Ruby Elizabeth Hunt stared up at the red brick institution that seemed to go on forever to the left and right of the main door. She could sense the darkness emanating from within and pulled back. Over the front doors read the words: *Women's Lunatic Asylum, Hart Island*. In her mind, she could read Dante's words about abandoning hope. Her throat went dry and her heart sped up to impossible velocity.

"This way, let's move on now."

She was jerked from her dreaded thoughts by a man with no heart.

Once inside the doors, Ruby gaped at the long dreary hallway. At the end were several steps. She was led up them into a large bare room, furnished with naught but hard wooden benches lining the walls. On these benches sat perhaps a dozen women, although it took a minute for her to recognize them as such. Animals more factual.

Each woman wore ragged, yellowed hospital gowns, torn and ill-fitting. Some rocked, some moaned, many just sat and stared into the fetid air, where, in many cases, an unfragrant puddle fouled the floor beneath their feet.

"What...what is this?" Ruby stuttered.

"Why, yer Majesty, this is the reception room where you will greet all yer guests." The man let out a loud guffaw, spraying saliva on her.

He pushed her down onto one bench and ordered her to stay put until the nurse was ready for her. Then he sauntered off back the same way they'd come.

Oh God, oh God, Ruby groaned in her head. *I must get out of here, I don't belong here, I don't...I can't stay...oh God, please.*

A giggle made her turn. On the bench next to her was a young woman, maybe Ruby's age of nineteen, giggling into her hands.

"Miss," Ruby said, and slid closer to her. "Uh, excuse me, miss?" She reached out to touch the woman's shoulder.

The woman screamed and jumped.

"No, no, sorry. I didn't mean to frighten you."

The woman turned to her then, and Ruby felt her flesh crawl. This girl looked like death. Her eyes were circled with black bruises, the irises a dark blue but with pupils so enlarged she could hardly see the color. Her skin almost shimmered, thin and pale as translucent snow. Her lips were chewed and chapped, a dark red from splotches of blood. But when she looked at Ruby, there was an intelligence that shone through the craze-cracked façade.

"Who are you?" the girl whispered and then spun her head around to be sure she wasn't heard.

"My name is Ruby. Ruby Hunt. What's your name?"

"Mm, Margaret."

"Margaret. That's a lovely name. What is your family name?"

"I, I don't...know." Margaret furrowed her brow. "Becket," she managed after a moment.

"Well, Margaret Becket, I'm pleased to meet you." Ruby reached over to take Margaret's hand. This time Margaret didn't flinch. She let Ruby take her hand but kept it limp.

"How long have you been here, Margaret?"

Margaret shook her head back and forth, back and forth.

"Do you not remember?"

"I, I..." The words hung in the air.

At that moment, footsteps slapped across the stone floor, and Ruby saw a woman in a white dress and squared-off cap, stalking down the hall toward her.

"What's this, then?" the woman said, glaring down at Ruby from her height of nearly six feet. "There's no talking here, only silence."

"No, uh, no one told me." Ruby turned to Margaret, but her new friend had moved to the end of the bench, eyes downward.

"Now you've been told. Silence is golden in this facility. Now you know."

"Are you a nurse?"

The woman grinned. "I'm your nursemaid, dearie. My name is Jane. Jane Himmler. Let's go. We must get you ready proper for your stay here."

Ruby stared up at her.

"Stand up, I said."

"But you didn't say..." Ruby stood.

"Follow me."

Ruby drew in a deep breath and followed the bulky attendant down the dimly-lit hallway, questions bursting from her mind but not her mouth. *Better just go along.* But as she hurried to keep up with Himmler, she felt a crawling sensation inching its way up her spine.

After a series of left and right turns, down mold-covered halls, Himmler led Ruby into a large cold and damp room. When Ruby walked in, her breath deserted her. In the room were stationed white, cracked and rusted tubs, filled with water, perhaps ten of them. Floating in the tub water were chunks of ice. Ice? In January?

"What is this place?"

"It's your bath, dearie. Take your clothes off."

"I will not." Ruby backed away.

Himmler shouted out, "Guards, here, now."

Two brutish male attendants in white uniforms rushed in.

"What are you doing? You can't...please... No, I won't undress in front of them."

"Your choice," Himmler said. "Take off your clothes or they will do it for you."

One of the men, whose tag read: *Frederick*, reached for her arm.

"No, no...I will, all right... I will. Leave, please. Please."

Himmler nodded to the men. They left.

Ruby began to undress.

"Hurry up, dearie. We don't have all day."

When her clothes were in a heap on the floor, Himmler picked them up and bundled them into a cloth bag hanging nearby.

"Now, in you go." She nodded toward the icy water bath.

"Why must I...? It's the middle of winter and—"

"This will refresh you and bring you to your senses. Patients have found it to be very invigorating."

Tears rolled down Ruby's cheeks and she lifted a leg over the tub and into the water.

"Come on, come on, you will get used to it." Himmler gave her a prod and Ruby jumped in, sat down, and shrieked in agony. "I, I, please, no, let me get out. It's so...so cold, please." Her teeth began chattering and she tried to curl up to get warm.

After an interminable length of time, Ruby stopped shaking, so numb with cold she didn't think she'd be able to move. Without even realizing it, she had urinated in the tub.

"Now, you shouldn't do that, you know," Himmler said. "Other girls will be using this water."

Ruby couldn't fathom her words.

"All right, out you go," Himmler said in a cheery manner. "Here's a towel to dry yourself, and over there is a gown for you to dress in."

Ruby had trouble moving her limbs, so Himmler helped dry her hair and body. Then she slipped the gown over her head and tied the straps around her waist.

"This way."

Ruby couldn't speak. Her tongue seemed swollen in her mouth.

"We're going to your room. It's late and you missed dinner, so you'll have to wait until breakfast."

Himmler shoved her out of the tub room and down the hall, up a set of stairs. She used a key to open a door on the second floor, then headed down another long corridor.

"Here we are. Home sweet home, dearie." She pushed a door open. "Your bed is under the window there. Say hello, to your new friend, girls."

Ruby stumbled into the room, blinking hard in the dim light.

Then she heard the most dreadful sound she'd ever heard in her life. The door crashed closed behind her with a metallic thud and, with deadly finality, a key turned in the lock.

Chapter 7

Detective Liam McCarty opened the door to his tiny apartment on Lafayette and Bond Streets in the Lower East Side. It was late and he was tired.

He removed the badge from his jacket pocket and stared down at it. Shiny, new. Detective Shield and the number, *6848, NYPD. New York Police Department, Homicide*. He smiled. He had earned it. Although politics was not his game, he knew how to play. And play it, he did. It paid off. Now he could do the job he was meant to do. Solve crimes and bring killers to justice.

The chirping had begun the minute he'd stepped into his home. Liam hung his jacket on a nearby coat rack and moved to the kitchen, the warmest room in the apartment, and where he would greet his two favorite pals. On the kitchen table was a tall cage which was home to two parakeets. One, a handsome sky-blue male with shades of purple in his wings. Budgie. The second, a delicate yellow-green female with an operatic voice. Tallulah.

"Hey, keets. Time for chow." He pulled out a bag of seed from under the sink, filled the food and water cups, and left the cage door open. Within a minute, both keets had hopped out.

"Ahh, freedom, right?" He grinned at them. Then he got busy fixing his own late-night dinner. While he heated up leftover corned beef hash, he fried up a couple eggs, and brewed some coffee. He wouldn't be sleeping much anyway. His mind was churning with the murder case he'd landed. The case of Ruby Elizabeth Hunt, young society girl, and the Hunt family, master barons of the insurance business.

"Wrap it up," his chief had ordered. "There's no investigating to do. Girl killed her family. Now she's in the loony bin. Where she belongs."

Liam shook his head. The whole case stank to high heaven. He had been sitting his final detective's exam during her arrest so played no role in the early days of the investigation. He regretted that bitterly. Now she was locked up and it was his job to wrap up the paperwork. At least, he had convinced the captain to give him some time to dot the 'i's and cross the 't's. But not much time. Certainly, not time enough to sleep.

He dumped his dinner plate in the sink then scrabbled in a kitchen drawer for a pencil and pad. Sitting back down at the tiny table, he began to make a list of the inconsistencies:

Doorman and elevator man both conveniently not at their stations.

Three bodies, throats slashed.

Chloral hydrate, knock-out drops, in the teacups.

Tea downstairs, bodies upstairs.

Ruby Hunt, nineteen, and awfully small to have moved those bodies.

Were the bodies moved or were they somehow lured upstairs as the drugs were taking effect?

Women don't generally slash throats.

Blood on her not spatter but smears, as if she held a body, her brother, in fact.

Uncle bullies his way in, decides what's happened and ships her off to an asylum without a trial.

Motive??? If not Ruby, who???

Liam started a second list. A to-do list:

Revisit the crime scene.

Interview neighbors.

Interview doorman and elevator man.

Interview Uncle—Thomas Randolph Hunt.

Visit Ruby Hunt at Hart Island Women's Lunatic Asylum.

Interview Ruby's friends.

Interview family friends, particularly her brother, Patrick's friends.

Talk to the Medical Examiner to get details of death and discuss possibilities other than Thomas Hunt's account.

Check with police lab to see if any physical evidence had been processed.

Liam leaned back in his chair, suddenly overcome by weariness. He spied the New York World and New York Herald on the floor near the front door. He had given up the Times—too expensive. He pulled himself up, stretched and wandered over to pick them up. On his way, he gazed out the window on the side of the building where the fire escapes were. They reminded him of a chase incident a month ago, when he was still a sergeant.

He'd been in pursuit of a suspect who took off down a side alley and up a fire escape, to finally disappear across the rooftops. He found him ten minutes later, squashed like a rotten pumpkin on the sidewalk. The suspect had tried to leap from one rooftop to another. Oopsa daisy.

Liam carried the two papers back to the kitchen table, then poured a fresh mug of coffee, the old one now going cold. He sat, drank, and began perusing the World. On the inside front page was the third in a continuing story of the Hunt murders.

"Now who the hell gave the press the story?"

Tallulah chirped in response.

He couldn't figure out why the chief didn't cut off the press, at least until the detectives solved the case. Oh right, because the chief believed the case was already solved. Ruby Hunt murdered her family. *What was I thinking?*

Liam threw the paper down and picked up the Herald. This time the story was on page three. In essence the words were the same. He picked up the World again, the Joseph Pulitzer yellow rag. Something nagged at him. Wasn't this the paper that made famous the reporter, what was her name? Nellie Bly? Not her real name, Liam recalled. There was something about a lunatic asylum there, right?

His mind was growing fuzzy with exhaustion. Just a few hours shut-eye, then he'd get back to it. But first, he wrote on his to-do list: Check out Nellie Bly.

At eight the next morning, Liam stepped off the 3rd Avenue cable car, and for the hundredth time, reminded himself he wanted to take a tour of the steam-power generator system downtown. It amazed him how the cable car could be powered by a source so far away. Finding time would be the trick.

He turned left and walked up East 72nd Street to Central Park, then right on Fifth Avenue to 910, the Hunt apartment building.

Inside he was greeted by the doorman, dressed in formal gray uniform with red and gold lapels. Liam held out his badge.

"Police, huh?" The doorman scratched his nose. "They already been here."

"What's your name?" Liam asked.

"Grady."

"That would be Henry Grady, right?"

"Yeah."

"You were not here to greet Miss Hunt when she came back home on the day of the murders, were you?"

"Look, I told the cops the whole story. Don't want to say any more."

Liam narrowed his eyes and moved closer to Grady. "Here's how it is, Mr. Grady." He spoke softly and Grady had to lean in.

"I'm the detective in charge of this investigation, and if I want to visit the apartment again, I will. If I want to ask you the same questions again, I will. And, make no mistake, if you're inconvenienced by this, I could take you down to the station and keep you around for a while, maybe long enough to inconvenience the tenants in the building here…who will, no doubt, complain and—"

"Okay, awright, aweady. Ask your questions." Grady huffed. "But if a tenant needs me, I have to respond. You get that?"

"I get it. Now, tell me exactly why you were not at your post on January third at four in the afternoon."

"Ya see, I was here when I smelled something funny. Then I seen it. Smoke. Coming up from the basement."

"Where exactly did you see the smoke?" Liam asked.

"Over there by the lift. It goes down as well as up and it's open to the basement below."

"Go on."

"So I run down the steps over there, ya know, and sure enough, some trash caught fire down there. And I—"

"Aren't you forgetting something?"

"Uh, whatcha' mean?"

"Were you alone?

"Oh no, no. I grabbed Jerry, ya know, Flynn, the elevator man."

"You mean that man over there, staring at me from the elevator cage?"

"Uh, yeah, that's him. He and me ran down the stairs and put out the fire."

"How did the fire start?"

"How the hell...I mean, how do I know? Trash just does that sometimes. Like simultaneous combustion or somethin'."

Liam cleared his throat. "How did you manage to put it out?"

"Doused it with a coupla buckets water. There's a big sink down there."

"And how long did that take?"

"Uh. Dunno, maybe twenty minutes."

"So, you and Jeremiah were gone for about twenty minutes, just when Miss Hunt came in."

"Yeah, yeah. Guess so. We didn't see her."

"Of course you didn't. You weren't here. How did she get upstairs then?"

"She used the lift."

"She knew how to operate it?"

"Oh yeah. All the tenants do. Ask 'em."

"I will." Liam smiled. "Now I'll need the key to the apartment, but first I'd like to see the basement."

Grady's face paled. "Whadaya' need the basement for?"

"Is there a problem?"

"No, I mean, well, it could be dangerous. Boxes and equipment, you know. We don't like people goin' down there."

"I'll be extremely careful, Mr. Grady. Now, the key to the Hunt apartment, please."

Liam decided to have Jeremiah Flynn escort him to the basement so he could question him. As expected, the elevator operator didn't have anything new to offer in the way of information.

Like Grady said, the basement was packed with various manner of stuff. From small tools to trash cans, stacks of wood to feed a heavy iron wood stove, and lengths of rope, different thicknesses and materials.

He pushed aside old screwdrivers and wrenches from a workbench and stumbled across a tin box that once held playing cards. He opened it and his jaw dropped. Inside were a half-dozen straight-edged razor blades. He picked one up. Sheffield "Silver Steel," with its unmistakable luster and sharp edge.

Liam noticed some rust marks in the middle of the blade. He sniffed the patches of discoloration. A coppery smell often indicated blood. Was that what he smelled? If it was blood, it was more than a chap would shed merely from shaving. He tucked it into his trouser pocket beneath his coat. The other razors seemed clean but well-worn.

Next, he examined a large battered metal can in the far corner. It had black sooty marks around the edges and down the sides. When he got closer, Liam saw the entire interior of the can was blackened. By fire. He bent over it and could smell the odor of fire, smoke and...something else. Oil?

A quick search of the room provided the answer. On a shelf near the back of the basement, hidden amongst jars, bottles, and cans, was a large gallon container of kerosene. Probably not unusual as it was used for oil lamps.

He prepared to lift it off the shelf, expecting it to be quite heavy, but it was light and he almost dropped it. Empty.

Liam opened the cap, smelled the container, then smelled the blackened trash can again. Same. Someone had set a fire here with kerosene.

But who? Were Grady and Flynn trying to save the building from vandalism? Accident? Arson? Or did one or both of them set the fire themselves to provide a distraction so they were not in the lobby when Ruby Hunt came home that day?

But why? Liam shook his head. He didn't think Grady or Flynn was smart enough to cook up such a conspiracy. He sighed and headed out of the basement toward the lift. This time Flynn took him to the top story where the apartment spanned the entire floor. He stepped from the elevator directly into the Hunt premises and stood agog.

Chapter 8

Spread out before him was an entryway larger than his whole apartment doubled, its floor a Carrera marble, gleaming white with exquisite black veins, like that used in ancient Rome. Or so Liam imagined from his readings about Italy, a place he longed to visit.

To his right, he noted an iron coat rack and from it hung a ladies' handbag, dangling by a gold chain. He knew from the initial investigation that this belonged to Ruby. He lifted it from the hook and brought it to a large table at the end of the hallway. On the table was a huge pottery vase filled with flowers. Flowers long dead, their stems wilting over the edge, petals strewn on the table and floor.

Liam dumped the contents of the bag on the table. Rouge, lipstick, handkerchief with the initials R.E.H. Ruby Elizabeth Hunt. A tiny purse with several bills and coins also contained a key, no doubt, to the front door. He sighed and put the contents back inside and hung it back on the rack.

To the left was a sweeping curved, carpeted staircase with scrolled iron banisters reminiscent of old European architecture he had seen in magazines. He would go upstairs where the bodies had been found, but first he wanted a sense of the family. How they lived, who they were as individuals and how they fit into the whole picture. He needed the frame into which the jigsaw puzzle pieces would fit.

He headed into the great room. Loveseats and settees barely filled the space. Across the expanse of polished wooden floors stood a fireplace, larger than Liam had ever seen, made of weathered brick with a rich, dark wood mantel. But this wasn't what caught his eye.

Above the mantel hung a painting. A family painting. He moved closer and gazed at the occupants. The matron, Laura Hunt, wore a gray velvet gown and pearls on her throat and ears. Her husband, Jonas Hunt, stood behind his wife, dressed in a black suit, starched white shirt and white bow tie. He wore a somber expression, no humor in his eyes whatsoever.

A younger man in the painting was Patrick. Poor lad was only sixteen when he was murdered. Patrick seemed to exude warmth and character from the one-dimensional representation. His attire matched his expression: lighter, more casual, almost sunny.

But the visage that held Liam's eye was the young woman. Ruby. Silky dark hair piled on top of her head. Dress of green silk to match her eyes, eyes which held a glint of humor. She did not want to pose for this portrait and her amused countenance said so quite clearly. Ruby wore no jewelry, but the color in her cheeks and lips didn't warrant any artifices. She was simply, naturally beautiful.

Liam felt himself holding his breath and let out a long exhalation. But he couldn't take his eyes off her. At that moment, he knew in his very bones, that Ruby Hunt did not kill her family. That she wasn't insane.

"Oh, get off, McCarty," he said to himself. "You don't know anything of the kind."

He did know, however, that he would meet her in person at the lunatic asylum and decide for himself.

For now, as chief detective, he needed to examine the murder scenes again. What he did know was that Ruby's uncle, Thomas Hunt, had made sure the only police allowed to question her was the captain himself and only that while her attorney was present. According to the records, the attorney insisted that her client remain mute. Did Ruby remain so? If not, what did she say?

Soon after, with the assessment of two doctors, Ruby Hunt was declared insane and shipped off to the Women's Lunatic Asylum on Hart Island.

It angered him that the rich could manipulate the law so handily. It angered him further that this all happened so fast--within a week the accused was condemned in the eyes of the world.

But that will change, Liam assured himself. Oh yes, that will change.

Finally, he turned from the portrait and began a thorough examination of the premises. He'd ordered nothing to be touched. What he would see now was exactly as it had been on the afternoon of the murders, January 3, 1902.

In the dining room, place settings for four, with teacups and biscuits rested on the table. A pre-dinner appetizer? Was Ruby to be the fourth? Did they not expect her?

Liam picked up one of the teacups and sniffed it. The liquid had gone to the police lab for testing and chloral hydrate, or knock-out drops, had been found. A common enough drug, often used in drinks and called Mickey Finns.

How did the drug get into the cups and who put it there? Clearly the killer wanted to sedate his victims and make it easier to slice their throats. But they weren't completely knocked out, maybe just woozy. Somehow, they had gotten upstairs on their own. Walked the gallows steps to their own demise. Unless there were two very strong men to carry unconscious victims upstairs, they would've gotten there under their own steam.

Then the question was why. What would have made mother, father and son all go upstairs at the same time? Another fire ruse, like the one in the basement?

Time to find out. He moved from the dining room and headed up the stairs to the scene of the crime.

The first room he entered was Laura Hunt's bedroom. French Provincial furniture cluttered the large space. A huge bed with carved headboard and footboard, wide vanity with cushioned seat, several armoires to hold dozens of dresses, each over seven foot. Plus, various end tables and lamps, vases and jewelry boxes.

Liam flipped open one box and saw it was empty. He knew, however, that Uncle Thomas had already removed the valuables in case of a robbery now that the apartment was empty of inhabitants. How efficient, Uncle Thomas. According to Thomas, nothing had been taken. Once again Liam wondered why Thomas seemed to know so much about the family and their belongings.

He stepped closer to the bed and forced his stomach not to flop at the vision. A large dark red stain covered the sheets in the middle of the bed. Streaks of blood splattered the pillows and feather comforter as well as the headboard and wallpaper behind the bed. Looking up, Liam saw blood spots on the ceiling. The killer had cut through the artery and blood spurted at high velocity. Must have been covered himself then, unless he wore special clothes that he might have removed.

When his stomach had quieted, Liam moved to the next bedroom, that of Jonas Hunt. *Why do rich people always sleep in separate bedrooms? Because they have more room?* He shook his head.

In the father's bedroom, two bodies had been found. Jonas and his son, Patrick. The scene was doubly gruesome. Blood splatters everywhere. But here, there was more than blood splatter and pooling.

Liam bent down to the floor near the bed. This was where Ruby was found, hugging her brother to her, smearing blood all over herself. The blood stains on the floor were streaks and smudges, not just drops and puddles.

Oh, Ruby, what you must have seen. The brother, whom you'd loved, gone.

He stood up and walked to the French doors and pushed the draperies aside. A small balcony with two chairs and a table were covered for the winter. Across the street, Central Park, one of his favorite places, spread out as far as the eye could see. A green space in the middle of gray concrete. He wondered if it was Ruby's favorite too.

So many questions. If Ruby was being framed for these crimes, how could the killer know exactly when she'd arrive? Timing was of the essence to pull this off.

He stood staring through the wavy panes trying to piece together the characters. The doorman, the elevator man, Uncle Thomas.

The most important missing puzzle piece...motive. Why would someone kill this family in such a brutal way? If he wanted them dead, why not just shoot them or poison them—certainly a lot less messy. And where did Ruby Hunt fit in? Did someone hate her so much that he would condemn her to a life of living hell in an asylum?

Could I be wrong? Is Ruby not how she appears in the portrait? Was she, indeed, mad? Was she hateful or vindictive?

Liam hated and loved this rollercoaster he was on. It got his investigative juices flowing. He would learn the truth and whoever was responsible for these awful crimes would pay full price.

New York City
2016

Chapter 9

May 13, 2016

Frank sat at his desk hunched over a stack of papers. His eyes, however, kept drifting to a small box to the right in which he'd stored Ruby Hunt's diary.

Will Jefferies strode in, brown bag in one hand, two diet Cokes in the other. "Corned beef, coleslaw on rye." He set the bag down, pulled out two sandwiches wrapped in white waxed paper and set one down near Frank.

Frank nodded. "Time to brainstorm." He opened his sandwich, took a bite, then swiveled his chair around and stood.

A large white magnet board stood on one side of his office. Frank had written notes all over it. Beside the scribbles were photographs pinned to the board with small magnets.

"First," Will said, "Tell me what the M.E. said."

"Not much, I'm afraid. The bullet that killed Sophie Hunt was a .22 caliber, likely a semiautomatic Ruger. The only trace evidence found were several short dark hairs on the carpet near the bed."

"Where the struggle was," Will said.

"Nothing else on or around the body and no fingerprints, except for Sophie's."

"So, what about those hairs?"

"Could've been a cleaning person, handy man, who knows? They're checking to see if the DNA is in database."

Will sighed. "A .22 Ruger is a typical gun for a woman, isn't it?"

Frank responded with a nod. "Which means the gun may have been Sophie's." He leaned over his desk, took a bite of his sandwich, and followed it with a swig of soda. "Check it out, Will. And let's follow up on those hairs."

"We know the killer or killers were looking for something. Maybe Sophie got in the way, unexpectedly. Perhaps she went for her gun—"

"They struggled, gun went off." Frank shrugged. "One possible scenario."

"Did the perp find what they were looking for, is the question."

"Nah. I'd bet my Beemer it was the suitcase," Frank said. "And that was no longer in Sophie's apartment."

"By the way, your mom still under protection?"

"Yeah, but she's kicking and screaming about it. She's probably right too. Doubtful the killer would connect her to the suitcase."

"If they did, they'd be smart enough to know it's in the hands of the police by now, anyway."

"What've you got?" Frank finished his sandwiched, crumpled up the wrapper and chucked it into the trash can.

"I canvassed Sophie's neighbors in the building and even a few next door and across the street." Will shook his head.

"I know. Nobody heard anything, nobody saw anything, nobody knows anything."

"Ahh, the Big Apple, a city of monkeys. Ain't it the best?" Will crinkled up his wrapper and tossed it in the waste can. "Seemed only one woman actually was friendly with Sophie and even she didn't have much to offer."

Frank looked at his watch.

"We going somewhere?"

"We're going to see Madelyn Hunt." Frank grabbed his sport jacket from a rack near the door.

"She's the one who gave the suitcase to Sophie, right?"

"Let's find out why."

Frank unlocked his silver 2012 BMW 328i, his pride and joy on the road. They got in and pulled away from the curb.

"Where we going?" Will asked. "And why take your limo?"

"David and Madelyn Hunt live on East 56th Street."

"Swanky."

"Yeah, one of those brownstones, no doubt renovated recently to the tune of beaucoup bucks."

"But from the direction you're driving, that's not where we're headed."

"You are very astute. Missus Hunt didn't want us to meet at her place, so she suggested a coffee shop nearby."

Will raised an eyebrow.

"Hence the luxury vehicle."

"Uh oh, can I afford this cup of coffee?"

Frank smiled.

"So, who is Madelyn Hunt to Sophie?"

Will gazed out the windshield as Frank drove. "Madelyn is married to Sophie's cousin, David Hunt."

Frank parked in a loading zone, directly in front of the café. He slid the police permit in the windshield so it could be prominently read, and they headed into the coffee shop.

Will stopped at the entrance. "You call this a coffee shop?"

The building was red brick with tan awnings, red and black bistro sets on the sidewalks, and waiters wearing white linen aprons.

"Hey, not me. She called it a coffee shop."

"Bet a cup is ten bucks."

Inside, an attractive woman, perhaps in her early sixties, waved to them from a table in the back corner, away from the windows. She had silver-streaked hair, expensively done to match her Bergdorf outfit.

She didn't stand as they shook hands and Frank introduced himself and Will.

A waiter appeared within a minute and the two men ordered.

"I'm sorry about your cousin," Frank said.

"David's cousin but thank you," Madelyn said. "I was much closer to Sophie than David was. They weren't close."

Frank waited while Madelyn sipped her drink.

She said, "I think Sophie's death was related to a suitcase that I found buried in the attic."

"Buried?"

"There were literally tens of boxes and suitcases piled on and around it. The only way I actually found it was..." She stopped. Her cheeks were pink.

"Missus Hunt?" Frank said.

"Uh, please call me Madelyn." She took a deep breath. "Here's the thing. I have a bit of a problem. I'm a cleaning nut, fanatic, actually, to the extreme. For years, I've wanted to go through everything in the attic but David, he, um...he said no."

"He stopped you from cleaning?" Will asked.

"I've been seeing a therapist, you see, for this, um, issue. OCD."

"OCD?"

"Obsessive compulsive disorder."

"Oh, yeah," Will said. "I've heard of it. That's when you can't stop washing your hands or...whatever."

Frank gave him an unhappy look. Will stopped.

"Yes. But in my case, it's not about washing my hands but cleaning my house. It's been making me very crazy, knowing the attic was such a mess, not knowing what was up there, stuff that had been there for decades, longer, maybe even since the earlier Hunts lived there a hundred years ago. Generations of Hunts."

"I thought they lived up near Central Park," Frank said.

"After the murders, Thomas Hunt, Jonas' brother, moved the family possessions out. You can understand why."

Frank nodded. "Thomas Hunt was Ruby's uncle?"

Madelyn nodded. "And Sophie's great grandfather."

Go on."

"So, a couple of weeks ago, when David was on a long trip, I went up there...and, well, I cleaned."

"And you found the suitcase?"

Madelyn nodded. "I looked through the other boxes, trunks, old valises, but this one, Ruby's, stopped me in my tracks."

"What did you think you found?" Frank asked.

"Well, you've seen what's in it, right? Sophie told me she was going to turn it over to her best friend, Lizzie, whose son's a homicide detective. That's you, right?" She looked at Frank.

"That's me and, yes, I did look through it."

"Well, don't you think the contents can help you figure out what happened to Ruby and her family?"

"We're not here to solve Ruby's case, Madelyn," Will said. "We're here—"

"I know, of course. To find out who killed poor Sophie. But, don't you see, there's got to be a connection, there just—"

"Let's back up a minute," Frank said. "Slow down. Tell me a little about the family, the Hunt family, so I can put everything into perspective."

Madelyn sipped her coffee. "David's great, great grandfather was Thomas Hunt. He was the founder of an insurance company at end of the nineteenth century. Hunt Liability and Assets. Made a fortune. His brother, Jonas, was Ruby Hunt's father."

"Ahh, Ruby's Uncle Thomas," Will said. "Her father's brother."

She nodded. "And, Thomas' son, Lowell, and *his* son, Harrison were also in insurance."

"What kind of insurance?" Frank asked. "Home, auto?"

"A little of that. For pin money."

Frank narrowed his eyes.

"I see you gentlemen don't know the insurance business very well."

"I guess not," Will said. "Tell us."

"Life, auto, home insurance. That's not where the real money is."

They waited.

"Nursing homes, assisted living residences, hospice, rehabs. Care facilities, in other words..." She gazed into her cup as if embarrassed to look at them.

"That's where the big money is," Will finished for her.

Madelyn gave a short jut of her chin in answer.

Frank rubbed the stubble on his jaw. "And lunatic asylums?"

Madelyn blinked.

"What about your husband?" Frank asked. "Did he continue the family's insurance tradition?"

"Actually, yes. As I said, the real money is in care facilities, so David decided to, er, branch out from home and auto insurance."

"To care facilities?" Will said.

"Yes." Madelyn blushed again.

What is she ashamed of? "How does that work?" Frank asked. "You answer an ad: nursing home for sale?"

"David is clever, ruthlessly clever. He experimented with a care facility that catered to the senior population, one that took care of all needs until the end of life." She paused to think, then, "Aurora Lifetime Living. The first one was set up on two acres in Scarsdale, New York." Madelyn snapped her fingers and a waiter jumped to her side. She ordered a new round of coffees for all. "Aurora offered everything. Assisted living apartments with occasional nursing care then full-on nursing care, then hospice, then—"

"Then funerals, cremations, etc. Convenient." Frank leaned back in his chair. "I assume it was a success?"

"Oh, yes," Madelyn cooed. "There are now fifteen Auroras around the country."

"Expensive?" Will put in.

"If you mean, could you afford it on a policeman's salary, definitely not. You buy in, like you would a condo or co-op. But with it you get medical services as needed."

"And what does a facility like this cost?"

"The base price for a unit is three million...goes up from there."

Silence hung for a few beats.

"What is David's role?" Frank asked. "Does he operate the local facility?"

"He hires a management company, New York Management, you might have heard of them? They oversee all the finances, the medical expenses, the housing, food, etc."

"Where does Social Security and Medicare fit in?"

"New York Management bills Medicare for some of the medical costs of the residents. In many cases, there are private insurance companies that handle the rest of the bills."

Will clasped his hands together. "How does a big company like New York Management keep track of individual patients, um, residents, for billing services?"

"Each facility hires an administrator to handle all that. He's often a medical doctor, qualified to make decisions regarding the residents."

"Life and death decisions?" Frank asked.

"Sometimes, I guess." Madelyn shrugged. "I would imagine it's in concert with the individual's own personal doctor. There is, however, one doctor who oversees all the others and has the final say-so. He's called a Superintendent."

"Like at Hart Island asylum," Will said.

Frank sipped his coffee and let it all sink in before he asked, "What do you know about Ruby Hunt?"

"Not much. No one in the family will talk about her. She's an outcast, shunned, exiled. An embarrassment to the Hunt name."

"Tell us what you do know," Frank said.

"Ruby was born in 1883, lived the life of a rich New York City girl, boarding schools and all that. I don't know this for a fact, but from little snippets I've gleaned, she was a decent person. A bit forward thinking for the time. Remember she'd come of age around 1900, a very repressed time for women."

"How did she get along with her family?"

"As far as I could tell, just fine. They seemed a happy lot…except—"

"Except for Uncle Thomas," Frank threw in.

"How did you know that?"

"Lucky guess." Frank gazed up at the copper ceiling. He realized Madelyn knew nothing of Ruby's diary. "How was it that Thomas seemed to have so much authority?"

She gave a faint smile. "I think it was simply his overbearing personality. Runs in the Thomas Hunt line. Whereas Ruby's father was a sweet but rather meek man. Also, Thomas was the financial whiz. He was really the moneymaker, not Jonas."

Will said quietly, "Do you think Ruby killed her family?"

Without a second's hesitation, Madelyn shook her head. "No, never."

"Why?" Frank said. "What makes you so sure?"

Madelyn reached into her purse and pulled out a small dark velvet photo album. She flipped it open. "If you look at these photos..."

Frank saw sepia-toned photos from another time.

"You'll understand. From the pictures, you simply *know*, in here," Madelyn touched her chest, "that Ruby was a kind and loving young woman."

Frank was about to say something regarding the faces of known killers, not all looked vicious and murderous. But when he stared down at one photo, he did understand. He touched his finger to her face.

"That was a family portrait. It hung over the mantel in the Fifth Avenue apartment in 1900. Besides the painting, the family had photos made as well to place in albums like this."

"May I hold onto this for a while?" Frank asked. "I promise to return it."

The photo stirred something in him that was hard to pin down. Ruby Hunt stood out from the rest of her family, almost as if the artist painted a glow around her.

No, Ruby Hunt did not murder her family. Frank was sure of it but did not voice his opinion. Will, for one, would think him a nut bar. Still, he trusted his gut.

That begged the question: If Ruby didn't kill her family, who did? And how does that relate to the murder of Sophie Hunt today?

Chapter 10

That night, Frank picked up Chinese take-out and went home with the sole idea of going through the news clippings from the Hunt family murder.

He shared some of his lo mein with Dexter, and the two sat amiably together on the couch.

"There's got to be more." A glance at his watch told him the New York Public Library was closed. He'd try their digital collection.

Frank threw the food cartons in the trash and retrieved his laptop from the bookshelf in the living room. He fired it up on the dining room table where Dexter hopped over and settled on the top of a chair.

"Why don't you try flying, Dex? I know your wings are clipped but you can stretch them a bit with a short flight. Birds do fly."

"Fy, fy, fy," Dexter mimicked.

Frank brought his attention to the screen. He called up the library digital archives and while he waited, his cell rang. Amanda. "Hi, sweetie", he answered. "What's up?"

"How's the investigation going?"

"Slow as always."

"I asked my editor to get me permission from the Department of Corrections to go back to Hart Island."

"Yeah?"

"We've got a pass to ferry over, but under tight restrictions. We can only check out the records building."

That made Frank's heartbeat jump. "When?"

"On Friday. I hope you can go."

"Try keeping me away. Any chance Will can come?"

"Yes, the pass is for three."

"That's terrific, Amanda. Thanks."

"I'll pick you and Will up at 8:00 a.m., your place."

"Say, while I have you on the phone, was the New York Times around in 1900 or 1902?"

"Checking out Ruby's murder?"

"Yup."

"The Times has been around since 1851. But it's likely you'll see more murder stories in the New York World and the New York Herald."

"Why's that?"

"The Times—too highbrow. They carried some follow-up articles to Nellie Bly's visit to the madhouse, like the grand jury investigation, but the real gritty stuff wouldn't be there."

"Which was Nellie's paper?"

"New York World. She worked for Joseph Pulitzer, the publisher."

"Thanks."

"See ya Friday." She clicked off.

He smiled as he likened his daughter to the famous investigative reporter, Nellie Bly, in the 1880s. After Amanda's piece on the hundredth anniversary of the Triangle Shirtwaist Factory fire of 1911 and the murders that occurred in 2011, she'd won several journalism awards. My daughter, a modern-day Nellie Bly.

Whatever happened to Nellie? He made a note to check.

Now, he clicked on his email to see if there was anything worth viewing. Nothing. He grabbed his cell and texted Will about their trip to Hart Island. Then he went back to the library archives.

He searched for the New York World, and the date of the murders: January 3, 1902.

A stream of articles came up, starting with January 3 and ending a couple of months later, nothing after March. The first two articles were the same ones that were in Ruby's suitcase, ones Bridget had saved.

Frank uploaded the first and opened it. Two photos stared at him from the front page under the headline: *Society Family Murdered in Fifth Avenue Apartment*. One photo was of Jonas Hunt, Ruby's father. The other was a shot of the front of the building. He knew from working with Maggie Thornhill on digital analysis of photographs dating back to the Civil War that the photochemical process for printing photographs in newspapers didn't exist until 1880. Before that, woodcuts or etchings were used. This was 1902. These were real images.

Frank rummaged in his desk drawer for a magnifying glass to better study the photographs. Jonas Hunt was impressive with slicked down hair parted in the center and a long handlebar mustache. The Fifth Avenue apartment was an elegant brick building that faced Central Park. The Hunts definitely had money.

The article itself was short. Reporters must have gotten wind of the sensational story right away but were given few details. Frank read the story:

Tragedy struck insurance mogul, Jonas Hunt, the head of Hunt Liability and Assets Company. Hunt, along with his wife, Laura, and teen-aged son, Patrick, were found dead in their Fifth Avenue apartment today. Nineteen-year-old Ruby Hunt found the bodies and was in a state of shock when the elevator man found her later. Cause of deaths not disclosed at this time, but New York Police Department homicide detective, Liam McCarty, has been assigned the case.

Frank chugged a bottle of water. He scanned the rest of the article but found only biographical information about the family.

"What happened to Ruby?"

"Oo-bee, Oo-bee." Dexter recited his rendition of *Ruby*.

He went back to the archives and uploaded the series. The next day's article ran two columns, one less than the first day's.

Details continue to unfold in the horrific Central Park Murder. According to New York World sources, Jonas Hunt, Laura Hunt, and son Patrick had their throats slit. It is surmised that they were caught unaware while having afternoon tea and perhaps drugged to render them compliant. Daughter Ruby Hunt was unharmed but found covered in blood. Investigation is underway and evidence is still being gathered.

The article went on to give more details about Hunt's business, Mrs. Hunt's charity work, and Patrick's schooling. There was only one line about Ruby and that was supplied by her Uncle Thomas, Jonas' brother. "Ruby has always been a sensitive and delicate girl, given to wild imaginings and crazy emotions."

"I guess Uncle Thomas had no sense of protection over his niece, eh?"

"Eh," Dexter murmured in response.

"Sounds like a set-up to me."

Frank looked at the follow-up articles, and the only new information he discerned was that Ruby was admitted to Hart Island Women's Lunatic Asylum for psychiatric evaluation. He'd have to look further for more stories.

He picked up his cell and dialed Will. "So, what do you know about chloral hydrate?"

"Isn't that the drug used to make Mickey Finns?" Will asked, yawning. "You think maybe Ruby drugged her family and then—?"

"It would have knocked them out. But how did they get upstairs after drinking it?"

"Maybe it just makes you drowsy, you know. Not like Rohypnol, which incapacitates one pretty damn quick."

"And where would she get it? Anyway, look into it, would you? And when it came into use."

"You mean like 1902?"

"Yup." Frank disconnected.

On a hunch, Frank Googled Liam McCarty, the detective in charge of the case back in 1902 and mentioned briefly in Bridget Monaghan's letter. He didn't expect to find much but was surprised when a stream of articles popped up. The headlines read in chronological order:

New Investigator Takes Over Hunt Murder Case. Frank scratched his head at the date. A week after the murders. Why on earth didn't McCarty handle the case from the start? His answer came a few lines later in the story. McCarty had just passed his detective exam.

Great, a rookie. No wonder why the case was never solved.

He went through a few more short stories which repeated facts he knew. But the fourth story caught his eye.

NYPD Detective Vows to Re-Open Hunt Murder Case. Frank learned that Ruby, now in the Women's Lunatic Asylum on Hart Island for two weeks, had been formally judged insane and would be committed to the asylum for life. Jesus.

In this article, a photo of Liam McCarty took up a tiny column inch. Frank hovered the magnifier over it. Only McCarty's head was visible. His face was gaunt, angled, his expression humorless, and his head was pale as if his hair was very light and shaved tight to his head. He was clean-shaven with a strong chin and piercing eyes.

"All right, Detective McCarty, you look like a man who means business." The detective was up against the odds. He had to find the real killers, with the crime scene a week old, and very little forensics at the time to assist him. He had to bump heads with Uncle Thomas Hunt, who apparently wanted Ruby out of the way. And he had to determine what Ruby's mental state really was. To do so, McCarty would have had to visit the asylum where Ruby resided and interview her.

Frank felt a burgeoning respect for the man. After all, according to Bridget, McCarty vowed to set Ruby free.

Dexter hopped down onto the desk and stared at him.

Frank asked his feathered friend, "So, what are the chances that Detective Liam McCarty kept a murder book?"

Chapter 11

May 15, 2016

The ferry swayed gently in the calm waters of Long Island Sound, off the dock on Fordham Street, City Island. A perfect day, warm, cloudless and dry for May in New York City.

Frank, Amanda, and Will leaned over the railing as thirty people hurried up the ramp, escorted by Department of Corrections employees.

"Jeez," Amanda said, "You'd think they were going to prison or something, rather than to visit a relative buried in a cemetery."

"Seems to be a stigma for anyone connected to Hart Island," Will said.

Frank felt his stomach lurch at that thought. These people had enough hardships in their lives. Now, they had finally located a loved one that had been buried on the island, whether accidentally or out of ignorance, and they must put up with further ignominy.

Will asked, "Who runs cemeteries that are not on church or private grounds?"

"The State, although I would guess Hart Island is the only one handled by the Corrections Department," Amanda said. "Probably because it's such a huge potter's field."

"Where did that term come from, anyway? Some guy named Potter, you know, like in 'It's a Wonderful Life'?"

Amanda smiled. "It's an ancient term, actually. A potter's field is a burying ground for indigents. Originally, it comes from the Bible, the book of Matthew in the New Testament. In chapter twenty-seven, Judas Iscariot returns the thirty pieces of silver the high priests gave him in exchange for betraying Jesus. The priests didn't return the silver to the temple coffers, however."

"Blood money," Will said.

Amanda nodded. "They used the money to buy a field to bury paupers in. The field was an area in which potters dug their clay."

"Hence, potter's field."

"Right. Around the 1700s, the term was used to mean any plot of land put aside to bury paupers."

"You've done your homework." Will stretched and yawned.

Frank stared out across the Long Island Sound to their destination, Hart Island, its long-unused power plant smokestack plainly visible above the trees.

"Lots of history there. A POW Camp during the Civil War, a boys' reformatory, a drug rehab facility, and a women's lunatic asylum. Now a burial site for a million forgotten souls."

"Dad? You okay?" Amanda put her hand on his arm.

"Sure, just thinking."

"Ah, yes, thinking." She turned to look out over the water. "Difficult to imagine, isn't it?"

He saw her eyes water.

"All those people who came here for such terrible reasons, and those who had no intention of ever coming here, but are now buried here in grim, crowded trenches." She shivered even though the day was warm.

"You're a very caring person, Amanda," Frank said.

"Because I cry at the drop of a hat?"

He smiled.

The ferry's horn blew three times. They had arrived at Hart Island. The dock was heavily fenced as was the rocky shoreline and tall gates at the end of the dock were manned by guards. Frank could see signs on the fences that read "Department of Corrections – Restricted Area" and "No Trespassing. No Docking. No Fishing."

They were met by a woman guard in a light blue, short-sleeved shirt with navy blue slacks, much like NYPD officers wear.

"Amanda Mead?"

Amanda stepped forward. "That's me."

"And, Lieutenant Mead?"

Frank nodded and introduced Will.

"This way, please. You'll all need to sign a few forms."

They followed the guard to the gazebo, where she had them date and sign paperwork on clipboards. Other visitors stayed behind while Frank and his party were escorted to their destination.

Ten minutes later, the Corrections Officer dropped them at The Pavilion. "You have the authority to browse through the building and the records room. When you're done, please call me on this radio and I'll pick you up for the ferry back." She handed him the radio.

"Right," Frank said. "What's the timeline?"

The officer looked at her watch. "Ten-thirty now. The ferry leaves at six."

Frank turned to his partners. "Let's go then."

They walked up the concrete steps to the red brick building. Grass grew in the cracks and the buckled steps were treacherous. The huge double doors were unlocked but needed both Frank and Will to push them open.

Dust danced in the sun rays coming through the windows.

"Whew, what a mess," Amanda said, clearing her throat. She reached in her carryall and brought out two other bags. "If we take anything with us, we'll need these."

"Clever," Will said. "Let's see what's what."

They walked through a second set of doors into a large hall lined with benches on either side. The walls were cracked; dark green paint peeled from them in large strips. The floor was comprised of old, beaten wooden planks.

They continued to a door on the right, which led down a long hallway with small rooms on either side.

Frank poked his head in several doorways. Metal bedframes with filthy mattresses still remained in a few. A rat scurried by.

Amanda grimaced. "Ugh."

"Now we know why it's not open to the public and there are no tours." Will sneezed.

"More likely the island is off limits because it's dangerous with all these dilapidated buildings." Then she added, "It's also hallowed ground on account of all the bodies buried here."

Frank moved to a small chest of drawers in one room. He opened a drawer and looked inside. Gently, he pulled out a sock. One, a blackened, originally white sock that a child might wear.

"Oh Dad," Amanda whispered. "Awful."

He dropped it back in the drawer and hurried out of the room and down the hall.

"Hey, check this out," Will called from the end of another corridor.

Frank and Amanda reached him and looked in the room. Grimy, streaked tubs with rusting faucets sat lined up in a row, space for one person to stand in-between each.

"Shit," Frank said.

"Oh my God," Amanda said, clenching her jaw. "These were the ice baths."

"What?" Will asked.

"Asylum patients were subdued, supposedly, by immersing them in icy water."

"Jesus," Will said. "Did it work?"

"What do you think?" Frank exited the vile room.

They came to a huge open space with only a few battered tables and chairs scattered about. Tall, structural columns lined up in the center of the room, supporting the upstairs stories. The windows still maintained their security wire cages.

"Judging from that long counter over there, I would guess this was the cafeteria," Will said.

Amanda shot some pictures.

"Let's find the records room, if possible," Frank said. "This whole place gives me the creeps."

"Let's try down here." Will led them down another hallway, this one lined with broken chairs and benches. "Maybe patients came to the office and had to wait here."

"Or were processed here," Frank said. "Like meat in a slaughterhouse."

"Yikes," Amanda responded.

Will shoved a door open into a large, dusty space. "Ahh."

The three walked in and stood gawking around. Old wooden and dinged-up metal file cabinets and broken boxes stood on the perimeter of the room; desks, chairs, and broken lamps were standing or lying in the center.

Astoundingly, file folders and molding papers were strewn everywhere.

"It's as if the place was burgled and someone was looking for something," Will said. "Why the hell would these files be all over the place?"

"Good question," Amanda said. "Shouldn't they all be in the file cabinets? I mean animals wouldn't have done this."

"Only the two-legged kind," Frank said, his lips tightly pursed. "What a freakin' mess. How will we ever find any kind of pattern here?"

They rolled their sleeves up and began going through the loose files on the desks and countertops. Next they tried the file cabinets.

"God," Amanda said. "Looks like a fire got some of these cabinets over the years." She looked around. "The files could be from the infirmary or the prison or the administration office. Where on earth would the asylum files be?"

"We've got a whole day to find something. Have at it." Frank shook his head.

Four hours later, Will said, "I think this is a waste of time." He wiped his forehead with his forearm and left a streak of dust across it.

Amanda uncrossed her legs from the seated position she occupied on top of an old desk. She jumped down and brushed off her jeans. "There's got to be something here."

Frank arched his back and stretched his arms above his head. "Nothing in the file cabinets, at least not in any kind of logical order. Tell you what. Let's do a quick look-see at the files on the floor." He shrugged. "You never know."

"And frankly, I don't want to come back here," Will said.

"It is rather repulsive." Amanda picked up a folder lying on the floor, then another."

The two men shuffled through papers on the floor, dust billowing into the dead air.

"Hey, hey, wait," Amanda said. "Bingo. Hunt, Ruby, here it is." She bounced to her feet; the others sprinted to her side.

Carefully, she showed them the writing on the folder tab then opened the cover. A photograph of a young woman stared out at them. Now yellowed and creased, the image was in surprisingly good condition.

"Oh, wow." Amanda sighed. "She was beautiful. But look at her eyes. So sad."

Frank stared at the portrait. Ruby Hunt pleaded with him through her eyes.

"Man, oh man," Will said. "That look…if that don't say 'get me the hell outa here,' I don't know what does."

They fell quiet.

Frank read what was legible under the photograph. "Ruby Elizabeth Hunt" DOB, October 18, 1883, address 910 Fifth Avenue, NYC. Admitted to Women's Lunatic Asylum, Hart Island, January 10, 1902."

"Only nineteen years old," Amanda said.

"Looks like water stains on this page. Can barely read it," Frank said. "Died, April 10, 1902, unknown cause."

"Unknown cause, my eye," Will said.

"Jeez, only three months after she was committed," Amanda said. "I might have killed myself if I thought I could never get out."

Frank looked up sharply. "According to Bridget, she was murdered, poisoned."

"But that was just a guess on her part, so who knows?" Will said.

"Right," Frank said. "Who knows?"

But I intend to find out.

New York City
1902

Chapter 12

January 11, 1902

Liam knocked on room 239 and sucked in several deep breaths. The mile-walk from his office to the Gilsey House on 29th and Broadway, a grand old dame from 1872, had taken only twenty minutes, but still he was out of breath from the cold. He could still feel its icy bite in his nostrils and throat.

The door opened and a woman smiled. She was not beautiful, not so much as pretty, really, but arresting. Her dark eyes sparked and an expressive mouth formed a broad grin.

"You must be Detective McCarthy?"

"McCarty, actually, ma'am."

"Hmm, I never heard of McCarty."

"It is said that my grandfather got the 'h' knocked out of him once or twice, so it seemed natural..." He shrugged with a smile.

She stared at him in disbelief, then burst into laughter. "Come in, Detective McCarty," she emphasized the 't.' "Please."

Liam followed her into the hotel room suite and she gestured toward a small sofa under the window.

"Can I get you tea or coffee?"

"Coffee would be nice."

"Good, that's my drink and already brewed." She walked to a dining table and brought over a tray with two cups, a silver coffee pot and a sugar and creamer.

"Thanks."

She poured him a mug. "So, how can I help you?"

He added cream to his coffee, took a sip and then looked at her.

Nellie Bly was dressed in a burgundy wool frock, with lace around the neck and wrists. Her hair was pinned up in a topknot, but wispy bangs over her forehead added lightness to the severity of the style.

"I'm working on a case that I hope you can help me with."

"Do you mean the case of Miss Ruby Hunt, who is said to have killed her parents and her brother and now resides at the Women's Lunatic Asylum on Hart Island?"

Liam's eyebrows shot up. "You are quite informed, Miss Bly. But that's not your real name, is it?"

"I was born Elizabeth Cochran, but I rather like Nellie Bly." She smiled. "It's my professional journalist name."

Liam relaxed. "Well then, Miss Bly—"

"Nellie, please, Detective." She batted an eye at him. "Or shall I call you, er—?"

"Liam. Of course, you may." He set his cup down. "I've read your book, *Ten Days in a Madhouse*."

She nodded, sipped coffee.

"Tell me, honestly. Was it as bad as you portrayed?" His mind darted to the memory of Ruby's portrait.

"You mean, is it an accurate picture of an asylum?" She set down her cup. "Or did I enhance it for dramatic effect?"

"You tell me." He pursed his lips, waited.

Her expression darkened as if the memory had sharp teeth. "Let me say first, that I pity Miss Hunt, particularly if she is innocent. An asylum is a horrific place to reside, especially for a young woman. No words can adequately describe the atmosphere, the treatment, the trauma that one faces upon entering. No words." She bit her lower lip and stared at her hands in her lap. "When I left the asylum, I felt utter despair. That I would never come to myself again. I had nightmares that lasted for months."

Liam shuddered. "I believe that answers my question."

She nodded.

"You tried to help some of the women attain their freedom, didn't you?"

"I did, indeed. To no avail." She paused to lift her cup and take a drink. "Do you know how simple it is to commit a woman to an asylum?"

Liam furrowed his brow. "What do you mean by *simple*?"

"A woman has no rights in this regard, as in many. None whatsoever. If she is married and her husband tires of her, or finds a younger woman more attractive, he can easily get rid of his wife."

"How?"

"He needs only the say-so of two psychiatrists, easy to obtain for men of means. The doctors visit the poor woman, take her pulse and pronounce her insane. On the spot."

"Surely you're not serious. I mean, how can a pulse determine—?"

"Exactly."

Nellie suddenly looked her thirty-eight years. Dark circles bloomed under her eyes as her recollections deepened.

"Good grief," Liam said, almost a whisper. His mind flashed again to Ruby. Could that be what happened? Did her uncle Thomas bring in two doctors and... Too dreadful to imagine.

Nellie interrupted his thoughts. "Some good did come of my exposé, however. Assistant District Attorney at the time, Vernon Davis, did investigate further, and a number of changes were made, including larger appropriation of funds for the asylums and the care of mentally ill patients, and..." Her voice trailed off and she looked at him intently. "Why are you really here, Liam?"

"I wanted a woman's perspective on, um, life in an asylum...before I—"

"Before you visit yourself?"

He nodded.

"Do you think Ruby is guilty of the crimes she's accused of?"

"I don't know. I haven't even met her." He moved to the edge of the sofa and leaned forward as if to convey a secret. "There are some, er, inconsistencies that don't sit well with me." Liam explained how he came to head up the investigation late and that his only role was to wrap up the paperwork.

"Are you going to abide by that?"

He stared at her, wondering how she read his mind.

Nellie jumped to her feet. "Paperwork, phooey. If Ruby Hunt is innocent, she should not be in that horrid place."

Liam rose, unsure of his next steps. "I didn't say she was innocent."

"No, we must get her out. We cannot let this injustice—"

"Hold on, now."

Nellie waited.

"First I must find out the truth about the murders. If, and I mean, if, I find out she is not the guilty party, then I will do all in my power to free her." He gave her a sad smile. "And, indeed, I will enlist your help."

She concurred with a fierce nod. "If you should need my help before then, please, please, call on me." Nellie held out her hand.

Liam took it and squeezed it in thanks.

Within two minutes, he was out the door and back into the cold.

Back in his office, Liam stopped by the desk of George Twombley, a British fellow who specialized in the latest crime forensics available in New York City.

"Hullo, Detective McCarty."

"What have you got for me, George?"

"Which would you like first? Blood or fire?"

"You Brits are always so dramatic." Liam grinned.

George blinked and a hint of a smile eked out. He moved his short but wide bulk in his chair and reached across his desk to retrieve a file folder.

"How long will this take, George?" Liam tried to contain his impatience as the other cop opened the file with maddening sloth.

"All right, then, blood first." George cleared his throat several times. "I examined the straight-razor you brought me from the cellar and compared it with the one from the suspect's."

"And?"

"First, we had to determine if the stains on the blade were blood, in fact."

"And?"

"It's not always simple. Even though there are tests to determine the stain is blood, like the fact that hydrogen peroxide will foam in the presence of blood, one cannot determine whether it is human or animal blood."

Liam sighed and leaned on the desk, resigned to hearing a lecture.

His colleague went on. "It seems that a doctor, Dr. James Blundell, at the end of the last century, began experimenting with transfusions." He leaned forward. "It had already been determined that mixing animal and human blood would cause a person to expire."

"Ah, yes."

"A German doctor, Leonard Landois, who, incidentally, just died, explained that if red blood cells from one animal were mixed with the serum—that's the liquid base of blood in which the cells are suspended, you see—if they were mixed with the serum of an animal of a different species, the red cells clump together like lumps in porridge, and could even burst."

"All right," Liam said.

"Further studies by a Karl Landsteiner from Vienna concluded that blood contains antigens and—"

Liam held his hand up. "Stop, stop. I am impressed by your research and knowledge, George. Just tell me the results, please."

George smirked. "The stains on the two razors were, indeed, human blood. Several types."

"Several types?"

"Either razor, or both razors, could have sliced the throats of one or all of the Hunt family members."

Liam felt like a balloon that someone had let the air out of. "And the fire in the basement?"

"There was clearly an inflammatory chemical used to hasten the flames, and to make it burn hotter."

"What sort of chemical?"

George shrugged. "Difficult to distinguish between kerosene or turpentine, mineral spirits or alcohol."

"Your best guess?"

"Kerosene would be the easiest to come by and the cheapest."

Liam remembered the kerosene smell in the trash can. He'd been correct. "So the fire could have been deliberately set to—"

"Nah, hold on." It was George's turn to hold up his hand. "It could have been a legitimate fire, you know, the janitors getting rid of old boxes, rags. Maybe got out of control or—"

"Or maybe they just said it did."

"In any case, there's no way to prove anything." George threw the folder down on the desk.

"What about fingerprints?"

"Ach, the only ones found on the razor in the apartment were Miss Ruby's. But..."

"But?"

"Probably nothing. There was a smudged print on the razor you found in the basement and it had a slice in it."

"What do you mean, *a slice*?"

"The finger had an imperfection, sideways, across the print."

"In layman's terms, George, please."

"The finger that made this print has a scar on it."

"A scar." Liam stared at his colleague, his mind wheeling with possibilities.

"But, as you know, it's a new science."

"It's all new, George. Blood, arson, fingerprints. But it's all we've got. Science."

George nodded, tapping his fingers on the desk. "And, the chloral hydrate that was used to knock out the victims..."

Liam waited.

"Could be purchased at any apothecary. Helps with sleeping, they say." He shook his head. "What's yer next step?"

Liam looked at George without seeing him. His mind was sifting through the forensic information. How did it fit with a young woman who by all accounts loved her family and had little, if any, knowledge about drugs and chemicals?

"Sorry, George, what did you say?"

"I asked what the next steps were."

"Ah, yes. A visit to the alleged murderer."

"Murderess," George said.

Liam's heart did a backward flip. "Next stop, the Women's Lunatic Asylum on Hart Island."

Chapter 13

January 12, 1902

Liam donned his warmest coat, wore a thick Irish wool sweater and vest underneath, plus a wool hat and gloves. Still he was freezing on the ferry that carried him to Hart Island. He refused to remain below deck, as he wanted to get the first clear glimpse of the island as the boat approached.

The day dawned bleak and icy cold, no sun promising even a degree of warmth or a ray of optimism. Even the towering power plant's smokestack billowed out black clouds of gloom. He felt as bleak as the day. His mind attempted to sort out a series of questions by which he could make sense of this case.

Face it, McCarty, you're nervous about meeting Ruby Hunt.

Her image in the family portrait floated in front of him, and a trickle of sweat ran down his back, even in the bitter cold temperature. He held up his hands. They shook. What would the asylum be like? Did Nellie Bly paint an accurate picture? Why the hell was he so nervous?

The air horn blew once, twice and again. The ferry began its docking process.

Liam hurried to the side of the boat where he would depart onto the island. He would be met by one of the asylum's attendants. Someone who, hopefully, was familiar with Ruby and her case.

The boat finally tied up at dock on starboard. The gangway was lowered and Liam hopped off. He started walking inland looking left and right. All he could see was brown dirt, puddles from a recent rainstorm, a few bare trees and gravel pathways leading in two directions. At the end of one path, he could see an imposing red brick building. From a distance, it seemed to tower over the landscape but couldn't be more than three stories tall.

A chill made him shiver. Suddenly he knew what was spooking him. He had an unrealistic fear that, once he stepped inside the asylum, he would not be allowed to leave. He would be captured and locked away, no one the wiser. Had he given George the details of his journey today? He couldn't remember. Shite.

Before dread could take hold, he spied a woman walking toward him from the direction he was heading. She wore a long black wool coat, black shoes and stockings and a dark red wool hat and matching gloves. She came directly to face him and he noticed grayish-brown hair under her hat and deep gray-blue eyes that wore a hopeful expression.

"Detective McCarty?" She held out a hand. "I'm Bridget Monaghan, Ruby's caretaker."

With the exhalation of a deep breath, Liam felt an overwhelming sense of relief. What had he expected? A dragon woman with talons and fire blazing in her eyes?

"This way, please." She turned and led the way back toward the asylum.

He walked at her side, feeling slightly less anxious.

"Are you a nurse, Miss Monaghan?"

"Aye, I've had some training. Mostly I'm an attendant, seeing to the needs of the, er, patients."

"Is that an Irish lilt I hear?"

"Aye, ye don't need much of an ear to hear the Dublin in me voice." She smiled.

Liam stopped to watch a large horse-drawn wagon carry its heavy load past a gate on their right. "Are those coffins in that wagon?"

"Aye, they are." She turned to look at him. "Do ye not know what Hart Island is?"

"I know there's a cemetery here for indigents."

"The isle of lost souls. Indigents, orphans, babies, those that no one gave a care about."

Another shiver ran through Liam. Potter's field for the thousands of poor, nameless human beings.

Bridget turned and moved more quickly down the path.

"Tell me about Miss Hunt," he said.

"I barely know the girl. She seems a sweet lass, utterly confounded by what has happened to her."

"Has she spoken of the murders?"

"She doesn't speak much at all, except perhaps to beg for release." Bridget walked up the steps to the large double doors. "She is desolate, cries the night in despair, is fearful of the other inmates, I mean, patients. Tries to keep to herself." She stopped but Liam believed she wanted to say more.

"Has she seen the doctors here?"

Bridget looked down at the stone floor. "Aye, she has. Once."

"Just once? I guess it's still early? She's only been here a few days, am I correct?"

"You are correct."

They reached a long corridor and Bridget ushered him into a small room off to the left. Inside sat a table and three chairs. Drab gray paint bubbled on the walls, and a smell of urine assailed him the moment he stepped inside.

"Wait here. I shall bring her."

"Miss Monaghan, is there no better meeting place?"

"None." She swished out the door.

Liam took off his coat and draped it over a chair then arched his back and stretched his arms over his head to release tension in his muscles. He circled the room once, twice, and again in the other direction, and then he moved to the barred window and looked out. In the distance, he could see men off-loading coffins from wagons. The graves, trenches really, must have been dug before the winter when the ground wasn't frozen hard. A terrible sadness caused his throat to tighten up.

The door opened and Bridget poked her head in. A young woman walked past her and entered the room, eyes on the floor. She wore a thin hospital gown in dark green, stained with bleach spots. A shawl was draped over her shoulders. The uniform befitted a woman of seventy rather than a girl of nineteen.

"Ruby, this here is Detective McCarty. He wants to ask you some questions, dear, if yer up to it."

Liam pulled out a chair. "How do you do, Miss Hunt? Please have a seat. We have a lot to discuss."

She tilted her head up and gazed at him with the most beautiful green eyes he'd ever seen. Beautiful but vacant. She sat in the chair offered. To Bridget she said, "Would you stay with me?"

Bridget looked at Liam in askance.

"Yes, of course," he said. "You are welcome."

Bridget pulled the third chair with Liam's coat draped over it to a far wall and sat as an observer. At that moment, the door opened to admit a short, stout woman whose fine mustache made Liam think of a pugilist.

Bridget jumped up. "Miss Barrows."

"What is going on here?" Barrows' mouth curled in a snarl.

Liam held up a hand to silence Bridget. "Good morning, Miss Barrows. I'm Detective Liam McCarty from the NYPD, investigating the case of Miss Hunt. This is my first interview and Miss Monaghan was kind enough to stay as a witness and take a few notes." He handed Bridget a small notebook and pencil. "Is there anything I can help you with?"

Frieda Barrows blinked, taken aback. "I should have been informed."

"Oh? And why is that? Are you the supervisor?"

"Well, er, no, but, I'm—"

"Are you in charge of Miss Hunt?"

Bridget stepped forward. "She is not. Miss Hunt is my responsibility."

The two women faced each other in obvious mutual dislike.

Liam scoffed. "Well, then, let's not waste any more time. I have an interview to conduct. If you would be so kind as to leave us, Miss Barrows." Liam pulled his chair out and sat across from Ruby.

Barrows' mouth opened then snapped shut and she stalked out of the room.

Bridget mouthed thanks to Liam and went back to her seat. "Shall I take notes?"

"That would indeed be helpful," Liam said, secretly stunned that he had pulled that off. Now he would have a written summary of the conversation.

"Sorry, Miss Hunt, for the confusion."

She looked at him and smiled.

The room was no longer grim and airless. Liam felt a sudden light-headedness. This woman took his breath away. Still, something was not right with her affect. "I'd like you to tell me, in your own words, what happened on the day of the murders."

Ruby's eyes closed and a tiny smile softened her face. "Ummm."

"What was that?" Liam asked.

She dipped her head from side to side. "I'm so tired. Can I go to sleep now?"

Bridget explained, "She's on powerful medications. I'm sorry, I should have told you."

"Miss Hunt, Ruby, can you hear me? Can you answer some questions?"

"Ahhhh, quest...quest...yons. Yes, answer some..."

"Oh dear," Bridget said. "This will never do." She went to Ruby and lifted her chin in her hand.

"Ruby, me darlin', can you make sense for the Detective? Can you, dear?"

"Sense and nonsense, sense, sense and nonsense." Ruby closed her eyes again. "So sleepy, bedtime now, thank you, please, please."

Liam sighed and leaned back in the chair.

Bridget pulled her chair over.

"How long will she sleep?" he asked.

"Hours. The nurse must have given her a strong dose this morning. Damn the woman."

"You think the nurse purposely gave her more because I was coming?"

"I dunno, but it's possible. Anything is possible here." Bridget tightened her mouth and her jaw clicked. "They knew you were coming. They know whenever visitors are coming."

"I suppose there's no point wasting my time today." Liam fastened his eyes on Bridget. "Do you think we can arrange another interview and this time make sure she gets no drugs?"

Bridget stared at him. "Yes, let me work this out somehow. I can mebbe arrange to give Ruby her medications meself."

Liam took his pad and pencil and scribbled some notes, tore off the scrap and handed it to Bridget. "This is how you can contact me. The telephone at my precinct and my home telephone. Or if you need to send a note, use this address."

Bridget nodded. "Give me a day and I will arrange another interview."

"You really care about her, don't you?"

"I care about them all, Detective. Only a few can still be saved. Ruby is one."

"You don't think she's guilty of murder, do you?"

She stood, smoothed out her skirt. "As I said, Ruby can be saved and deserves to be. She needs a strong ally."

Ruby's head was on the table now and she was snoring softly.

Liam donned his coat, hat, and gloves.

Bridget's parting words as he exited, "Will you be her champion, Detective? Isn't that what the Irish name Liam means? A guardian protector?"

Chapter 14

January 13, 1902

She stared at the insect making its way across the ceiling, down onto the far wall. The room was dark but a beam of moonlight seemed to follow the creature as if a spotlight was aimed at its hard carapace. Ruby shivered beneath the thin blanket and felt a rivulet of water drip down her cheek and onto her neck. She was crying and didn't realize it.

With a groan, she sat up and draped the blanket around her shoulders. She slid her feet into wafer-thin slippers and stood. Surrounding her were other beds and other women, snoring, moaning, whimpering in the night. As if her plight were not grim enough, she had lost her privacy as well. She could not pee without an audience. All bodily functions were monitored, if not by staff attendants, then by fellow inmates.

Yes, inmates, she admitted to herself. We are not patients; we are prisoners in a horrid jail, with no chance of parole.

Ruby sat at the edge of her cot and her thoughts wandered foggily back to the day, yesterday, and the detective that came to see her. What was his name? Something Irish? McElroy? McDonald? Would he come back? Did he believe she was hopelessly insane?

Oh, why did they give her those pills? She couldn't think straight. Couldn't answer his questions, couldn't make sense of anything. But she had to tell her story. Surely, if she did, they would understand. They would let her go home.

Home. No such thing now.

Ruby could not stop the flood of tears that burst out. Her mother, father. Patrick. Gone. Forever.

She dropped her head into her hands and prayed that this was a dream and she would awaken at any moment. Yet, moments ticked by and still she was caught in the nightmare.

With a deep sigh, she rose from the bed. A bit lightheaded, she stumbled to the huge, grimy mullioned window and gazed out between the bars. A layer of snow blanketed the entire landscape...a flat, desolate terrain fractured by a few run-down buildings in the distance. Was that the Long Island Sound she saw beyond? A large freighter steaming by? In the wispy moonlight, the grounds of her prison appeared surreal. Perhaps this was a dream after all.

She turned and walked to the door, turned the knob. It wouldn't open. Of course, she was locked in. Could not even go to the toilet to relieve herself. That's what the pail in the corner was for. No. She would wait, hold it until morning.

Suddenly, she remembered. Under her mattress was a pad and pencil. To begin a journal. Dear Bridget had gotten her the implements to keep track of her life in words. So, she would stay sane, not succumb to the conditions of the place, and go mad. Bridget had said insane asylums created insanity.

Ruby pulled out the diary and pencil and sat on her bed, angled so the moonlight would reflect on the pages. What is the date? January 13. She began to write.

When six a.m. came, and the winter sunlight took over for the weak light of the moon, Ruby tucked away her diary and scrambled into bed. The attendants would be unlocking the doors any minute. Today, however, she would meet her doctor. She looked forward to it. He would understand immediately that she, Ruby Elizabeth Hunt of the New York Hunts, was sane. Perfectly, wholly, unquestionably sane.

Now, however, she would have to deal with the morning ablutions. First, to the toilet, next to the bath. She cringed at the thought of the icy torture, but she had learned in the few days she'd been confined, that it was best to endure than object. It was dangerous to report an attendant to the doctors, for those same attendants would eavesdrop to hear what the patients said, and then they would watch for opportunities to seek revenge on the patients.

One patient, Louise Rosenkrantz, who had dared speak to her in secret, confided that an aide had held her under the water until she nearly drowned...and more than once, too. Ruby was appalled. She knew the tubs were heavy cast iron and she'd wondered why some of the women patients had a variety of bruises, all colors and shades, when they returned from the baths. A struggle in that trough would explain the injuries. In other instances, particularly cruel attendants would yank the hair of a patient, pulling it out in clumps, as they dragged the women down the hallway, kicking and screaming.

Ruby made up her mind to behave in accordance with the rules while she was a resident there. For, surely, she would be released soon. Just as soon as she talked to the doctor today.

Following a meager breakfast of hard bread, lukewarm oatmeal and weak tea, Ruby was permitted to visit the *day room* along with a number of other patients. Her first experience taught her quickly that this area was a potential powder keg for mayhem. There were no reading materials and sewing and knitting supplies were a danger to the residents. Thus, the only occupation a patient could engage in was daydreaming, gazing out the windows, walking in circles, and, if lucky, whispering a few words to each other under the watchful glare of the caregivers.

Ruby spied a familiar face across the large space—Margaret Becket, the woman she'd met on her first day. Margaret sat in a caned-back chair, head down, arms folded loosely in her lap. Her hair was matted and greasy and the dress she wore, thin and patched. Her lips moved, but there was no one near her to listen.

Ruby headed toward her, then snapped her head around to see if anyone watched. She sat down next to the woman who had aged several years in several days.

"Hello, Margaret. Remember me?" Ruby touched her elbow. "I'm Ruby. We met when I first arrived here. Do you remember me?"

Margaret flew from her seat with a scream. "Don't touch me, don't touch me." She raced across the room, trying to get through the door, but was stopped by a male guard.

An attendant hurried over to take her back to her room. Or at least, Ruby hoped that's where she went. She had heard whispers of some electrical device in a locked ward that would calm patients.

A tall, thin woman approached Ruby. "She's a bit nervous, Margaret is."

Ruby looked at her. "You know Margaret?"

The woman shrugged. "I know pretty much all of 'em..." she narrowed her eyes, "'ceptin' you. Who are ya, then?"

"Who are you?" Ruby shot back.

"Ah, feisty? Well, I'm Francine, Francine Gaspard."

"Sounds French."

"Yeah, *oui, oui,* I'm French. Right from the French Quarter of the *Le Bronx*. Heh."

Ruby half-smiled.

"So, you?"

"Ruby. Ruby Hunt."

Francine nodded. "Yeah, I heard about ya. Murdered your whole family, right?"

Ruby's eyes popped. "What? No, no, I didn't...I would never..." She stopped with a gasp.

"Awright, awright, don't get yourself in a blather."

"How did you know about, about the murders?"

"I got my ways."

"How long have you been here?"

"Dunno. Maybe six, maybe seven years?"

"Seven years? Oh God. Why, how—?"

"My husband found a new little tart. Lot younger, prettier than me, ya know?"

Ruby opened her mouth but no words came out.

"He decided right then I was crazy. Had me checked out by some doctor friends of his, and bam, quick as a slick, in I went."

"But—"

"That's the way of it, Missy. We women got no rights. None a' t'all."

"What about the law? How can they lock you up without reason?"

"Law? What law? There be no laws for women, Missy." Francine put her hand on Ruby's shoulder.

A loud shout from across the room caused her to drop it.

"Hands off, Francine." Jane Himmler stalked across the room in three steps. Although small in stature, the supervisor had no trouble bossing everyone around. Her whiny voice sounded like it came through her nose. She sported a short, unattractive hairdo, wispy facial hair, and beady eyes that seemed to follow her even when Himmler's back was turned.

Ruby stepped backwards.

"You two split up before you wind up in trouble."

Ruby turned and moved away from the two women. When she looked back at them, she saw Himmler poking her finger into Francine's chest, none-too-gently. She hoped Francine didn't get into trouble because of her. Her lips trembled of a sudden, and she could not stop the tears from falling. She turned to the wall and sobbed. An arm went around her shoulders and she leaped away.

"'tis all right, Ruby. Aye, it's just me."

"Oh, Bridget, I'm sorry, I didn't mean—"

"I know, dear. Come with me. I'll walk you back to your room so's you could get ready for your doctor's visit."

"Yes, please." Ruby walked a few steps with Bridget then stopped. "He will help me, the doctor? He will, won't he? He must, mustn't he?"

Bridget tightened her lips and stared at Ruby with sad eyes.

That's when Ruby realized the truth. She would never be leaving Hart Island.

New York City
2016

Chapter 15

May 15, 2016

The sky had turned steel gray, presaging an imminent storm. Frank decided there was no better time to do some research at the New York City Public Library and then comb the stacks of archives at One Police Plaza.

He arrived at the library in time to escape the deluge that promised to wash away the dirt on the streets of mid-town Manhattan. One could only hope. In his briefcase, he had a legal pad, several pencils, a Samsung tablet, and several ancient file folders.

One of the file folders he'd found at the records building on Hart Island was that of the staff at the asylum. In it, he found a photograph and information about Bridget Monaghan. He'd begin with her.

Bridget Mary Monaghan, born 1867, Dublin, Ireland. Immigrated to U.S. via Ellis Island, 1891. In 1892, with nursing training, she landed a job at Blackwell's Island Asylum, which was later moved to Hart Island. Left 1902. No forwarding address or job information. The photo did her no justice, but those file-photos made everyone look like a criminal.

Frank took some notes. Ruby entered the asylum on January 10, 1902, died April 10, 1902. Just three months later. When in 1902 did Bridget leave? Right after? Where did she go? He turned on his tablet and began Googling PeopleLooker, PeopleFinder, and TruthFinder. Will Jefferies would tackle Ancestry.com and the heritage sites. Amanda would check the Times archives.

As Frank perused the websites, he felt his frustration build. How would he ever find out what happened to Bridget? Then something caught his eye on the PeopleFinder site. A Bridget M. O'Malley from Dublin, nursing aide in New York City, passed away on September 15, 1920. Could the 'M' be Monaghan? He read on. Mrs. O'Malley was survived by a husband, Joseph, and one sister, Angela, both residing in Brooklyn, New York.

What was her date of birth? Why doesn't this article say? Frank rose from his seat and headed toward the librarian. He asked her, in an official capacity, to track down the obituary in the papers and get the missing information. The librarian was only too happy to help an NYPD Lieutenant.

Frank returned to his seat and began tracking the O'Malleys in Brooklyn. He found Joseph right away but without kids, that was a dead end. Bridget's sister, Angela Monaghan, or whatever her married name would be, was elusive. He did locate an Angela Monaghan Watts, married to John Watts, in 1910. They had six children and nine grandchildren, according to an article about health care 'families.' Evidently Bridget's sister, if this was indeed her, was also in nursing. And maybe her kids and grandkids? He would have to find an address for the grandkids, or great grandkids. He texted Will for that task.

The librarian returned with the obit on Bridget. Frank read the three simple lines and sighed.

"Not what you wanted?" the woman asked.

"No, actually, it is. I wanted the date of her birth and her full name. And there they are." He pointed. "Bridget Monaghan O'Malley, August 9, 1867." The year, location, and occupation were right. This had to be the right Bridget Monaghan. He texted the info to Will.

Frank turned to the librarian, who hovered nearby. "Do you think you can help me again? Sorry to be a bother."

"That's my job," she said and smiled.

Frank looked at her and realized she was an attractive woman. He especially liked her voice. It was rather musical. He smiled and stood. "Frank Mead, and you are?"

"Rachel. Rachel Bejarano. I'm happy to help the police. Sounds like an interesting case…cold case, I assume, from 1900?"

"Yes. Thanks. I could use some help."

Rachel waited.

Frank gestured to a seat. She sat across the table from him. He handed her a pad and pen. "I'm trying to track down an NYPD cop from 1902. His name was Liam McCarty, no 'h.' I have no idea if he moved or died, but he seems to have gone off the grid sometime in March of 1902."

She jotted notes. "Anything more you can tell me?"

He showed her the articles he had found about Liam in the early days of the investigation when he was appointed lead detective.

"Ah, this will help. Thanks." Rachel stood. "How long will you be here?"

"Probably only a half-hour. But you can call me." He gave her his card then grabbed it back. "This is my cell. Call any time, day or night."

"Wow, this really is important, isn't it?"

"Maybe important enough to treat you to dinner. That is, I mean—"

"You've got a deal."

The room had gotten warm all of a sudden.

Rachel waved his card and left.

Man, am I out of practice. He shook his head.

⁂

Outside, the rain had stopped and the sun was painting a rainbow across the street. Frank smiled. *My lucky day, I guess.*

Before he could reach his car, Will texted that he would pick him up in front of the station house in thirty minutes. He had tracked down Bridget's descendants in Brooklyn.

Frank checked his watch. *1:30.* Good time to drive to the boroughs. Beat the rush. He hustled to his car and drove to the precinct in time to meet Will. He hopped from his car into Will's.

"Where are we going?" Frank asked, settling into the passenger seat and turning the air vents on him.

"25 Stratford Road, Flatbush section of Brooklyn."

"Flatbush?"

"Yeah, I guess it's quite gentrified these days. Not to worry, I'll protect you."

"Gee, thanks. So, who are we going to see?"

"A woman by the name of Sally Ann Robards. Great, great grandniece of Bridget Monaghan."

"No kidding. Will, you're a genius."

"Tell me something I don't know."

"Did you talk to her? Does she have any information on Bridget? After all, it's—"

"Yeah, a lot of years have gone by." Will glanced over at Frank and grinned.

"What?"

"You're going to be ecstatic."

"I am?"

"Yup. Not only does Sally have stories to tell. She's got a letter from her ancestor, written back in 1920 just before Bridget died."

"Seriously?"

"Would I lie to you?"

"What's it say?"

"Now that I don't know. We'll see when we get there."

Frank tapped his fingers on his knee. "If Bridget left a letter for her sister's kids and it got passed down all the way to today, it must have been important."

"My feelings too." He slowed the car and turned from Church Avenue onto Stratford Road. Number 25 was an old but elegant apartment building. No doubt expensive co-ops.

They got out and entered the main lobby. A doorman called upstairs to the Robards' flat.

"Go on up. Third floor, number 307 on your right." The doorman pointed to the elevator.

Sally Robards answered the door and invited them in and offered them coffee, which they declined.

When they were seated in the living room, Frank explained why they were there.

With delicate fingers, Sally pulled at the chain around her neck. *Maybe she played the piano?* She wore a pink short-sleeved top and a denim skirt. Frank guessed her age to be mid-sixties, which would jive with being the niece of Bridget, twice removed. Her eyes were huge and she wore little makeup, didn't need any. The reddish blond hair, now shot with gray, bespoke her Irish heritage.

"I can't tell you how glad I am that the police are finally looking into this case."

"Wait, what case?" Frank said, aiming a glance at Will.

"The case of Ruby Hunt, of course. It was a travesty of justice, locking her away for something she didn't do, confining her to an asylum..." Sally shuddered.

"Miz Robards, let me clarify why we are here. A descendant of Ruby has been murdered recently."

"See, I knew it, it's all related to the Hunt murders."

Frank held up a hand. "That's what we are trying to ascertain. Now, may I ask you some questions?"

"Yes, yes, sorry. Of course." Sally wiggled in her chair, antsy to be of help.

Frank described the situation in 1902 as he understood it. "Finally, your great, great aunt suspected that Ruby was poisoned. Now, we have no evidence to substantiate this but—"

"I may have that evidence." Sally reached for a small yellow five-by-ten envelope resting on the coffee table. "Bridget left this to be passed down through the family."

"What is it?"

"Open it."

Frank opened the envelope and retrieved what looked like an old large document folded up in small squares. Very gently he laid it on the coffee table in front of them. "Looks like a map."

"Of what?" Will asked.

"A cemetery."

"It is," Sally said. "It's a map of Hart Island's potter's field."

Frank's mouth fell open. "What?"

Sally nodded. "Bridget somehow got a copy and marked Ruby's burial place. Bridget explains it all in this letter that came with the map."

Frank held his hand out for the letter.

"If she was poisoned," Sally went on, "you can have her exhumed and, and do whatever you do to test for poison. Right?"

Will looked at the key written in flowery script at the bottom of the map. "Bridget must've handwritten the plot number at the bottom." He ran his fingers across the map and stopped at a red dot. "X marks the spot."

Frank opened the folded letter.

"Read it aloud," Will said.

"To future generations,

Although it is far too late to save the physical being of Miss Ruby Elizabeth Hunt, for she has gone to God, I beg you to please try to prove her innocence in the death of her family so she may finally rest in peace. I have tried to make her life in the asylum a wee bit better under such horrific circumstances, but she was so desolate, perhaps her death was best in the end.

There was a police detective, Liam McCarty, who tried to help prove her innocence as well. I believe he was a bit in love with Ruby. He was unable to buck the corrupt system that favors the wealthy above all. Sadly, he disappeared sometime before her death. No one knows his whereabouts.

I have tried many times to contact the police in charge of the case, but no one will respond to my appeals. In light of the untenable circumstances, I have resigned my position at the asylum on Hart Island.

To whomever reads this letter, I enclose a map of Ruby's burial site. I pray to God that someone will help vindicate her.

Bridget Monaghan, April 30, 1902

The three of them sat in silence with only the clock on the mantel ticking in the room.

"Holy crap," Will said. "The cop disappeared?"

"What are the chances that was coincidence?" Frank said.

"Will you exhume the body?" Sally asked.

Frank looked at her, then down at the map. "Yes. We'll find Ruby's remains and set her to rest."

He kept his next thoughts to himself. *And, we'll find out what happened to Detective Liam McCarty and his murder book.*

Chapter 16

"Where to now?" Will turned the A-C on in the unmarked police car.

"Drop me at One PP. I want to check the records on Detective McCarty."

"Right." Will pulled out from the curb. "I'll check on the procedures for exhuming a century-old body." He turned to Frank. "You do want to exhume Ruby, correct?"

"Absolutely. It may be far too late to get any forensics, but it's worth a try. And make copies of that map and letter so you can log them into evidence."

At One Police Plaza, Frank checked in at the front desk and asked to visit the archives. A few minutes later, he was two stories underground in the Records Department.

He recognized the woman at the desk. This is my lucky day, he mused. "Hey, Melinda, how are you doing?"

Melinda Barkas broke into a wide smile. "Look what the cat dragged in. Frank Mead. How the hell are ya?"

Melinda Barkas was a blond knockout, and every cop in the city who hadn't hit on her wanted to. She, however, only had eyes for a vice cop named Sara Chumsky. Ah well.

"Doing great, Melinda. But will do a lot better if you can help me track someone down."

"Sure, Frank. Who?"

"A detective named Liam McCarty, no 'h.' The catch is that he was on the force in 1902."

"You're kidding, right?"

"Nope."

"1902, huh." She stood up, displaying a tall, thin but athletic body. Frank sighed to himself.

"What you want is Personnel records. The newer ones are on microfilm, but the older... Come with me."

Melinda led him down a hall, pressed a key code and entered a room full of library stacks. The stacks moved with a flick of a wheel to allow visitors into the aisle they desired. She kept walking until they reached the far end of the immense room.

"Here you go. This row begins with 1900." She turned to him with a gleam in her eye. "Have at it."

"Great."

"I'll be outside if you need something. Use these desk phones to call this number." She gave him a card, smiled, and headed back the way they came, calling out, "Good luck."

Frank spun around and walked down the first aisle until he reached 1902. "I hope to Christ these are alphabetized."

They were. Frank ran his fingers over the giant log books starting in January, 1902. A-C, D-F, G-I, J-L, M-O. Bingo. He pulled out the last one and carried it to a table at the far end of the aisle. He set it down, turned on a table lamp and, without sitting, began to turn the pages.

Let's see, the murders were January 3. McCarty didn't start his investigation until he got his shield so that would be the tenth, when Ruby was committed. Frank flipped the pages. Yes. Liam McCarty, born, December 8, 1876 in New York City. That would make him, what in 1902? Twenty-six—still pretty damn young to take on a case like this.

Some history? Parents emigrated from Ireland, no info there. Lived in New York City. Obviously. Not married. So, what happened to him?

Frank's cell went off. He couldn't believe he could get any reception in this bunker.

"Mead."

"Hello, Lieutenant?"

He knew her voice right away. "Rachel?"

"I thought you'd want to know this right away."

"Go ahead."

"This Detective McCarty? I found some information. He died on March 15, 1902. Very sad. The article states he fell in front of a train. Killed instantly."

"He fell in..?" he whispered.

"Awful, isn't it?"

"What train?"

"The 9:05 a.m. to Scarsdale, New York. Maybe he planned to take it for some reason."

"Scarsdale, hmm?"

"He may not have been going all the way to Scarsdale," she said. "The train stopped at several places in the Bronx."

"Do you have an address for him, Rachel?"

"I don't. But he could have been going to visit a family member, maybe one of his brothers, or a friend."

"Right."

"The article says it appeared to be an accident."

"Accident, right. Can you scan that and email it to me right now?"

"Of course. Just take a minute."

"I really appreciate your help."

"Anytime."

"How about tomorrow night? Dinner, I mean."

"You don't have to—"

"I want to. What time do you get off?"

"Tomorrow, around six."

"I'll pick you up at the front steps."

"I look forward to it, Frank."

"Me too."

He stood between the gloomy stacks and their dust-covered files, brooding on Liam McCarty's tragic death. His cell beeped with Rachel's email:

> *Detective Liam Francis McCarty was born December 8, 1876, to John and Mary McCarty of New York City. He is survived by two brothers, Collin and Sean, also in New York City, and their sons. McCarty was lead investigator on the Ruby Hunt murder*

case. Tragically, he was killed on March 15, 1902 as he stepped in front of a moving train heading into Grand Central Station. The train was on its way north to Scarsdale as its final destination. It is unclear whether McCarty was intending to board the train. His death was ruled accidental. He hadn't yet finished the investigation into the Hunt murders.

Rachel had added a note: *And, coincidentally, a month following his death, Miss Hunt herself died in the Women's Lunatic Asylum on Hart Island.*

Coincidentally, my eye. Could he have committed suicide? Hell, no. If anything, he was pushed. From the little Frank knew about McCarty, the detective wouldn't quit the investigation until he had vindicated Ruby.

Frank had to find that murder book. Outside the records vault he asked Melinda once again for help.

"Find what you wanted?"

"I did, thanks. Now I need something else."

She waited.

"This cop, you know, from 1902, how can I find his notes from one of his cases?"

"You mean his murder book?"

"Man, you are uncanny."

"Come with me."

Frank followed her into another room with different files. Crime case files.

"1902? Names in the case? Accused, convicted, whatever."

"Ruby Hunt."

Melinda sat at a computer and began typing. After a minute, she jumped up and hurried down the hall to a room with metal bookshelves stuffed with banker's boxes. Thousands of them.

"Check alphabetically for Hunt. Should be there."

She left him to it.

Frank scanned the shelves, found the "H" box and pulled it down. Inside was the Ruby Hunt file. His heart ratcheted up a notch. Finally, he'd get some answers. He flipped open the file and one piece of paper drifted out, landed on the floor.

His shoulders slumped when he picked it up to find one line written on the page: *Confidential file. Not for public consumption.*

He stormed out and nearly bit Melinda's head off.

"Sorry, sorry, I didn't mean to take it out on you. But where the hell is the file? And the murder book?"

"Jesus, Frank, I don't know. It should be there. She clicked away on her keys to do some checking. "It should be there. Crap. I don't get it."

"What do you suggest?"

She stared at him with deep blue eyes. "Is it possible he took the files himself, the murder book? You know, thinking it wasn't safe to keep them here?"

Frank stared back at her with weary gray-blue eyes. "You might have something there. But where would he have stashed it?" He gazed into the distance.

"Hey. You're the detective."

At seven that night, Frank sat at his desk, compiling a list of follow-ups. The most urgent was to check into David Hunt's finances to see if there was any hanky panky in the insurance businesses that he ran, and any solid connections, one, to the old murders in the Hunt family and, two, to Sophie in the last few weeks.

The second lead was to track down Liam McCarty's family, if anyone was still around. Collin and Sean McCarty and sons, hopefully, grandsons. The only good news here is that McCarty is not as common as McCarthy. Maybe he'd catch a break.

He leaned back and spun around in his swivel chair. He called his mother and gave her an update. Now he dialed Amanda.

"Hey, Dad," she answered.

"I wonder if you can do me a favor." He told her he wanted to track down the McCartys. "You have any quick way to do that?"

"I might. What's it worth to you?"

"How about Chinese take-out with Dexter?"

"You mean, like now?"

"Now's as good a time as any."

She let out a huge exasperated sigh.

Frank tempted her with: "Sesame chicken, brown rice, wonton soup?"

"Give me a few hours."

"Love you."

"Yeah, I bet you do." She hung up.

He smiled as he grabbed his laptop and flicked the lights off in the office. For the third time that day he realized he was a lucky guy.

At ten that night, Amanda knocked at the door of his apartment. Dexter screeched out an excited welcome.

"I hope the chicken's not cold," Amanda said, unhitching her backpack and dropping it on the floor. "I'm starving."

"It's warm," Frank said. "Table's set."

Amanda held out her arm for Dexter and the parrot jumped on. "Hi, you handsome devil."

Dexter preened and bobbed his head, feathers fanned out like an exotic dancer.

They sat and ate but Frank questioned his daughter during the meal, impatient for information. "Did you have any luck?"

She gulped down her food, swallowed some water then wiped her mouth. "Jeez, Dad."

"Sorry."

Amanda reached for her bag and pulled out loose papers. "I had some luck. Liam McCarty's great grandnephews are alive and living in Manhattan. All three of them. The oldest, Connor, is the grandson of Liam's brother, Collin, so, in my opinion he would be the most likely to have any info that was passed down."

"Sounds feasible."

She handed him a page with names and addresses. I've sent emails to all of them to see if I am, indeed, right, but it's late and probably won't hear anything until tomorrow."

"What do you know about this Connor McCarty? What's he do for work?"

"Oh, you'll love this. He's a homicide cop. 9th Precinct." Amanda grinned. "Am I good or what?"

Chapter 17

May 16, 2016

Connor McCarty met them at the 9th Precinct on East 5th Street in Manhattan. His firm handshake and no-nonsense manner made Frank feel more confident that he was close to finding out the truth about Liam McCarty's fate over a hundred years ago.

McCarty led them into his office and closed the door. "Sit." He gestured to two rickety chairs in front of his government-issue gray metal desk.

Frank gave him a briefing on the Sophie Hunt case, including a mention about the suitcase that belonged to Ruby.

"I heard about the case you snagged. Sophie Hunt." McCarty stared into space. "The name brought back memories."

"Memories?" Frank asked. "You can't be more than fifty."

McCarty smiled. "Forty-seven."

"You mean memories of Ruby Hunt?" Will asked.

"Yeah." McCarty leaned back in his chair and ran a hand over his bald head. "They say it's all about timing, right? So, would you believe, me and my wife are in the process of moving. She's always wanted to move to Long Island. Go figure. Anyways, we're packing, you know, going through all our stuff. And what do I come across in the attic?"

Frank waited, white knuckles gripping the arms of the chair.

"Yup. A box full of my great, great uncle Liam's shit from his days on the force." He leaned forward, both elbows on the desk. "Patrolman for six years, passes his detective's exam and winds up dead after three months with the shiny new shield. Lousy deal."

"What can you tell us?"

"If he was anything like the rest of the McCartys, he would've been stubborn to the point of pig-headed. He never would've quit a case he found hinky, ya know what I mean?"

Frank nodded.

McCarty turned behind him and pulled up an old beat-up carton from the floor, set it on the desk. "There's some personal stuff, a few photos of the family and all, but then there's this file." He pulled out a brown folder and handed it over.

Frank opened it to find documents on Ruby Hunt.

Will stuck his nose in. "What's there, Frank?"

"Ruby Hunt's committal papers, her medical records in the asylum, her death certificate—"

"Death certificate? How did her death certificate get into Liam's belongings?" Will asked. "He was dead before Ruby."

"I can explain," McCarty said. "There's a note in here from a George Twombley, Liam's sergeant, who added it into the case file later."

Will nodded.

Frank squinted at the writing. "Cause of death, congenital heart disease."

"Bullshit," Will shouted.

"Lots of ways to make it look like heart disease," McCarty said.

"What else?" Will asked.

"Looks like a burial order for her to be interred on Hart Island."

"There's also a photo of a painting of Ruby," McCarty added. "Nice looking lady, eh? But the *coup de grâce* is—"

"Liam's murder book." Frank had already found it at the bottom of the box. A simple composition book used back then.

"Yup, his murder book. Pretty extensive notes on what he found, too."

"Did you read it?" Will asked.

"Yeah, I did."

"What's your take?"

"I think there was something seriously wrong with the whole case."

"Meaning?"

"When you finish, I think you'll agree with me. Ruby Hunt didn't kill her family. Someone wanted to pin it on her, get her out of the way."

"In the suitcase, there was a letter from her caretaker, Bridget Monaghan...." Frank began.

"Oh yeah, Liam mentions her. Tell me about the suitcase."

Frank did. He ended with, "Bridget thinks Ruby was murdered."

"I think she was right." McCarty looked at Frank. "I also think Liam was murdered."

"He didn't fall in front of a train."

"Hell, no, he didn't. He was bloody pushed."

Frank looked at Will, whose eyes were on the murder book in Frank's hands.

"Did Liam have a suspect?" Frank asked.

"He did," McCarty said. "I don't want to be a spoiler. Read it yourself and tell me if you agree."

Someone knocked on the closed door.

"I gotta go for now. Take it all with you."

"Thanks, Connor. Really appreciate it."

"If I can help, just call." He walked to the door, opened it. "I want to know who killed my great uncle."

∞

At two in the morning, Frank sat at his desk at home. Dexter snoozed on the sofa arm while Frank read Liam's murder book twice and was making notes on the third go-round. He had to hand it to the young cop–he was thorough, meticulous in his details and, the best part—Liam McCarty wrote down his impressions and theories about the case. This was not usually done in the murder book. A murder book was reserved for facts, for the courtroom, to be precise. What the hell, he was a rookie. But a clever one.

Frank jotted down some of the key points that Liam made. All pointed to the conclusion that Ruby was not the killer. Liam questioned: how did she get the family members upstairs, how did she attain chloral hydrate, why would she use a razor in such a brutal manner to slice their throats, and the biggest question is why? Why on earth would a nineteen-year-old girl murder her family?

The simple answer, Liam suggested, is that she's insane. However, his visits to the asylum proved beyond a doubt in his mind that Ruby Hunt was not insane.

What about the money? Frank mused. Follow the money. Was there a will? Who would inherit the Hunt fortune?

Liam had conducted an investigation into Thomas Hunt, who, in Liam's words, was considerably less than cooperative. He did learn, however, that Thomas was appointed as Ruby's guardian.

Unfortunately, it appeared that Liam's boss wanted the case closed immediately. Frank was pretty sure that the police captain and Thomas Hunt had a connection. Much of the investigation was done on Liam's personal time, not the department's. That would not have set him in good stead with the force.

Frank reviewed the section of the murder book where Liam mentioned the forensics of the case. A joke, pretty much. CSIs were able to determine that the blood on the Sheffield razor blades, one Ruby held at the murder scene, and one Liam found in the basement, was, indeed, human blood. But there was no way to match it with the victims.

The fingerprints on the blade that Ruby held at the crime scene were hers, naturally. But they did find a print on the blade in the basement that had an interesting artifact. On the print was a slice that cut across the print. Which means, Frank realized, the owner of the print had a scar on his finger.

Liam didn't...or couldn't take that any further. But he did indicate that Thomas Hunt was a likely candidate as the murderer. Once the family members were dead, possibly by bribing the doorman and elevator man for their assistance, he could frame Ruby for the crimes.

Frank rubbed his eyes. So why didn't he just kill Ruby too? Why go through the whole committal process to get rid of her? *Liam gives me no clue.*

Frank's mind was shutting down. Right before he went to bed, he decided to read a few paragraphs of Ruby's diary. Getting into the mind of the victim always gave him inspiration to work harder...even if it was too late for Ruby.

New York City
1902

Chapter 18

January 30, 1902

Ruby writes in her diary:
I first met Dr. Franz Uber two weeks after arriving at the madhouse. That's what I called the Women's Lunatic Asylum of Hart Island, for it is, indeed, not a place for those of sane mind.

Dr. Uber is head of this madhouse and I prayed that he would be astute enough to see through the terrible error of my committal. As an eminent psychiatrist, he surely would recognize that I am not crazy. My wish, however, was brutally shattered, when after only a few moments of discussion, the doctor rose to his feet, jerked me up from my chair by the elbow, and marched me to the door. The dialogue before went thus:

Doctor: "Miss Hunt, can you tell me why you murdered your family?"

Myself: "But I did not, sir, I never would. I loved them terribly."

Doctor: "The evidence is quite compelling, Miss Hunt. You have no way to explain the blood, the fingerprints, the fact that you were the only one present with the corpses."

Myself: "Good God, no, Doctor, but someone else, someone—"

Doctor: "Yes, yes, they all say the same, someone else, someone else. Will you not take responsibility and confess? I assure you, your physical and mental well-being will benefit by releasing this burden from your conscience."

At this point, I was dumbstruck. I could not speak. My mouth opened and closed and, no doubt, the doctor found me a fish out of water. The interview was abruptly ended and I was led back to my cell, numb to my very core.

Ruby dropped her pencil and notebook onto her bed. She could not see to write through the tears. How could this be? Wasn't the doctor a friend of Uncle Thomas? Why didn't he help her, get her released, freed?

She knew at that blinding instant she must see her uncle. He had not visited once since her incarceration, and only then to sign endless paperwork. Was he really responsible for this monstrous deed? Did he hate her so much that he would just throw her away like so much garbage? How could she get word to him?

A scuffling outside her door brought her up short. She tucked the book and pencil under her mattress and jumped onto the cot, pretending sleep. Through slitted eyes, she spied the hallway light angling into the room and a figure standing in the doorway. The figure scurried in, closed the door, and came to stand over her bed. Bridget.

"Oh, thanks be to God," Ruby said, sitting up.

Bridget reached for her hands. "Are you all right, little dove?"

"It was so awful, Bridget. Dr. Uber...he didn't believe me, didn't even listen, never heard anything I said. I tried to explain, that I am innocent but—"

"I know, dear, I know. He is a hard man, Dr. Uber." Bridget sat next to her on the bed. Another cellmate from a nearby bed murmured to them and Bridget shushed her.

"Bridget, I must see my uncle."

"Thomas?"

"Yes, I must. This has to be a mistake. He would not leave me here like this without trying to rescue me."

"Are you sure about that?" Bridget said, mouth a straight, tight line.

Ruby stared at her. "I don't...how can...why would he do this to me?"

"I don't know. I do know he has been here to see Dr. Uber several times."

"But he didn't visit me."

Bridget simply looked at her.

Ruby's eyes went dark. She stared into space for a long moment then turned the flinty green marbles on Bridget. "I want to see Detective McCarty. How do I get word to him?"

A series of bells clanged outside in the hallway, causing Bridget to cringe. Ruby did not blink. Her body felt encased in glacial ice and she wondered if she would ever thaw. What did it matter?

Bridget led a stiff and uncommunicative Ruby to the cafeteria where lunch was being served. She sat her down on a bench at the end of a long table.

"I'll get you some food. You stay here."

Bridget worried that Ruby was getting lost inside herself, as she'd witnessed so many patients doing. She hurried to the line, grabbed a tray, and pushed through to get a hard loaf of bread, a bowl of warm oatmeal mush and a cup of watered-down tea. When she returned, Ruby was sitting in the exact same position.

"Eat." Bridget set the food in front of her. "Eat, Ruby." She leaned into her ear. "I will contact the detective today, I promise. But you must keep up your strength or he, nor I, will be able to help you."

Ruby nodded without looking at her and picked up her rusty metal spoon.

Bridget stood near her, although her job required she keep watch over several patients. Her thoughts, however, were only on Ruby. Dr. Uber, that cruel, arrogant imbecile. He cared not a whit for the patients. He certainly knew that Ruby was not insane. This was about money. It had to be. What was Thomas paying him to keep his niece locked up? Could she find out? Perhaps there was some clue in Uber's office? Dare she sneak in and search?

Bridget straightened her back and rolled her shoulders. Tonight. Yes, tonight, she would attempt to break in the head doctor's office and search for evidence of his collusion with Thomas Hunt.

For now, true to her promise, Bridget wrote a note to Liam McCarty, urging him to visit. She headed toward the asylum's mail room and stopped before dropping the note in the outgoing slot. Better to give it directly to the ferryman when the boat docked, rather than risk the mailroom.

Later, on that miserable rainy day, she jogged to the ferry landing, raincoat flapping in the wind, hood over her white cap. She never noticed Jane Himmler following her to the dock to hand off the letter.

At two in the morning, Bridget tiptoed down the administrative hall on the second floor. Directly in the middle of the corridor was Dr. Franz Uber's office. As expected, it was locked. She came prepared with two slim ice picks to jiggle the lock with. Growing up in Dublin, she'd had a number of opportunities to do just that, and successfully.

A smile brightened her grim countenance when the lock clicked and the knob turned. With a glance over her shoulder, she stole into the office and flicked on a small torch she'd brought with her. No sense alerting anyone by turning on those damn electric lights.

She stood still and beamed the pale, yellow light around the room. Bridget still marveled at this clever invention, only a few years old. A miracle of science.

Immediately she switched it off and stood still a moment to get her eyes accustomed to the sudden dark. When she could see, she moved to the curtains behind the desk, and yanked them closed. Only then did she turn the torch back on.

She scanned the room for possible places where she might find financial documents. The room was lined with bookcases, floor to ceiling. Impressive. An antique Persian rug covered the wood floor while three handsome arm chairs stood on it, facing the desk.

That's where she would begin. Bridget hurried to the desk and began opening drawers, which, surprisingly, were unlocked. She quickly flipped through folders and notepads, but could find nothing pertinent. Where would he keep bank statements? She kept looking, carefully putting papers back in their exact place so Uber wouldn't notice they'd been disturbed.

Frustrated, she closed the last drawer. To the left of the office door was another door. A closet. Bridget opened the door to find a large file cabinet, heavy oak with a set of four drawers. All locked. Damn, damn. She hustled back to the desk to find keys, but to no avail.

The flashlight was fading as her fear was mounting. She turned off the light, pushed the curtains open, and slipped out of the room. She did not take a solid comfortable breath until she was back in her own room on the first floor. Her hands shook badly.

I guess I'm not cut out for detective work. Or burglary, for that matter. She shook her head and flopped exhausted on her bed. "I'm sorry, Ruby."

Chapter 19

February 2, 1902

Liam knew he was in trouble when he got the message. He had been hounding Thomas Hunt for an interview but the man proved elusive. Finally, this morning, he received a message, hand-delivered by courier to the station house.

Please join me for lunch, 12 noon today at Delmonico's, 56 Beaver Street. Yours truly, Thomas Randolph Hunt

Delmonico's? He must be joking. Or clever. Hunt knew very well that a policeman could not afford a restaurant whose prices did not even appear on the menu. That was, if one could read the menu, which was in French. He would order coffee and beg off lunch.

At 11:15, Liam brushed off his suit jacket, straightened his tie, and headed out. He arrived at Beaver Street by streetcar at two minutes before noon. Perfect. Damn, though, he was hungry. Katz's Deli would have been much more to his liking.

He stood gazing at the façade of the most elite restaurant in New York. Founded in 1827, the elaborate entrance, a Renaissance revival style with ornate marble pillars, graced a corner of two streets. Liam remembered reading about the pillars, famous because John Delmonico had them brought from Pompeii, Italy. Or some such story. There should be a red carpet rolled out in front of such a place for visiting royalty. And he, a lowly policeman. Ha.

He entered and was greeted by the maître de, who led him directly to a table near the far window. On his way, he passed white-clothed tables, dark wood wainscoting, and polished oak floors. He recognized the mayor at a table with several other well-dressed men. Liam ducked his head to avoid scrutiny.

Thomas Hunt sat with a drink in front of him. Scotch, Liam guessed from the color. Or whiskey.

To Liam's surprise, Thomas rose, shook his hand, and both men sat.

A waiter bustled over and handed both men menus.

Liam waved his off. "Sorry, I only have a few minutes."

Thomas smiled. "Of course, you're a busy man." He turned to the waiter. "I shall wait until my friend departs, then order lunch." To Liam, "Will you have a drink?"

"Nothing for me, please." The waiter curled his lip and took back one menu.

Liam settled in his seat and studied the man in front of him. Dressed in dark wool suit, white shirt with high neck collar, and a bow tie matching the suit's color, Thomas Hunt presented the picture of wealth and success.

"Now, Detective McCarty, how can I help you?" Hunt's voice was deep and eloquent with a slight British accent.

Liam had prepared a long list of questions in his mind, but all words now escaped him. He cleared his throat. To buy himself time, he pulled out a notebook and pencil from his jacket pocket.

"I wonder if you could tell me in your own words, what happened on January 3, of this year. As you know it, of course."

"Yes. I planned to meet with my brother, Jonas."

"Ruby's father?"

"Uh, yes. The family always gathered for tea, at least most weekdays, around four o'clock."

"Did they expect you for tea?"

"I assume so."

"There were only four place settings, not five," Liam said. "Was someone else not expected?"

Thomas blinked. "Ruby often shows up late or not at all. It may be the fourth place was actually for me."

"Why does she show up late?"

Thomas set down his drink and shook his head. "Ruby, Ruby. She's a dreamer, always has been, since she was a child, likes to visit museums, art galleries, libraries, shop at the department stores—"

"That makes her a dreamer?"

"Not per se. She has no occupation, just wanders hither and thither, doing whatever she fancies."

"For instance?"

"She goes to Central Park to visit the zoo. I mean, a girl of her age and intelligence really should find something worthwhile to do besides visit the monkeys at the zoo."

Liam smiled. "I find the monkeys rather enjoyable."

"Hm, yes." Thomas swigged his drink and waved to the waiter for another.

"What would you have her do, then? If not wandering hither and thither, that is."

"Well she could take up a worthwhile cause. Work at a hospital or a school."

"I see, charity work."

"Of course, charity work. She needn't get paid," Thomas said.

"She will have money in her own right, now? I mean without the rest of the family to share in the estate?"

Thomas froze in place.

Liam stared at him. "Did I strike a nerve?"

Thomas reached into his jacket pocket and pulled out a cigar, nipped the end off, and took his time lighting it, puffing without looking at Liam.

"I said—"

"I heard the question, detective." Thomas cleared his throat. "Ruby will not be entitled to her inheritance."

"Because she is incarcerated?"

"Correct."

"Who inherits her father's estate?"

"Really, detective, is this relevant to the murder investigation?"

"Money often is a motive for murder."

"I will be appointed her Executor until such time as she is able to handle her own affairs."

"Of course." Liam eyed the whiskey glass, wondering if he could nab it for the fingerprints. It was impossible to get a good look at Thomas' thumb to see if it bore a scar. The glass would tell. "So, tea was set and you got to the apartment at what time?"

"I was a bit late. Thank God or I might not have lived to see the sun rise." He stopped. "I guess it was around five or five-thirty."

"Were the doorman and elevator man there to greet you?"

Thomas raised an eyebrow. "Why yes. Aren't they supposed to be?"

"Yes. Tell me, were there any life insurance policies on family members?"

Thomas coughed out cigar smoke. "What? Are you insinuating that they were killed for the—?"

"Not at all." Liam stopped writing and stared at Thomas. "These are just routine questions."

Thomas regained his composure. "There was, indeed, an insurance policy on all family members. Standard, since we are in the industry."

"And who are the beneficiaries?"

"I haven't looked into that yet. We've got funerals, you know."

Liam didn't see a lie in his eyes. "Go on, please. It's five or five-thirty…"

"The elevator man took me upstairs, where I found the most appalling scene of my life." Thomas sat forward in his chair and put a palm against his forehead. "It was ghastly. Blood everywhere, my brother… God, I get sick thinking about it."

"I understand. Take your time." He waited while Thomas sucked on his cigar.

The waiter delivered Thomas's new drink.

He took a hearty swallow.

Liam was done waiting. "Tell me how you found the bodies."

"My brother and nephew…both were dead in Jonas' room, just lying there…sprawled in their own blood."

"And Ruby?"

"She was clutching Patrick, crying, howling. Pathetic."

"Do you mean her crying over her dead family was pathetic?"

"Of course not. She had every right to cry. It's just, she acted, well, inappropriate."

"How so?" Liam scribbled in his pad.

"She should have gotten help. Called a doctor, or the police? How did she know they were dead?"

"How did you know they were dead?"

"It was plain to see, man. Certainly, they were dead." He waved a hand as if shooing off a fly.

"What about Mrs. Hunt?"

"Laura was in her own room, dead, on her bed. The blood...awful." He bit his cigar as if that would dull the horrific memory.

Liam kept him talking. "What prompted you to go upstairs to the bedrooms?"

"Tea was set, man. Nobody was around. I called out. No one answered. I went looking for them."

"How did you and Ruby get along?"

Thomas threw down a swallow of booze. "We weren't particularly close...but she was a young girl and..." He paused as if taken aback by the question. "Look here, Detective McCarty, it seems to me you would do better with your time than waste it with me. I can't give you any more—"

"If you don't mind, I would like your opinion on something."

"Be careful what you imply, detective. My lawyers will eat your balls for lunch."

"Off the record. Okay?"

Thomas settled back in his chair. "Of course." He blew smoke in Liam's direction. "Shoot."

"Do you really believe Ruby murdered her family?"

Thomas set his black eyes on Liam. "She has always been unstable. One never knew what would set her off."

"Set her off?"

"As a child... Here's an example. Laura got Ruby a kitten when she was about six or seven years old. Unfortunately, the cat got sick, poisoned, somehow. Ruby wouldn't eat or sleep for days. Cried until she drove everyone crazy."

Liam clenched his jaw. "Yes, I see. Definitely unstable." He had trouble forming the next words. "And the doctors agreed with your *unstable* assessment?"

"They most assuredly did. After the cat died, Laura sent Ruby to see a therapist. Don't know if it did any good."

"What about this time? I mean with the murders. You had a psychiatrist evaluate her mental health?"

"Indeed. *Two* gentlemen, eminent in the field of psychiatry agreed she was in a serious state." He paused to crush out his cigar. "Hence, my niece is in an asylum."

"You don't believe her mental state was due to the gruesome murder scene and the fact that she lost her family? Must've upset her much more than a dead cat."

"Her hysteria went far beyond that which is normal. My niece is mentally unfit to be on the streets."

Liam nodded. "Do you think she can, um, get well, recover there on Hart Island?"

"If anyone can help her, Dr. Franz Uber can. I have the utmost faith in him."

"And he is the head doctor?"

"The Superintendent of the women's asylum on Hart Island, yes." Thomas downed his drink. "Now, I'd like to enjoy my lunch, if that is all, detective."

Liam flipped the notebook cover down. "For now. I thank you very much for your time." He stood and as he did he deliberately tipped the table. The empty glass from which Thomas drank pitched off and rolled into the aisle.

"So sorry. I'll get it." Liam picked up the glass by its base and pretended to set it on a nearby waiter's tray when in fact, he stuffed it in his jacket pocket. He turned to make sure Thomas didn't notice the sleight of hand.

Thomas was busy examining the menu.

Liam arrived back at his office just minutes before a winter storm rolled into the city. He took off his coat, hung it on a coat rack and stared out the window at the fluffy white flakes falling thickly from the sky. Getting home tonight would be a nightmare.

He stepped to the outer office, where only a few employees milled about.

"Quiet day, I see," Liam said to no one in particular.

"There's coffee, Liam," a young patrolman called.

"Thanks." He strode to the counter and poured himself a hot cup.

George Twombley moseyed into the room. "I've been looking into the insurance the family held, as you suggested."

Liam sipped coffee and waited.

"Both Thomas and his brother Jonas were in the business, as you know. Hunt Liability and Assets. Seems Jonas took out a very large policy on the entire family."

"The entire family?"

"Yes. Should something happen to Jonas, Laura would inherit. If Laura died, Ruby would inherit, and then Patrick."

"Is that unusual?"

"I doubt it. If you have money, why not ensure your family's future well-being?"

"What about Thomas?"

"Ah, here's where it gets interesting."

Liam shifted in his seat.

"Thomas took out a policy as well. On Jonas and his family as well as his own family. His wife's name is…" George thumbed through his notes. "Frances Sykes."

"Any offspring?"

"Two sons, Lowell and Harrison."

"Do you think Jonas knew his brother had a life insurance policy on the entire family?"

"Doubtful, but then unless Jonas made a concerted effort to look, he wouldn't necessarily know."

"Wouldn't he have had to sign the papers if the policy was on him?" Liam asked.

"Good question. I'll keep digging. Then again, forgery would have been easy for a family member in the insurance business."

Liam blew out a breath. "If Ruby was the only one left alive, she would inherit the Hunt fortune, right?"

George nodded. "However, it's my guess that if Ruby was either locked up in jail or an asylum, she would forfeit any claim to that estate."

Liam stood and stretched. "Let's not guess, let's find out exactly what would happen to that money and the insurance payout."

"What do you think the odds are," George said, "that with Ruby out of the picture, the beneficiary of the Hunt estate would be—?"

"Thomas Hunt."

Liam took home the file case folder that night. He read through it page by page, and by one in the morning he was half-asleep. That's when he noticed an anomaly. On the pages related to the insurance company of Hunt Liability and Assets, were several mentions of the asylum on Hart Island. He read them again and a third time.

Unless he was so tired he couldn't make sense of it, it appeared that three patients, in addition to Ruby Hunt, were insured by the company. All of them were institutionalized within the last two years.

Liam brought the pages under the gaslight so he could read the beneficiary's signature. *Henry Flynn.* Could that be a combination of Henry Grady, the doorman, and Jeremiah Flynn, the elevator man, or just a coincidence? "Don't get carried away," he told himself. Common name, Henry Flynn.

He turned to another policy. This time the beneficiary was Jeremiah Grady.

Liam broke into a wide smile. "Gotcha."

Chapter 20

February 6, 1902

The storm dumped six inches of snow on New York and brought the city to a virtual standstill. Liam tried for four days to board a ferry to Hart Island without luck.

This morning, Saturday, brought sunshine and cold temperatures so he decided to give it another try. The homicide captain had made it clear he was to get this case officially closed and soon. Now, he investigated on his own time.

He rose early, fed himself and his parakeets, and donned his heaviest jacket. On his way out the door, he grabbed his notebook and pencil then jerked a gray and blue striped wool hat snugly onto his head. He'd take the silly looking thing off when he reached his destination.

Flashing his badge, he boarded the ferry to Hart Island. From a distance, he could see another boat at the dock. Squinting, he could read the words on its bow: Riker's Island. This was burial day. Great. Inmates from Riker's Island would be unloading coffins and burying bodies in the giant potter's field. Liam shivered but not from the cold.

He spied the red brick building that served as the woman's lunatic asylum. What was Ruby doing right now? Since he'd met her only a few short weeks ago, he'd had trouble getting her out of his mind. The letter he had received from Bridget Monaghan depressed him and cheered him at the same time. Ruby was not doing well. But, she wanted to see him. Ruby was clear-headed enough to ask for him. She wanted his help and he intended to give it to her.

The ferry blew its horn upon landing and the boat bumpers jolted against the dock. Liam made his way down the ramp and onto the dock. Several inches of snow blanketed the island but the pathways were clear. He strode up the main path to the brick building.

When he entered the main lobby, he yanked off his hat and tucked it in his jacket pocket then strode toward the main office door. An alarm blared, making him jump. The loud, insistent bell kept clanging, and before he could take another step, three men in white jumpsuits shoved him out of the way. Orderlies? Caretakers? He backed himself to the wall and watched. The three raced out the front door and down the steps, and then each flew in a different direction.

Liam thought his head would split when the alarms finally stopped, to be replaced by a voice over a speaker system.

"All security to Gate Six. All security to Gate Six."

At that moment, a number of nurses burst through a doorway that led upstairs. They, too, headed out the main door. One of them was Bridget Monaghan.

She saw him and rushed over.

"Detective, we have an escaped patient and all hands are on deck, so to speak." She touched his arm. "I shan't think we'll be long. This is a...well, a routine escape." She gave him a faint smile. "Normally you would need me to escort you to Miss Ruby, but perhaps—"

"This is a good opportunity to see her alone?"

"She's on the second floor, third door on the left. I shall be back within thirty minutes." And she was off at a run out the door.

Liam smiled to himself and hurried to the staircase. He took the stairs two at a time and found the room. Should he knock? No. He turned the knob and peeked in, then entered. Three women were in the room. Two were asleep in their beds. Ruby was at the window, staring out through the wrought iron bars.

He cleared his throat and she turned, hand at her throat.

"Oh, Detective McCarty." She hurried to him, put her hands on his. "I'm so glad, so glad you've come."

"There seems to be some emergency going on and I took advantage of that, per Bridget's instructions, to visit with you alone for a few minutes."

"Yes, old Mary Broderick escaped again. It's said she does that every two or three days." Ruby shook her head.

Liam noticed her hair was a tangled mess, probably not washed in weeks. Her face looked gaunt and her lips drained of blood. In all, she did not look well. He felt a clenching in his chest.

"Come sit here." Ruby pulled up a chair to her cot.

He sat in the chair.

She sat on the cot, nearly knee to knee with him. "Detective—

"Call me Liam, please."

"I did not kill my family. I found them..." She swallowed. "I believe you."

"Do you, really?"

"I'm a man of science, Ruby. Scientific evidence points in a direction other than you."

"Can you help me?"

He pulled out his notebook and pencil. "I have questions for you, if you are up to it."

"Yes."

"Tell me in your own words what happened." He needed to find discrepancies in the stories between Ruby and her uncle.

After Ruby's account, Liam asked, "Was your Uncle Thomas expected for tea?"

"He sometimes came, but I don't know about that day. I never saw him."

"You saw four tea cups set out, three had liquid in them. You were to be the fourth?"

"Yes." She smiled. "I was often late for tea. I so enjoy visiting Central Park. Do you?"

"Yes, in fact, I do."

"An oasis in the city of concrete and stone." She dropped her head. "Silly, right?"

"Not silly. Perceptive," he said, feeling his face heat up.

"When I arrived home, the house was so quiet, unusually so. Patrick always had music playing on that new contraption of his." She looked at him. "I went into the kitchen to see if anyone was about and there was a pot boiling on the stove. I turned it off."

"Was that odd?"

"Mother always cooked dinner when the servants were gone. They were gone that night." She frowned. "But she would never let the pot boil like that. She was very careful." Ruby stared at the wall.

"Ruby?"

"I can't believe they're gone."

"I'm sorry," he said.

"No, I'm sorry. I dither. Ask me more questions, please."

"Tell me about Thomas." He prepared to take notes.

She looked up at the water-stained ceiling. "He was, frankly, not well-liked by any of us. Even my father made fun of his pompous attitude. Patrick thought he was far too serious, and I, well, he gave me the creeps."

"What do you mean?"

"Always staring at me with those black, cold eyes. He never smiles, you know. Patrick thought he was born without a sense of humor."

"What about business? Did he work with your father in the insurance business?"

"He did."

Liam looked up from his scribbling. "Do you think Thomas is trying to get your release?"

She pursed her lips, stuck her chin out. "I think he wants me to remain here all the rest of my days."

"But, why?"

"I...am not sure..." She broke off.

"You must have a guess."

"Thomas thinks I'm a scatterbrain, a dolt. After all, I'm a woman and he has little regard for female intelligence. He doesn't know I have knowledge of my father's affairs. I was made privy to his will, a year ago, on my eighteenth birthday." Her eyes glittered.

Liam uncrossed his legs and sat up. "Tell me about that."

"If anything was to happen to my father, the entire estate was to go to my mother. Yes, even as a *woman*." Ruby emphasized the last word. "Father believed my mother could handle the family financial affairs. And she could. My mother was brilliant."

Liam nodded.

"If anything were to happen to her, I would be next in line, then Patrick."

Liam looked up at her, saw the beginning of tears in her eyes.

She leaped up. "Oh, why wasn't I killed too? Death would be better than . . .this." She stopped. "Why Liam, why am I not dead?"

"You weren't there. If you had come home early from the Park, Ruby, you might be dead too."

Ruby collapsed onto the cot, tears streaming down her cheeks.

At that moment, the door squeaked open. Bridget stole in. "Sorry, I don't mean to intrude." She saw Ruby's tears. "Oh, Miss Ruby, what is it? Are you okay?"

Ruby moaned aloud. "I'm all right." But she continued to cry into the threadbare blanket.

"There's only a few minutes before your next treatment, my dear. I'm so sorry."

Ruby sat up, her face a mask of shock and tears. "No, please, please."

"I'll be with you, pet. I promise."

Liam asked, "What is this treatment?"

"It's the very latest in psychiatric treatments," Bridget said. "Electroconvulsive shock therapy. It's been proven successful in a number of cases. But it can be a bit, er, uncomfortable."

Liam stared at Ruby. He had read up on this treatment. Barbaric. Patients were strapped down onto a hard board while wires were hooked up to their heads. A stick was placed in their mouths so they wouldn't bite off their tongues, and then a switch was thrown...my God. My God. Liam wanted to protect Ruby but he could think of no way. If only he could stuff her in his pocket and escape.

Ruby cried into her hands. "No, no, please, Bridget. I cannot bear it. My very self disappears after the shock...I am no longer me. Please." Tears came rapidly now. She turned terrified eyes onto Liam. "Arrest me, Liam, so I can go to jail instead of this horrid place."

"I have no jurisdiction here...no authority..."

Bridget took her hand and pulled her up from the cot. "We must go now."

"Or better yet, Liam, kill me, please. Kill me, Liam."

He felt his heart punch his ribcage.

Bridget stood above still-seated Liam. "You'd better go, detective, before we all get into trouble."

Liam took Ruby's free hand. "Be strong, Ruby. You must be strong. I will return, I promise. Bear up to the treatments as best you can. I shall help you."

❧

When Ruby left the room, Liam grabbed Bridget's arm. "I must speak with you. Alone."

"Out near the ferry, there are some benches. I'll be about an hour." Then she hurried down the hall after Ruby.

Liam walked in circles around the benches, the cold dousing his burning anger. He sat, perused his notes, stood and paced. To the dock and back again and again. Finally, he saw Bridget approaching him at a fast pace.

"How is she?"

"For the next day and a half she will be nearly comatose. Sleeping most of the time." She looked at Liam and saw in his face shock and angst at Ruby's plight. "But, she will be calmer after that. Better able to cope with this horrid place."

"I need to ask you to do something for me."

She opened her mouth, then closed it and waited.

He pulled out his notebook and flipped pages. "There were three other patients here in the last two years that were committed and..." He stopped when he saw Bridget's eyes get big around. "You know who I'm speaking about, don't you?"

Bridget stared at the distance over his shoulder. "Yes, I know exactly the women you mean. They weren't my patients, but everyone gossips around here, so..." She shrugged.

"Why do you remember them specifically?"

"Their situations were very much like Ruby's. They were discarded by their husbands or families on the pretense they were insane."

"Aren't many women brought here under that pretense?"

"Actually, there are patients who do belong here. They are, indeed, mentally disturbed. These three women *were* different."

"They weren't crazy?"

"Ruby isn't crazy." Bridget shook her head. "They weren't crazy either."

"Do you know their names?"

Bridget's bottom lip quivered. "Yes, but what does it matter? They all died within a few months of arriving here."

Liam stared at her. "How? How did they die? They were young, no?"

Bridget wrung her hands. "Aye, they were young. Like Ruby. They were not in my care, so I cannot say exactly, but I'm told they took sick in their stomachs...I doubt from the horrid food."

Liam felt his own stomach clench. This did not bode well for Ruby. Not well at all.

New York City
2016

Chapter 21

May 17, 2016

The day had been sunny, dry and spectacular, and the evening carried the same theme. Frank's step was light and it was due to more than the weather.

Rachel Bejarano, librarian extraordinaire waited on the library steps next to Patience, the lion. Or was it Fortitude? He could never remember which was north and which was south. Rachel would know. She looked as sunny as the day in a yellow top, white skirt and white jacket. Her dark hair was loose and swung around her shoulders. Gladiator sandals were on her feet, and even from here he spotted red paint on her toenails. More important, there was a bounce in her step. Like his.

"You made it," she said. "So where are we going?"

"I'm ashamed to say I used my clout with the NYPD to get us reservations right around the corner."

"Bryant Park?"

"Yup."

"Wow. I'm impressed. A day like this, tourists in droves and you get a reservation for us...I'm impressed."

"So you said."

"Doubly impressed. Not bad for a first date, mister."

They both laughed and walked side by side around the block to the outdoor area of the Bryant Park Grill where dozens of wrought iron tables, chairs and colorful umbrellas sat below the level of the library. Flowers abounded in pots all around. A woman greeted them, showed them to a table, and gave them menus. Once they ordered, both sat back with sighs of pleasure.

They small-talked for a few minutes before their drinks arrived. Rachel had ordered a Cosmo, Frank a draft beer.

"Tell me about Frank Mead. Just a little so I know who I'm dealing with."

"Fair enough. I'm forty-nine, a native of New York, lower east side, to be exact. My mom still lives there. I have a brother and a sister here." He paused, unsure of whether to mention his wife, then: "I was married. My wife died sixteen years ago. I have an amazing daughter, Amanda, who is a reporter for the New York Times."

"I'm impressed again." She laughed.

He nodded, a proud father. "Let's see, what else?"

"Have you always been a cop?"

"Family tradition. My father and grandfather were cops. Here in this great city. I graduated John Jay College of Criminal Justice back in, well, never mind." He swigged his beer. "I was in DC for a while but then came back when my mom was going through chemo..."

"Oh, sorry."

"She's okay. Doing well, in fact. You'd like her. She's a feisty old gal."

She smiled. "What's her name?"

"Lizzie."

"Sounds feisty."

"Okay. Quid pro quo. Tell me about Rachel."

She sipped her drink. "Not terribly much to tell. I'm 42. Grew up in Brooklyn, Prospect Park. Married and divorced, no children." She stirred her Cosmo with the swizzle stick. "Always been a bookworm. Read all the Nancy Drew and Hardy Boys books by the time I was in third grade. Then it was the classics—"

"Hey, the Hardy Boys were classics."

"Ha, they sure were...are. I went to NYU for undergraduate and graduate school in the library sciences and, about ten years ago, landed this cushy job at the greatest library in the world since Alexandria."

"Better than the Library of Congress?"

"Of course, because I work here and not there."

"Now I'm impressed." He gazed into his amber brew, thinking she might be a valuable resource. "You must know a bit about research."

"A wee bit."

"Would you be interested in helping me on this case?"

Rachel practically bounced in her seat. "Would I? I was hoping you'd ask."

The waiter came with their orders and they ate quietly, both in their own heads for a while.

"Let me tell you about it," he said.

Her hazel eyes sparkled and he felt a jolt of desire. He tried to swallow but found his throat so dry he had to drink some iced water from a glass on the table. He hadn't felt this attracted to a woman since Maggie Thornhill.

Pull yourself together, Frank.

He gave her a full summary of the case, beginning with Sophie's death and ending back in 1902 with the Hunt murders.

Rachel blinked. "So, Detective Liam McCarty was heading up the investigation?"

"Yes, but his hands were tied. The boss wanted him to wrap it up, but he wasn't satisfied with the rush to justice, so he continued the investigation on his own time."

"How do you know that?"

"From his murder book."

"What's that?"

"His case files on the murders," Frank explained. "Somebody had killed him for that book."

"Are you suggesting that Liam was thrown under the train…that it wasn't an accident?"

"Exactly."

The waiter came by, removed their plates. They ordered desserts and coffee.

"I'm in," she said. "What can I do?"

He pulled out a notebook and pen. "There are several family trees I need to track. Most of them people related to Hart Island and the Women's Lunatic Asylum in the early 1900s. We managed to track Bridget

Monaghan's descendants and that was a coup, but we're having trouble finding any other heirs from the hospital staff, that is, the nurses, doctors and caretakers. Do you have access to that kind of information?"

She finished her drink. "There are archives from all the institutions on the islands. Blackwell's Island, City Island, Hart Island. You know, of course, there is a major movement on Hart to allow people who believe they have relatives buried there to visit?"

"I do. In fact, Amanda is writing a story on it."

"That's great. Let me check into it. I'll find those descendants for you."

"You're a peach."

The waiter set their desserts on the table.

"Wait 'til you see what else I can do." She winked.

The next morning, Frank's first stop was to the Office of the Chief Medical Examiner. He needed a favor and Dr. Serena Oliver was the person who could provide it. After he parked in front of the building at 421 E. 26th Street, he threw his NYPD placard in the windshield and looked at his watch: *7:10*. No problem. Serena would be there.

A young man, with a name tag that read Raoul, sat at the entry desk where Frank showed his badge and asked to see the Chief. Raoul called up, gave Frank's name and nodded.

"She's on her way."

"Thanks." While Frank waited he wandered over to a plaque on the wall that read: *OCME serves public health and the criminal justice system through forensic science. Our independent investigations of deaths and analysis of evidence provide answers to families and communities during the most challenging of times.*

If he recalled correctly, OCME had been around about a hundred years and was the largest medical examiner's office in the country.

"Frank Mead, to what do I owe this pleasure?" Serena Oliver stepped out of the elevator, smiling. She wore a dark brown suit, white shirt and no jewelry but an expensive-looking watch.

He grinned back at her and they clasped hands. Old friends and colleagues, they'd shared many a grim murder story.

"Come on, let's get a coffee," she said.

"Oh, yes." He followed her out the door and down the street to Starbuck's. "What no cafeteria coffee?"

"You got that right." She turned to order for them and Frank picked up the tab. They sat at a table near the window.

"By the way, nothing from DNA on those hairs found at the scene. No match in the system."

"That was quick. I wasn't expecting anything for a month or two."

"You know how many cases we've got?" She smiled and sipped her caramel latte. "There was a mix-up and your case went to the head of the line."

"Serena, you never cease to amaze me."

"What do you want to talk to me about?"

"I need a body exhumed."

"Oh? Do you have the family's permission?"

"The body is on Hart Island and was buried in 1902."

"You ought to write novels."

"I'm serious."

"The Hart potter's field is off limits, you know that. Besides, 1902? Could be nothing left but dust, if that much."

"I'm working on the Sophie Hunt murder."

"Ouch. How's a body from 1902 going to help?"

"Over a hundred years ago, the family of Sophie's great, great grandfather, Thomas Hunt, was murdered. Allegedly by the nineteen-year-old daughter of the same family. Ruby Hunt. She wound up in an insane asylum on Hart Island and died there, somewhat mysteriously."

"Are you saying these two murders, a century apart, are connected?"

"Yes. And I need your help to prove it."

Serena sighed. "All right. If I buy this connection, how will we find her body on Hart? There are a million graves on that island, Frank."

He pulled out Bridget's map and explained. "It's right here."

Serena's eyes went wide. "What is this, Treasure Island?"

"I believe this map is more authentic." He put his finger on a marked location. "I believe this is where Ruby Hunt is buried."

She looked down at the map then up at him. "Okay, let's say that's the case. Are there any descendants left alive to approve such an exhumation?"

"There is a great, great, grand-nephew, but I don't believe we need his permission. This is a full-on homicide investigation, and I can get a court order if need be."

"Of course, my office would conduct the exhumation."

"Of course. That's the good news." Frank grinned.

Serena set down her coffee. "So, what do you want from me?"

"Answer me this. What can a hundred and fourteen-year-old dead body give up as far as evidence?"

"Do you have a few hours?"

"How about a few minutes?"

She breathed out a long exhalation. "All right. Let's say we find the body in the spot marked on the map. Let's also say the body is not so deteriorated that there are only bone fragments or nothing at all."

"What are the chances of that?"

"Small, but it's possible some bone fragments or hair strands could've survived. Depends on conditions in the ground and exactly how she was buried. I assume she wasn't embalmed?"

"In a mental institution? A hundred years ago?"

"Hmm, good point. If there are skeletal remains, we'd try to pinpoint certain attributes: gender, approximate age, height, etc. That's the easy part. Then we need to take DNA samples from any tissue remaining, or bones."

"Right, and match it with a family descendant to prove it's Ruby."

"Is there a descendant?"

"Yup. David Hunt. He'd be Ruby's cousin, three generations removed."

She nodded.

"So, we ID her. How do we determine if poisoning was the cause of death? Toxicology?"

"Most toxins which were in the tissues would be lost to decay, but the heavy metals like lead, mercury or arsenic, would likely survive in the bones or, better yet, the hair."

"Arsenic," Frank said. "Probably easy to come by then in rat poison or--"

"Yes. Another poison, however, is not so easy to identify." She paused, finished the last sip of her coffee. "The other variable is this: in order to find the poison in her hair, Ruby would've had to have ingested poison in small amounts over days or weeks. A single dose wouldn't find its way into her hair. The bones may or may not hold the remnants either."

"Cumulative effect?"

"Precisely."

"Hell, I'm betting that's exactly what we'll find." Frank jumped up. "Thanks, Serena, I'll be in touch real soon."

"Where are you off to?" Serena asked.

"I've got to go dig up a grave."

Chapter 22

May 18, 2016

Madelyn Hunt took a breath and surveyed the chaos in her kitchen. She had emptied the pantry. Cans, boxes, plastic bags, and condiment bottles of all shapes and sizes cluttered every counter surfaces. She shook open a large black trash can and began examining each food item, one by one, for the expiration date. Those that even came close to expiring went into the bag.

"Jesus Christ, Madelyn, what are you doing?" David Hunt stormed into the kitchen and ran his hands through his dark gray-streaked hair.

Madelyn stopped, turned. "I'm cleaning. What do you think I'm doing?"

He shook his head. "Why?"

"Because the pantry needs cleaning." Her voice dribbled to a squeak.

"That's what we pay cleaning people for, Madelyn, so you don't have to do it."

She looked at him, then at the clutter, then back to him. "I don't mind doing it. It will save money."

David let out a deep exhalation. "We don't need to save that little bit of money. Why would you think we do?"

"I've heard you talking to Ronnie," she said, referring to their accountant. "Tell me the truth, David. Are we in financial difficulties?"

"Of course not. I would tell you, Maddie. Sometimes we just have to move money from one account to another. But there's no problem, really. Really."

"I'm not stupid, you know." She smiled. "Just crazy."

He smiled back half-heartedly. "Have at it then." He left.

Madelyn watched his back. It used to be tall and straight, now it was bent and shorter. Not from age, but from the weight he carried on his shoulders.

What is that heavy weight? And how can I find out?

At ten that night, David still worked in his office downstairs. Madelyn had already turned in when she heard the doorbell. She donned her robe and went to the top of the stairs and peeked down. David opened the door to the *Doctor*. That's what she called him, anyway. Dr. Roger Steinberg, Superintendent of Aurora Lifetime Living facilities.

Why was he here so late? Something was wrong, she knew it, felt it in her bones.

David led Steinberg into his office, but did not completely close the door.

Madelyn tiptoed down and crept close to the light that angled from the room. She could hear every word.

"HCFA is on my ass, and I promise you I will not be the one to go down," Steinberg said.

HCFA? Madelyn did not know what that was, although the acronym sounded familiar.

"Relax, Roger. I'll handle it."

Madelyn heard a match strike. David was smoking again.

"You can't handle it. Clearly. That's why we're in this mess."

"There's no mess—"

"Oh, but there is, David. The last, er, account is under investigation."

"You mean, the Sandfords?"

"I do. The family wasn't happy with the death certificate. They want a post-mortem."

"Shit," David whispered.

"Shit is what we're in. Deep."

"What will they find in the autopsy?"

"That old Mrs. Sandford took too many meds."

"That's not unusual."

"Except for the fact that she was never prescribed those meds to begin with."

"How did—?"

"We picked the wrong patsy this time," Steinberg said. "The old lady was perfect. Ditzy, losing it, all her organs were going to shut down soon, but..."

"But what?"

"The family was ruthless in their interference."

David said, "Too many pompous asses trying to prove they were right. And no doubt fighting over her fortune."

"Believe it or not, it was her granddaughter who caused all the stink. The meek little mouse really loved the old bag. She wouldn't accept the cause of death.

"Her own insurance company had no problem."

Roger scoffed. "Wouldn't have been if not for the Medicare billing. That's why HCFA is getting involved. Her own insurance company had no problem."

Madelyn heard Roger sit down on the couch. The leather squeaked.

"Maybe we should cut back, you know, for a while, until this cools down," David said.

"I intend to."

Silence lasted a full minute and Madelyn shifted on her feet, afraid she was missing some of the conversation.

"There's something else we need to discuss," Roger said.

"What's that?"

"Sophie Hunt."

David jumped up, and his chair rammed into the bookcase behind him. "What about Sophie?"

"The cops are still investigating."

"Of course they are. That's their job. They want to find her killer."

"But we know who the killer is, don't we?"

"What are you talking about?"

"Let's say, I have my theories. Theories that the cops would love to entertain," Roger said.

"You're nuts, you know. What theories? You're a detective now?"

"Relax, my friend, your secret is safe with me. As long as we, um, work together on this."

"I don't know what the hell you're talking about."

"Look at it as your insurance policy, David."

Madelyn heard her husband collapse into his chair.

"What do you want, Roger?"

"A bigger cut of our business arrangement."

"I see. So this is blackmail."

"Ugh. Ugly word. Nah, this is just a new, call it updated, contract. I continue to oversee the facilities, bill Medicare for those special cases…and I promise to make sure we dot every 'i' and cross every 't'. For that I get a bit more of the proceeds."

"How much, you god damn backstabber?"

"Now don't be crass, David."

"How much?"

"Let's just turn the figures around. Instead of forty-sixty, let's make it sixty-forty."

"You are fucking out of your mind."

Madelyn held her hand over her mouth to prevent a gasp from escaping.

"I think that's eminently fair, with all the information I have at my fingertips. You cannot afford to lose me, David. Let's be realistic."

A loud thump caused Madelyn to back up a step. But evidently David had only slammed a book on the desk.

The couch leather squealed again and Roger said, "Think about it, David. This is the best deal you're going to get from me."

"I can end your contract here and now, you know. You can't afford to go to the cops with this fraud scheme since you are up to your eyeballs in it."

"Correct. But I'm not up to my eyeballs in murder."

"I had no part in any murder."

"Even an accidental shooting gets substantial jail time, I believe. How would you handle prison, my friend?"

Madelyn heard footsteps moving toward the office door. She dashed to the stairs and flew up them two at a time.

The two men walked out into the entry hall.

Steinberg opened the front door. "Think on what I said. It's a good deal to stay out of prison."

The doctor slammed the door behind him.

David leaned his head on the door, trying to calm his heart. He turned and paced the hallway, wringing his hands. His breathing was uneven and he felt sweat run down his back. He wiped beads of it off his upper lip. What could he do? There must be some way out of this. Damn that Steinberg. What did he really know about Sophie?

Could I risk him blabbing to the cops? Feeling unsteady, he went to the steps and sat down on the third one from the bottom. He sat for long minutes contemplating his future, gazing into his life behind bars. That's when his eye caught it.

Madelyn's slipper lying on the first step.

Chapter 23

May 19, 2016

Frank, Will, and Amanda stood below deck on the ferry to Hart Island. A storm had blown in, the leading edge of an early season hurricane now battering the coast of the Carolinas, Georgia, and Florida. Sea spray on the windows blurred their vision and the boat rocked uncomfortably.

"Shit," Will said. "I hate funerals. But I really hate funerals in the rain."

"This isn't a funeral," Amanda said. "Although, maybe after this, Ruby Hunt can get a real funeral...if the family, that is, would claim her body... never mind."

Frank put his arm around her shoulder. "Yeah, I think they'll give her a proper burial." He was thinking of Madelyn Hunt. "But let's not get ahead of ourselves. We've got to make sure it's her, first. Hopefully, there will be enough remains to—"

"Okay, okay," Amanda said. "I know the process."

"Somehow it seems even more morbid on Hart Island," Frank said.

The rain whipped across the windows, blurring their view. Temperatures hovered in the eighties, so at least they weren't chilly.

"The M-E's office should already be there," Will said. "They took an earlier ferry with their equipment."

"Serena should be thrilled at the prospect." Frank smiled to himself.

"I hope I don't barf," Amanda said.

"At the exhumation?" Frank asked.

"No, on this rocking boat. Jeez."

A few minutes later, they docked, crashing into the pier several times before they could tie up. A member of the M-E's team met them and introduced himself as Carlos. Frank helped Amanda off. Will followed, none too steadily, and they ducked their heads into the fierce wind and pelting rain and headed inland behind Carlos.

"Good thing Carlos was here," Will shouted in the wind. "How the hell would we ever find that X on the map?"

"I'm surprised Dr. Oliver didn't opt to postpone," Amanda yelled.

"That would just mean a long wait for our investigation," Frank reminded them.

They pushed forward. In the distance, they could see a large white tent, its flaps blowing. The tent looked big enough for a White House party.

"Hope that thing is laced down good," Will said. "Can't afford to raise the dead and have them blown into dust."

"Ugh, thanks for that," Amanda said.

Will smiled. "Sorry."

They reached the enclosure and ducked underneath the flaps.

"Zip up," shouted Serena. "We're all here now."

A man in white coveralls zipped the flaps closed and suddenly the wind and rain were shut out. It was almost quiet.

Will looked around. "This is a serious tent."

"This is serious business," Serena said.

"Oh God," Amanda said, her voice hushed.

"What?" Frank turned to see what she was looking at. In the middle of the tent stood a long, narrow mound of dirt. "What...I mean, is that it?"

"From the map you gave me, Frank, I couldn't determine the exact location of the grave, so I tented over the general area. Part of a very long trench. I think we're in the right vicinity of that X." She took a breath and turned to them. "Be clear. I can only hope the body of Ruby Hunt is one of the ones we'll dig up."

"One of the...oh, my God," Amanda said.

"Remember, this is a pauper's cemetery. There could be a dozen bodies that've been buried here, over who knows how many years," Frank said.

"The best we can do, is find remains that seem to fit her description. And go from there."

A strong gust shook the tent.

Serena pointed to a pile of white garments. "Now put on those suits and let's get going. I can't guarantee how long this tent will stay intact."

When the three of them were dressed in white uniforms, complete with hoods and masks, they stood waiting.

Serena gave the signal to her team and they grabbed their shovels.

"Wouldn't a backhoe have been easier?" Will asked.

"This is an archaeological dig, Will," Serena said. "You have to move the earth in a meticulous manner. You don't want to jumble all the bones, you see."

Will shuddered. "Right."

"Also," Serena said, "These bodies were buried without ceremony, without family members, without a box—"

"Wait," Will said. "Without a box, you mean a coffin?"

"In 1900, they were just rolled in a shroud, a sheet most probably. Cheaper, easier, lighter weight," Amanda offered.

"And you could fit many more bodies in one grave," Frank added.

"Ugh," Amanda said.

"Careful, Carlos," Serena said. "Just remove the top layer and then probe below every six inches or so."

Carlos wiped his forehead. Despite the storm outside, temps were high. Several fans, powered by a generator, were blowing in the tent, but it felt like a furnace inside. He bent down and began to cautiously dig into the earth.

"*Madre Dios*," he said and jumped back.

"What?" Serena asked.

"I hit something, she soft."

"You mean like a corpse?"

"Mebbe, yes, a corpse."

"Go on, Carlos, gently, gently," Serena said.

"Yes, ma'am." He lowered the shovel into the grave and began moving dirt.

Serena said. "Get another helper to get in and see what's there."

Two men came closer. Carlos stepped carefully into the trench, his face scrunched into a grimace. "There's something here, wrapped in a sheet or something," he said.

"Well, bring it up, then," Serena ordered.

The men did. They rolled the shrouded body above ground and climbed out.

Serena bent to uncover it. Within a few minutes, she covered it back up. "Nope, this is a male."

Frank coughed and stepped forward to look.

"Uh, I'll stay back here," Amanda said.

Serena shouted orders. "Let's go, back in, boys."

Carlos began moving dirt again in the trench. Within a minute, his shovel hit a hard surface. Everyone heard it. Metal on wood.

"Whoa," Carlos said.

Frank, Will, Amanda and Serena, along with two other work men rushed to Carlos' side.

Carlos touched his shovel to the dirt again, this time, scraping from side to side.

He tapped on something solid.

"Shit," Frank said. "A coffin?"

Carlos dropped his shovel and got to his knees. He began moving dirt with his hands, throwing it off left and right. Before long, he leaned back. They could all see it. A pine box, worn, blackened by years of dirt.

"I don't get it," Amanda said.

"Okay, calm down, everyone. This is a graveyard, after all. Some bodies may have been buried in coffins. Boys, let's raise this box...carefully."

The three men cleared the box of dirt entrapping it and with thick, heavy straps wrapped around two ends and the middle, aided by the others, pulled the box from its ancient grave.

A smell came with it. A smell of long confined ash and dust. Not the smell of new death, but of musty, century-old decay.

They set the coffin on the ground near the trench. All stood looking down at it, deep in their own thoughts. Carlos made the sign of the cross.

"I don't see any markings on the box," Frank said. "Nothing to indicate who's buried here...or when."

Serena said, "Gentlemen, please open the casket. Frank and company, please stay back for now."

Frank was ready to jump out of his skin. He knew Will and Amanda felt the same.

Carlos reached for a pry bar and gently pried the top loose. Finally, when the top was no longer nailed down, the other two men helped him lift it off.

Frank, Amanda, and Will rushed to the edge of the box.

"Okay," Serena said. "This is more promising. Remains of a female, probably young." She kept probing. "Wearing a torn, filthy hospital gown. No surprise there. Her hair was dark, almost black."

Frank leaned in and saw the strands of hair crisscrossing her body. He looked across the coffin at Serena. "What the hell?"

"She was well-preserved," Serena said, in a whisper. "Someone cared about her enough to bury her in a coffin."

Frank had no doubt who that someone was. "Bridget."

Serena started giving orders, jolting Frank out of his reverie. "I want this box going back in exactly this condition. Nothing gets left behind."

"The whole box goes back?" Amanda said.

"There could be evidence in it," Frank said.

"And, we need to move," Serena barked. "If we don't get her back within seventy-two hours and chilled down to four degrees, she will decompose rapidly and we'll have nothing, no one to examine."

The men hurried to move the coffin to a truck and drove down to the dock. This time a special Coast Guard boat awaited them.

"I called it in," Serena said. "No time to waste."

She turned to Carlos. "Stay behind and examine that trench for any more remains that might be the girl. Just in case this coffin holds someone else. Be gentle, Carlos. We don't know how many more corpses are in there. Then close it up and—"

"Say a prayer for the dead. *Sí*, chief."

By the next morning, Frank had most of the answers he needed from the post-mortem. Serena, true to her word, worked through the night.

At eight a.m. she and Frank sat together at her favorite Starbuck's in the Village.

"So, the body is that of Ruby Hunt?" he asked.

Serena sipped her latte. "DNA will take a while, as you know, so we cannot jump to conclusions that it will match."

"It will match," he said. "I know it will."

"I tend to agree with you, based on her size, age, and coloring. But, Frank, I will not declare the body to be Ruby Hunt until the DNA is confirmed."

"Right."

"And, before you ask, I will confirm how she died. Arsenic poisoning, slow and methodical. In her tissues and her hair."

"Someone knew what they were doing?"

"If Ruby Hunt arrived at the asylum middle of January and died just three months later, the poisoning had to have begun almost immediately."

Frank stared at his cup of java. "Jesus. Someone wanted her dead, not just out of the way."

"I'd say that was a good bet." Serena shook her head. "What could this poor girl have done to have someone want her dead so badly?"

"I doubt it had anything to do with her. I think it had to do with the almighty dollar."

"Hmph."

They fell silent.

"What now, Frank?"

"Now I have to connect Ruby's death to Sophie's death. It wouldn't surprise me if the motive behind both murders is the same."

New York City
1902

Chapter 24

February 7, 1902

As she was awakening, for a miraculous moment, Ruby believed she was home. In the safety of her own room, surrounded by her possessions. Her musical jewelry box, which played Handel's Messiah when the lid was lifted, her collection of buttons from her wardrobe, and her most precious treasure, her books.

She closed her eyes again, allowed her thoughts to settle on those wonderful stories. *Alice of Vincennes, Unleavened Bread, Sister Carrie*, and her favorite, *The Wonderful Wizard of Oz*. Oh, if only the Wizard would save her.

Ruby was shaken from her musings at the sound of a door slamming and voices screaming across the hallway. Her eyelids were melded together with a fine web of tears. When she wrenched them open, she wished she hadn't. Nothing had changed. The paint still peeled off the walls. Roaches still scurried across the ceiling. The window, covered with metal bars and wire mesh, still threw no light on the room. She shifted in bed and felt a sharp stab where a broken spring jabbed her.

She sat up, felt light-headed, and dropped her head back onto her pillow. *Oh God, oh God. I am still here. Why do I feel so utterly fatigued, so weak? Did they give me more drugs? Wait, no, I remember. The treatment. I had the dreaded treatment that Margaret had told me about.* Margaret, the first patient she'd encountered here, her only friend in this

God-forsaken place besides Bridget. Where was Margaret? Why hadn't she seen her recently? She must ask Bridget. The thought skipped away to the far reaches of her mind.

Ruby pressed the sides of her head with her hands, probing her brain to remember. The treatment had done this to her. But what was the treatment? Glimmers came back like tiny pinpricks on her skin. Memories that flitted like dreamscapes, just out of reach. She remembered lying on a hard table, wires attached to her head. A nurse held her shoulders, another her legs. They pinned her knees down, shoved a stick in her mouth. Then someone shouted 'now.' A jolt went through her from her head to her toes. And she shook and shook until her body felt like it would convulse into a pile of broken bones. Then...all went black.

How long ago? How long had she been asleep? Comatose. Hours...a day...more? Bridget, Bridget, where were you? Why didn't you help me?

"Oh, shut up, already," a voice nearby said.

"What?"

"I said shut up. You been shouting and mumbling away. I need ta' sleep, fer God's sake."

"But I was thinking. I didn't speak aloud...did I?"

"Shut up," her roommate shrieked.

Ruby pulled the covers up. Her body started to quake. She could no longer tell what was real. She lapsed into a stupor, neither awake nor asleep. In this depressed limbo, she was jolted awake by someone shaking her.

"Ruby, get up, wake up." It was Bridget.

Ruby struggled to open her eyes and push herself into a sitting position on the bed.

"Whaaa?"

"Get up, dove, the doctor wants to see you." Bridget helped her stand and walk about the room a few paces. "This could be a good thing, my pet. Come on, now."

The doctor? This notion shot a stream of adrenaline into her body and Ruby came alive. She shook herself, moved around the room faster.

"Let's fix your hair, then." Bridget brought a brush out from her apron and began to brush Ruby's tangle of hair. Soon, it looked smooth but so much had fallen out from her ordeal, that the thick locks were now wispy and fine.

Bridget wiped Ruby's face with a wet cloth, but the bluish circles under her eyes wouldn't wash away.

"There, you look lovely, my dear. Let's go, the doctor is—"

The door burst open and Jane Himmler led Dr. Uber into the cell.

Bridget jumped to attention. "Wait now, we were coming to your office, Doctor. There's no need for you to come here."

"Never mind," Uber spat. "I'm here now." He looked at Ruby who stared at him. "Sit down, Miss Hunt."

Ruby sank down onto her cot.

He sat next to her, put his thumbs under her eyes and pulled down the lower lids. "Yes, I see."

"What do you see?" Ruby asked. Her body tensed with anticipation.

"I believe a new treatment can help you."

"The only treatment that can help me is release. I must get out of here." Ruby pushed away his hands.

"Ahh, I see I was right. She is much too volatile to be on her own."

"No, I am fine. There's nothing wrong with me, nothing." Her voice rose an octave.

"You are getting agitated."

"Yes, I am getting agitated. This is frightfully unfair. I do not belong here." Ruby practically shrieked.

Bridget placed her hands on her shoulders to calm her. "What new treatment, Doctor?"

"It has been developed by a colleague and has shown promise of success with patients such as Ruby."

"No, no..." Ruby began to cry.

"It helps the mind relax."

"What does?" Bridget said.

"Insulin therapy. It will induce a coma which will calm the entire nervous system."

Ruby glanced up at Himmler who smiled.

"But," Bridget said, "a coma...how does she come out of a coma?"

"There's every chance," Uber said, "that she can recover. Every chance." He stood. "Yes, I think that is the next therapy for Miss Hunt." He turned to Himmler. "Miss Himmler when is the shipment of insulin arriving?"

"It should be here in a week, Doctor."

"Good. We will see you then, Miss Hunt."

He flew out the door with Jane Himmler on his heels.

Ruby clutched at Bridget's hand. "Don't let them give me this treatment, Bridget. Please, please, don't let them..." her voice cracked into sobs. "I didn't kill my family."

Bridget stood there, helpless, not knowing what to say to comfort her. Finally, she left. She prayed that she would hear from Detective Liam McCarty soon. She could not help Ruby alone.

Two days later, Liam scribbled in his notebook until three in the morning. He had to organize his thoughts.

Bullet point 1:

Ruby would, indeed, lose her inheritance if she were locked up, either in jail or in an asylum. Good old Uncle Thomas would be the sole beneficiary of his brother's estate.

Bullet point 2:

Three young women had died of stomach ailments at Hart Island in a short period of time. All were healthy. All were wealthy. The names of their beneficiaries were a suspicious amalgamation of the elevator man, Henry Grady, and the door man, Jeremiah Flynn.

Liam was convinced the two had deliberately set the fire in the basement as a ruse to disappear from their posts prior to Ruby's arrival.

Bullet point 3:

Stomach ailments could be induced by poison. But what kind of poison? All his research showed that arsenic was a good bet. If given a little over several weeks or months, the victim would manifest stomach ills and eventually die. Arsenic was easy to come by and could be readily mixed in food, certainly in the horrid food the inmates were fed.

Bullet point 4:

Ruby was in imminent danger. They could already be slowly poisoning her, but according to Bridget, the barbaric treatments the doctors were applying could ultimately kill her. First, electroconvulsive therapy, now, according to Bridget's latest note, something called insulin therapy. And finally, the most gruesome of all: a frontal lobotomy, where portions of her brain would be surgically removed.

Liam had learned that this treatment would cause permanent personality aberrations. Ruby would no longer be Ruby, but a walking vegetable.

Liam rubbed his head in despair, and his two parakeets whined in sympathy.

He threw down the pencil, stood up and paced his living room.

How could he get her out of there? Could he appeal to a judge, a lawyer? That would be difficult with a powerful man like Thomas Hunt opposing him. Could he dare 'steal her away' from the island? How could it be done? Even if he could secretly abduct her from the asylum, both of them would be hunted forever until captured.

No, he had to find a legal way. And that way was to catch the real killer.

Chapter 25

February 12, 1902

Early the next morning, Liam fidgeted at a long oak table in the reference section of the New York Public Library. It was a warm, dry, and safe place to meet with Bridget Monaghan.

Within five minutes, Bridget rushed in and slid into a seat next to him. She looked around the room, over her shoulder several times, and kept her voice low. "I was so glad to hear from you, Liam."

"How did you manage to get away from the island on such short notice?"

"Ach, I told them my poor mother was sick and they gave me a day pass."

"A whole day? How magnanimous of them," Liam said with a smirk.

"Oh, Liam. I am terribly worried about Ruby. You know that insulin treatment that I told you about will start in a few days. She will not survive it, I am sure, I am so—"

Liam grabbed her hands, which were gesticulating wildly. "Ssh, Bridget. I know, I know. That's why I'm here. To help save her."

"How? How can we save her?"

"We must get into the asylum records."

She gasped and tried to pull away.

He shook his head and squeezed her hands tighter. "No, listen, listen. I have information about those other three patients that died from stomach troubles. I believe they were poisoned."

Bridget's eyes popped. "Jesus, Mary and Joseph."

"I believe they were victims of an insurance fraud perpetrated with the help of the asylum doctors and staff."

"And Ruby's uncle is in insurance..."

"Exactly."

Bridget rubbed her head. "Oh, dear God."

"Listen to me, please." Liam looked around the room. "I need to get into those records, find the death certificates, see the insurance papers. Find any possible connection with Hunt's insurance company and these women's institutional commitments and deaths." He paused. "Now, do you know where these would be kept?"

She nodded, tipped her head and gave him an odd look.

"What?"

"Believe it or nay, I tried to get those papers...well, some sort of evidence anyways...to help Ruby."

"What did you find?"

"I broke into the Superintendent's office one night but I couldn't find anything. The bloody file cabinet was locked and I couldn't find the key."

He took her hand in his hands. "You are an amazing woman, Bridget. And very brave."

She looked down at her hands. "To be honest, I was scared to death."

He shook his head. "No, you are incredibly brave and loyal."

"But I didn't find anything," she said.

"You didn't know what to look for." He held her gaze. "Are you up for another attempt?"

"Can it really help Ruby?"

"I believe so."

"Then, yes, I am up for it." She shook her head. "But how will you get onto the island after hours?"

"I won't. You will have to do it. I will tell you what to look for."

Bridget's face fell. She rubbed her hands together. "But how will I get into the file cabinet?"

He smiled. "One of the things I learned as a young lad growing up in a poor New York City slum was how to get into anything with a lock. Now you evidently have some of those skills, am I right?"

She blushed. "Indeed. I managed to get into the office."

"Good. I will teach you how to get into the file cabinet."

"When? I have to get back tomorrow and—"

"Now. Come with me."

"Where are we going?"

"I am going to introduce you to two delightful parakeets." Her mouth fell open.

In the early morning hours of the following day, Bridget walked the hallways at the asylum. She was on night duty, which would play perfectly into her break-in attempt on the Superintendent's office. As she patrolled, her fingers unconsciously followed Liam's directions in picking the cabinet lock. Turn, up, twist, down, again.

When Jane Himmler finally retired for the night into her room on Ward 2, Bridget took a deep breath to pump up her lungs and her courage and headed to her destination. With several backward glances and the torch in her pocket, she repeated her moves of the last break-in. She easily gained access to the office, closed the curtains and headed directly for the file cabinet.

This time, armed with instructions and practice, she popped the lock on the cabinet in only a few minutes. She let out the long breath she was holding and with the torch propped up on a shelf nearby aimed at the drawers, she could thumb through the files.

"Thanks be to God, these are in alphabetical order," she whispered.

Within a few minutes she found the file of one of the poisoned girls. Another two minutes brought her to the second girl's file, and then a third. She was about to close the drawer when she decided to have a quick look for Ruby's file. Before she could locate it, she heard a noise from the hallway.

Bridget closed the drawer as quietly as possible, clicking the lock in place. She grabbed the other files and tucked them under her left arm beneath her heavy woolen sweater. She then switched off the torch and tried to still her heart from pounding out of its chest.

The footsteps came closer, seemed to stop at the door. Bridget squeezed her eyes shut. Then the footsteps continued down the hall and disappeared around the corner. Bridget sank to her knees, hoping she didn't soil herself, she was so terrified. She waited an interminable moment, rose, checked that she locked the file drawer, opened the curtains, and relocked the outer door behind her.

She continued down the hall to her own room, sweat dripping down her back and turned the key in the door behind her. She threw the files on the bed, wiped her face with a wet cloth and tried to quell the shaking. But with all the fear, anxiety, downright terror she'd just been through, Bridget felt a profound sense of achievement. She had done it, by God. She had saved Ruby.

Two weeks went by and a frustrated Liam McCarty knew he was too late to save Ruby from the insulin treatment. His Captain had assigned him to a new murder investigation that consumed his daytime hours. Plus, the boss made it clear that he was to sign off on the Ruby Hunt case in another week or there would be hell to pay.

His contact with Bridget was minimal, but he'd learned from her messages that Ruby had her treatment and survived. She had remained in a coma for seven days, but then revived. She was now in the depths of depression and on a suicide watch. Bridget was distressed. The documents she had stolen from the Superintendent's office had not been noticed missing so far, but she worried that they would come back to haunt her.

By the end of a dreary, snowy, and freezing week in February, Liam finally managed a ferry trip to Hart Island. Bridget met him and they walked on ice, in more ways than one. Bundled up they sat on a bench looking across at City Island. Sullen clouds hovered above as the wind picked up and bit into their faces, a threat of prospects to come.

Both felt as somber as the weather.

"What now? Did those documents help?" she asked.

"They will. I just haven't had the time to follow up. I'm sorry."

"I understand, luv, you have a job to do. Can't afford to lose that."

"Problem is my captain doesn't want to hear about Ruby's case. As far as he's concerned, it's solved and Ruby is as good as dead." He shook his head. "So now my daytime hours are completely taken up with new cases. Always new cases."

"So, what now?"

"I wish I had a plan."

They fell silent.

"How is she, by the way? Should I stop by and see her?"

"She won't know you, I don't think."

Liam squeezed his eyes shut.

"She's in her own little world now. It keeps her safe, you see." Bridget turned to him. "But then again, maybe that's just what she needs, to see you, a friendly face. Yes, why don't we try?"

"I'd like that, really. To see her."

"I know, I know."

"How about now?" he said.

"Well, why not?" She stood and he followed her to the dismal red brick building.

Inside, he gave his badge and identification to the clerk at the front office and sat an hour, waiting for the okay to see Ruby.

What will she be like? Will she know me?

A moment later, a door at the far end of the corridor opened and Bridget walked toward him with a young woman at her side. She looked familiar but not familiar, and Liam almost choked on a breath. Ruby Hunt was a mere ghost of herself, with bone-thin arms and legs, emaciated beyond imagination. Her hair was stringy and damp, her eyes circled with indigo-blue skin. She appeared half-dead.

Liam almost cried out, but held his tongue. Then she looked up and saw him. A smile came, transforming her face.

"Liam, you've come. You haven't forgotten me."

The sun emerged from the clouds and the world seemed right again.

Chapter 26

February 24, 1902

Liam spotted her the minute he walked in the door of Schrafft's. Except for the large letters in the name on the front of the building, he might have mistaken the restaurant for a movie theater with its fancy marquis. As he entered he eyed luscious-looking candies in colorfully decorated boxes on display. When was the last time he had a chocolate?

He pulled off his wool cap and made straight for the far end of the lunch counter where she had saved a seat for him.

"Well, hello," he said to Nellie Bly. "Thanks so much for meeting me."

"I'm happy to see you again, detective. And this is my favorite place to dine."

He looked around, smiled. "You dine here often?"

"Whenever I'm in the neighborhood." Schrafft's was a candy store and luncheonette at Broadway and West 36th Street. It had opened a few years before and created a sensation in the city.

"Try an egg cream." She pointed to a tall glass with a milky-chocolate looking drink.

"What is it? Eggs?"

"Oddly enough, it has neither eggs nor cream," she said. "It's milk, chocolate syrup, and soda water. Delicious."

He grinned. "I'll try one." He sat on the stool next to her and ordered one.

"Now," she said. "I hope you are enlisting my help in the case we previously discussed. I have done nothing but think on it."

"Oh? Have you solved it then?"

She laughed, a pleasant tinkle. "Not yet, but together, we have two times the chance of doing so."

"I think with you at my side, Nellie, we may have ten times the chance." Liam tried the egg cream set in front of him. "Hey, this is good."

She turned to him, waiting.

"What is that perfume you are wearing, if I may ask? It smells like flowers."

"You may ask and the smell is that of violets. It is the newest *eau de toilette* from Paris, called *Violettes Celeste*." Nellie pursed her lips in a wry smile. "But you are procrastinating, sir. Now tell me why we are here."

"I do need your help." He paused, unsure how to begin. "This case of Ruby Hunt...I'm officially off it, but I cannot let it go."

"Yes, I completely understand. I would not be able to drop it either. Tell me."

"Whatever I say must be in confidence. You cannot write a story about this. Do you understand?"

"Of course. But when you solve this case, I get an exclusive."

"Done." He sipped his soda. "I believe Ruby's Uncle Thomas Hunt had something to do with the death of her family. And, certainly, he is the man who had her committed."

"Thomas Hunt is the insurance man, right?"

"The head of Hunt Liability and Assets. His office is housed in the New York World Building. Where your newspaper—"

"I know the New York World Building very well." She narrowed her eyes. "What are you suggesting?"

"I want to know your thoughts on getting into the building at night, particularly the Hunt offices."

Nellie swiveled around in her seat to stare at him. "My thoughts? Are you asking me if I have a key?" She grinned. "You're not planning what I think you're planning, are you?"

He shook his head with a smirk. "And what might that be?"

"A break-in to find documents...incriminating documents in this case. To find out whether he had special policies on the family, on Ruby..." She trailed off.

Liam didn't speak for a moment. "You think I'm mad, don't you?"

Her answer came after a long hesitation. "Yes, I do. There's all kinds of security in the building—"

"I've checked into all of that and I know I can get in between the security rounds."

"And if you get caught, you realize your life is virtually over?"

"I do."

"You really care about Ruby, don't you?"

He looked down.

"This is personal, not just professional," Nellie said. "I see."

"Will you help me or not?"

"I'll do more than that. I'll go with you."

At two in the morning, Nellie Bly and Liam McCarty entered the back door of the New York World Building. He marveled at her tenaciousness. After a lengthy argument at Schrafft's that almost got them ousted from the restaurant, she had convinced him that he could not do this without her. Hence, here he was, following this brave woman into perilous waters.

Getting into the building was easy. Nellie did, indeed, have a key.

"Being a reporter, I'm here at all hours of the day and night," she said with a wave of her hand. "You never know when a story will break."

They walked down a dark corridor and into the main reception lobby. Marble pillars held the upper stories, three ornate brass cages held the lifts, and black and white floor tiles shone with a high-polished wax.

Liam tried to swallow his fear when he saw a guard at a large desk.

"Oh, Miss Bly, how are you?"

"Just fine, James. This gentleman is my assistant on a project. May we sign in?"

"Of course, of course." James spun a log book around for them to sign.

Nellie signed and she turned the pen over to him. She had already instructed him to sign as Charlie Jones. He did.

"Let's go, Charlie, lots of work to be done."

Liam nodded, tried not to let James get a good look at him and followed Nellie to the elevator.

Inside, she moved the lever to five. "That's the floor my office is on. We'll use the stairs to go up to the Hunt office." She closed the door to her office, then went to her desk where she kept a flashlight.

He looked at his pocket watch. "We have eleven minutes before the guard is on the seventh floor."

They stole quietly to the staircase and walked up the two flights. Liam held his watch in his hand and gave her a signal.

Nellie opened the door slowly. They scurried like thieves to the door at the end of the hall. Liam dropped to his knees with his tools at the ready. Nellie held the beam on the lock. In less than a minute they were in.

"I'm impressed, detective. Is that part of police training?"

He frowned but didn't answer.

"All right, let's both get to looking. I'll let you know if a file cabinet needs lock-picking." She smiled and hurried across the room.

The office was smaller than Liam expected, with a waiting room, complete with three chairs and a reception desk, plus an inner office, with a desk and four chairs. Both rooms were elegantly furnished and Nellie stopped to run her hand along a chair.

"Lovely, Victorian," she said of the narrow, high-backs with tapestry seats.

"Come on." Liam headed straight for a bank of file cabinets, which he quickly unlocked. Together, he and Nellie combed through the files for four minutes.

"Shush, what's that?" she whispered.

They both stopped moving and held their breath. "Nothing," she said. "Keep going."

They kept searching. "Here it is," Liam said. "Hunt. The entire family file." He started looking through, but Nellie said. "No time, let's just take it."

"Wait a minute," Liam said. "I want to check one more thing. Yes, here, here." He couldn't contain his excitement.

"What?"

"An entire folder on the Women's Lunatic Asylum at Hart Island."

"My God," Nellie said. "Why on earth would he have so much interest in that awful place?"

"Looks like a number of women committed there were insured by Hunt Liability."

"Follow the money," she said. "Isn't that always the case? Follow the money."

"We'd better get out of here."

Too late. The sound of footsteps.

Liam put his fingers to his lips. She turned off her torch. He gently closed the file drawer, clicking the lock, then he grabbed Nellie by the arm and they dashed to the large desk. Dropping down behind it, they held their breath and waited.

The outer office door opened, and they could see a beam of light flash around. Footsteps moved to the inner door, Thomas' office. Same beam shot around the room.

The guard was humming to himself. Liam prayed he'd continue. Finally, the beam of light switched off and the musical security guard left, relocking the outer door. His footsteps headed down the corridor. Now he was in full voice.

Nellie drew in a deep breath. "God, I thought we were done-for."

He took her hand and squeezed it. "He was singing my favorite song."

"My Blushing Rosie?"

"Yup. But I'd prefer it sung by Harry MacDonough."

She giggled. The tension of the moment dissipated.

"Got the files?" he asked.

She patted her jacket. "Right here, near my heart."

They couldn't see in the dim light but each guessed the other was smiling.

New York City
2016

Chapter 27

May 21, 2016

The office was warm and muggy, and he was tired, but Frank Mead could not get it out of his head that he was missing something. He stood, walked around his desk, and moved closer to the white board. Photos of Sophie, the crime scene, and her apartment were posted. So were Bridget's letter from the suitcase and the 1902 photo from the asylum. He moved closer to that old creased photograph.

Why did Bridget include this one? Doctors, nurses, staff, and patients. Three patients. Ruby was not one. Who were these women? They had some significance, Frank was sure. He sighed, turned away.

In his gut, he felt that David Hunt was at the center of it all. Was Madelyn involved too? If not, did she know about her husband's role and was protecting him?

His cell blared out a popular Latin song, *Despacito*. *Thanks for the ringtone, Amanda.* She had thought he needed to slow down, take it easy. Whatever. As if a cell phone ring was the answer.

"Mead." He listened a moment then smiled. "Sorry, I didn't mean to bark." Frank sat down and listened again. "I'd love to. The photograph? Yes. I'll bring it." He gave directions to his favorite watering hole. "Give me thirty minutes."

He clicked off, feeling lighter and happier. In half an hour, he would meet Rachel Bejarano for a drink. She had some information for him, but that was not what made him smile. Before he flipped off the lights, he grabbed that old photograph and put it in his pocket.

Rachel arrived a few minutes after him and he waved to her from a small table in the back.

"Wow, where'd you find this place?"

"McSorley's Old Ale House is one of the most storied taverns in this great city."

"Really?" She smiled and looked around. "It is definitely old."

"1854, to be exact. My great grandfather came here after he arrived from Ireland."

"He was a cop too?"

"The first of a line of Meads in the NYPD."

"Ahh, so you come by it legitimately."

He smiled. "What can I get you?"

"Is that a Guinness?"

"It is, lassie. Would you like one?"

"Indeed, I would." She settled into her chair after draping her shoulder bag over the back. "I have information which I hope will be helpful to the case."

"Tell me." He studied her face. Alluring eyes and kissable lips. He swallowed and looked away.

Rachel pulled out a file folder from the shoulder bag. She opened it, flipped through pages. "I checked on the staff at the Hart Island asylum and found nothing really untoward." She took a long draw on her Guinness. "No police records, shady businesses or anything like that."

"What about the Superintendent?"

"Doctor Franz Uber had an exemplary resume. Well-educated, lots of papers in journals, that sort of thing."

"How about his bedside manner?"

"No idea."

"Go on."

"Right after Ruby's death, Uber was transferred to an institution in Chicago."

"That would be after April 10, 1902."

"Correct. Newspaper articles just carried an announcement. There's no reason given for his leaving."

Frank frowned.

"Similar stories with the staff. They all moved on within a year but no surprises. And you know, of course, that Ruby's caretaker, Bridget left soon after too."

"So, we have a patient dead from poisoning, a cop who stepped in front of a train, and a caretaker who was clearly suspicious of both situations. The staff had to have been up to their necks in all of this."

"There's more," Rachel said. "Do you have the photo that Bridget left in the suitcase?"

Frank pulled it out of his pocket and set it in front of them.

"First of all, what does this seem like to you? A group photo of happy folk in front of a lunatic asylum?"

"To me it looks like the kind of stunt the Nazis would pull when they tried to convince the Red Cross everything was honky dory at the ghetto."

Rachel smiled. "Exactly."

"Okay, so they faked it for the press."

"There's something else. I am taking a wild stab at this, and it will have to be verified, but I believe these three women, the patients standing there with fake smiles, were poisoned like Ruby and buried on Hart Island."

"What makes you think that?"

Rachel cleared her throat. "In my research into the patients at the asylum, I came across three death certificates that seemed suspicious to me. They all died within six months of arriving. They were all young. They were all seemingly healthy. Like Ruby."

Frank picked up Bridget's photograph. "You think these are those women?"

"There is a way to find out. I was able to get photographs of the women from their intake processing at the asylum." Rachel reached again in her bag for another folder. She pulled out images of three women.

Frank stared down at three sad, disheveled young women in standard booking police photos. "Christ, they look like prison shots. Like today, but this was 1902."

"Is there any way the police can match these photos with the women in that photo? You know facial recognition programs or something?"

"Not the police, but I know someone else. She's probably the best digital photographer in the country. She can certainly do it."

"Great."

He winced. "Problem is she's in D.C."

"Scan these and e-mail them to her."

Frank smiled at the idea that he'd be working with Maggie Thornhill again.

"This is quite a conspiracy."

"Poisoning, insurance fraud, cop-killing. Not much different than today."

"Has the M-E gotten a DNA match for Ruby?"

"Not yet. With all the requests in a city this size, takes a while. Any articles come up on David and Madelyn Hunt?"

"Only in the society pages. They attend a lot of charity functions. But, as law enforcement, *you* can look into the company's finances."

He nodded.

Frank's cell went off.

Rachel laughed at the ringtone.

He shrugged and answered. "Yeah, Will."

"We got another murder, Frank."

Frank sat up, brow furrowed as he gazed down at his empty glass. "Where?"

"The Charles Building."

"Damn." He disconnected and looked up at Rachel, disappointed he couldn't spend more time with her.

"You've got to leave, right?"

"Sorry."

"A homicide?"

"Yup." He dropped a twenty on the table for the beers and tip.

"May I ask where?"

He stood. "West 79th, the Charles Building."

"Really?"

"Why? You know the place?"

"There's something familiar about it." She scoured through her notes. "Something to do with your case."

Frank sat back down, watched her.

"Here it is. Doctor Roger Steinberg lives there."

"Who is Roger Steinberg?"

"His name came up in my search of all these insurance companies. He's the Superintendent of the Aurora Lifetime Living care facilities." She shot him a wide-eyed look.

"David Hunt's right-hand man."

⁂

The crime scene team swarmed Roger Steinberg's apartment with their cameras, brushes, tape, mini-vacs, and other evidence collectors.

Frank walked into the bedroom where the victim had been killed. Steinberg lay on his bed, fully-dressed, with two bullets in his chest. Will was already there.

"Got a guess on the gun the killer used?" Frank asked.

"It's not a twenty-two caliber. That'd be too easy."

"So, it's not the gun that killed Sophie." Frank said.

"That'd be my bet. You know, we never did prove that Sophie owned the gun that killed her. Nothing registered to her, anyway."

"My mom said she did, she was sure," Frank said.

"They're not hard to come by, but how would she know where to get one?"

"Ask Lizzie." Frank smirked.

"Yeah, I guess your mom would know, wouldn't she?"

"So, here's the thing. The vic is Doctor Roger Steinberg. Do you know who he is?"

"I think you're going to tell me," Will said.

"David Hunt's chief administrator."

"Holy shit. That means this murder and Sophie's murder must be connected."

"Right," Frank said. "Now all we have to do is prove it."

An hour later, Frank was back at his desk looking at a large yellow envelope that had been couriered over from a friend at the Assistant District Attorney's office. Sheldon Reynolds was a longtime assistant DA, and for whatever reason, never aimed for the top-dog position. Frank was happy about that. They often exchanged favors.

He opened the packet and pulled out a sheaf of papers. It was almost eight p.m. and his energy was fading. Through blurry eyes, he started reading the notes on Hunt Liability and Assets. The company's history went back to the original Hunt family insurance firm, and here was proof that, indeed, several Hart Island patients were insured, and payouts were made upon their deaths. Were they the same patients that Rachel found—those three women?

He flipped through Rachel's pages to find the patients' details. All young, all wealthy, all committed by their husbands. The beneficiaries of their life insurance policies were listed as Henry Flynn and Jeremiah Grady.

Wait. Jesus. I know those names.

Frank jumped up, unlocked a cabinet drawer, and pulled out Liam McCarty's murder book. He read the pages and let out a long, low whistle.

The doorman of the Hunt apartment building was Henry Grady. The elevator man was Jeremiah Flynn. How transparent could they be? Dumb asses. He'd think Thomas Hunt would have known better than to use those names.

Frank smiled as he leaned back in his chair. *Liam, my young man, fellow detective, astute judge of character, you were absolutely, positively correct. There was a major insurance scam going on in 1902. It was all about fraudulent policies. And Thomas Hunt was at the center of it all, orchestrating his two puppets to do his bidding.*

Too bad he couldn't dig up the other women's bodies and check for poisoning. No need. He knew in his gut they were murdered. Just like Ruby. How could he find out what happened to Flynn and Grady?

Rachel Bejarano.

Chapter 28

May 22, 2016

At quarter to eight the next morning, Frank was in his office, on his second cup of coffee. Will walked in, stopped short. "You're early."

"Got a conference call," Frank said.

"Yeah? With who?"

"Maggie Thornhill."

Will stopped pouring his cup of coffee from the Mr. Coffee pot in Frank's office. "What's that about?"

Frank pushed some papers around on his desk until he uncovered the photographs that Rachel had given him. He held them out to Will. "Do these women look familiar?"

"Hmm, old photos. 1902?" Will squinted at the faces, from one to the second and third and back again. "Wait a minute. Are these the women in Bridget's photograph?"

"Bingo."

"Holy shit. How'd you get these?"

"Rachel Bejarano is a research librarian. She did some digging."

"That's cool. But can you prove these are the same women?"

"Hence my call to Maggie. She's an expert at facial recognition technology."

"I remember. Good idea."

Frank looked at his watch then picked up his cell. "Showtime." He hit one button.

"Maggie's still on speed dial, eh?"

Frank shooed him out of the office.

"Hello, Maggie?"

"Hi, Frank. How are you? How's life in the big city? And death?"

"Busy. Landed a case that has a historic component to it. Right up your alley."

"I hoped this was a social call."

He could hear the smile in her voice. "How about you? Keeping busy?"

"This is Washington, D.C. the capital city for crime."

"I remember it well."

"So how can I help?"

"Here's what I've got." He gave her a synopsis of the case.

"So, you want me to compare the photos of the three patients to the women in the group photo from 1902?"

"I need proof they're a match."

"When do you need them?"

"Yesterday."

"I figured. Okay, there are a few things that come to mind."

"Go on," he said, leaning back in his chair.

"There's a newly emerging trend in facial recognition software that uses a 3D model."

"3D? Maggie, this is 1902."

"I can digitally scan the existing photo and convert it to 3D. The results should be revealing."

"Yeah?"

"3D facial recognition measures distinctive features of the face, where rigid tissues and bone are most apparent, such as the curves of the eye socket, chin and nose, then extrapolates those measurements into a perspective view, giving the face a third dimension of depth. Very useful in identifying a subject."

Frank waited. Maggie was on a roll.

"It could prove particularly valuable when working with old photos because there's the potential to recognize a fuzzy or sepia subject from different angles."

"Meaning?"

"If the subject is tilting their head or their head is slightly turned left or right, as was often the case in old photos, people couldn't stay still that long, you see, the 3D model can assess the head's position and--"

"Okay, okay, you win. Try the 3D if you can. What do you need from me?"

"Scan the images as jpeg files and email them to me. Also include an official NYPD letter requesting exactly what it is you'd like me to do...for my boss. That's it."

"How much will this cost me?"

"Cheap for you, Frank. And I'll get to it right away."

"Thanks, Maggie."

She clicked off.

Frank grabbed the photos and headed into the administration area to find the IT person. He asked her to immediately scan and send the photos, with the best resolution possible, and gave her Maggie's email address. Then he let out a deep sigh of relief. Maggie would get back to him quickly...and with the answers he needed.

Later that day, Will caught up to Frank. "Hey, have a seat. You're not gonna believe this."

"I'll believe anything at this point."

"I've been running background on Steinberg. Got his prints from the ME, and guess what? He's not Roger Steinberg. In fact, *Doctor* Roger Steinberg has been dead twelve years, in a grave in Minnesota."

"What? Then who the hell is our victim?"

"Glad you asked. His real name is Theodore Jessup, con-artist extraordinaire from the West Coast. Apparently done a bit of time in The Country Club."

Frank scratched his head. "Lompoc? Holy shit."

"Funny thing, though, he is, was anyway, a doctor. Lost his license some years ago for shenanigans with drugs. Evidently stole Steinberg's identity and credentials and passed well enough to get a job with Aurora facilities."

"Do you think David Hunt knows?"

Will shrugged. "If he's on the up and up, no. He simply hired himself a doctor slash administrator to run the place. Probably didn't bother to do a background check."

"Pretty foolish not to," Frank said.

"Ten years ago, employers were a lot less cautious."

"Right."

"What now?"

"Let's go visit the Hunts."

The sun was at four o'clock in the sky when they arrived at the brownstone on East 56th Street. Ash and Maple trees lined the gentrified street, and Frank found a parking space half a block away.

"Did you call ahead?" Will asked.

"Nope. Let's see how hospitable they are when we show up on their doorstep unannounced."

Will snickered.

They climbed the four steps to the front door and rang the bell. Moments later, Madelyn opened the door. She wore a white pantsuit with a blue silk blouse. Frank noted a tiny spot on her jacket collar, and her well-coifed hair was slightly askew. Quite different from the Madelyn he'd first met.

"Oh." She stepped back.

"Is this a bad time, Missus Hunt?" Frank said, remembering she had suggested him calling her Madelyn at their first meeting, but he didn't feel comfortable with that under the present circumstances. "We have a few more questions for you."

"Now?"

"Unless you'd rather come down to the station," Will put in.

"The station? Seriously? Is this about Roger?"

Frank nodded. "We have a few questions for your husband, too."

She opened the door wider. "Come in, please. My husband's not here. He's at the office."

Frank walked into the main room, the living room, he assumed. "May we sit?"

"Yes, of course." Madelyn gathered her wits about her. "Would you gentlemen like some coffee?"

"No thanks," Frank answered for the both of them. "We don't want to take up much of your time."

She sat on a plush gray nubby wool loveseat. Frank and Will sat opposite her in two cushy chairs that matched.

"Nice," Will said, looking around the room filled with expensive antiques, curios, and fine Persian rugs.

"What can you tell me about Roger...the poor man?" She sat forward on the edge of her seat.

"First of all, we're sorry about Doctor Steinberg. You were probably close."

She rubbed her hands together then on her slacks as if they needed drying.

"Were you close?" Frank asked.

"Not really. He worked for David so I didn't see him all that often."

"How long did you know him?"

"Oh, about eight or nine years, I think. David told me Roger was a good doctor."

"Did he practice much, working for Aurora facilities?" Frank asked. "He was more of an administrator, right?"

"Well, yes, I guess." She stared at her hands.

"Are you okay, Missus Hunt?"

"Uh, fine, yes. Just very distressed to have someone I know die... like that."

"Like what?" Will said.

"Well, murdered, for God's sake. Right in his own home."

Frank leaned forward. "It must be distressing to have two people you were close to murdered in a short period of time."

"Yes, poor Sophie, of course. Just terrible." She looked at Frank. "Do you think the murders are related?"

"It's too early in the investigation to say."

"They must be, mustn't they?" she said to no one in particular.

Frank looked at Will then turned to Madelyn. "Is there something you want to tell us?"

Madelyn didn't answer.

Frank softened his voice and crossed his legs as if he planned to stay a bit. "Tell us a little about Doctor Steinberg."

"I don't know all that much about him, really. He was in family practice, I believe. You know a GP, not a specialist." Her words came faster. "Came from California or Oregon or someplace out west. He wasn't married, had no family that I know of." Her eyes filled. "So sad. And now he's dead."

"We're sorry for your loss."

"Thank you." Madelyn pulled out a wrinkled tissue from her pocket and dabbed her eyes. "Is that all?"

Frank and Will rose.

Will said, "Tell us where you were when the doctor was killed?"

She swallowed hard. "Last night? Ah..?

"Between ten p.m. and two a.m.," Will prodded.

"Here. David and I were both here. We had dinner then read a bit, watched a movie, and went to bed."

Frank's turn: "Do you own a gun, Missus Hunt?"

She blinked several times as if trying to process the question. "What, no, of course not. Why would I? What are you implying?"

"We have to ask, please understand." Frank walked to the door, turned around. "What about your husband?"

"No. David doesn't own a gun. I would know if he had a gun."

"All right. Thanks. I appreciate your help." Frank opened the front door. "We'll be in touch."

They made it down the front steps when Will said, "What's your take? Does she know about the real Roger? Or not?"

"Hard to say." Frank walked toward the car. "She seems clueless, but she may be an accomplished actress."

"I assume you didn't tell her the truth about Steinberg because you want to get the husband's take first."

"Yeah. He's another one that's hard to read."

"I agree."

"Let's go talk to David Hunt," Frank said. "See if he's as contradictory as his wife."

"Or an equally good actor."

Chapter 29

May 22, 2016

The Towers on East 60th Street was a high-rise office building that hurt Frank's eyes. Constructed in the 70s, a period of the least attractive architecture, in his opinion, it was an attempt at modern décor that completely missed the mark. Gray concrete broken with narrow windows rose twenty stories into the dusky sky. The interior carried the gray and dull browns ad nauseam into the lobby areas.

"Looks like someone puked there," Will said.

Frank glanced at a large dark splotch near the elevators. "Ugh, thanks for that."

They rode up to the twelfth floor and exited the elevator. On the right was the office suite of Aurora Lifetime Living.

"If I had to work here every day, I might puke myself," Will added.

The door was unlocked but the reception desk was empty.

"I guess Steinberg's office was cleared as a crime scene already," Will said. "Quick work."

"Yeah, I have friends in high places."

They walked farther into the reception area and saw evidence that the crime lab had been there. Furniture moved, lamps on, file and desk drawers open.

"Guess no one came to work today," Will said.

"Maybe in deference to the boss' death."

"Strange the outer door is unlocked."

"Someone's here." Frank walked around the desk and peered down a long hallway.

"Hello? Hello?"

A door opened at the far end of the corridor and David Hunt stepped out. "Sorry, we're closed for the day."

"Police, Mister Hunt." Frank held out his I-D.

"Oh yes, yes. It's rather late, though. Can it wait?"

"This is a murder investigation, sir. It really can't wait."

"All right, yes, come in, then." David turned and re-entered the office.

Frank entered behind him and stopped short. He might have to revise his opinion of these ugly buildings. The view was magnificent. The city and the river spread out below and with the sun broaching the horizon, the colors were surreal. Aurora must be quite profitable to afford such lavish views, he mused.

"Sit down, gentlemen, please." David had removed his suit jacket and his tie hung loose around his collar. Perhaps he didn't need to be as formal with no one in the office.

"You're here to talk about Roger, of course. Horrible, simply horrible. I can't believe he's dead."

"When did you last see him?" Frank asked.

David leaned back in his chair. "Sometime yesterday morning, I think. Yes, we had a meeting about some changes in policies."

"And where were you last night?" Will asked.

"What are you implying...that I killed him?"

"We have to eliminate people from the investigation, to narrow the field of suspects," Will said.

David stared at Will, mouth open.

"Last night?" Frank asked.

"Yes, yes. Well, Maddie and I were home last night. Didn't go out at all, just watched some TV and went to bed."

"Did you speak to Doctor Steinberg last night?"

"No."

"How did you hear about his death?" Frank said.

"His cleaning lady called me."

"When?"

"When did she call?" David steepled his fingers under his chin. "Maybe seven this morning."

Frank squinted at David. "Why would she do that? Call you, I mean?"

"Oh, she called the police first, of course. Then, I guess she figured I needed to know."

"Do you know this cleaning lady?" Will asked.

"Yes, well, she cleans for us too."

"Ah," Frank said. "Tell us, please, a little about Roger Steinberg. Background always helps our investigation."

David stood. "I need some water. This is very upsetting. Can I get you some?"

At their negative response, David stepped out of the office and trod down the hall.

"Nervous?" Will said. "Buying time to get a story together?"

"He's had all day to do that."

"With his wife."

David returned with a glass of water, drank some, sat back down. "Okay, right. Roger. I've known him maybe ten years. Good doctor, great mind. Very organized. That's why I hired him to administer the Aurora facilities. Excellent with numbers, understands the insurance business, knows the Medicare system inside and out." He stopped, drank more water, which he spilled on his shirt and barely noticed.

"How did you meet?"

"I advertised for the position ten years ago. He applied and I interviewed him. We got along well. I thought he was the most qualified for the job. I hired him."

"Did you do a background check?" Will asked.

"Of course, I did. Do you think I would just hire someone for a position like that...right off the street?"

"So, who did this background check? Dick Tracy?" Will asked.

"What? What do you mean?" David sat up.

"The doctor Steinberg you've known for ten years has been dead for twelve years and buried in Minnesota."

David's jaw dropped. "No way."

"The man who worked for you is Theodore Jessup, a con artist who's spent some quality time in prison in California."

David leaped to his feet, sending his chair crashing into the credenza behind him. "Are you crazy?"

"Fingerprints don't lie," Will said.

"Sit down, Mister Hunt," Frank said.

"There's got to be some mistake. He's...it's not possible. I know him, knew him. Roger...Jesus." David reached back for his chair and wheeled it to the desk where he sat down heavily.

The men fell silent for a moment.

"What does this mean?" David said. "He was with me for ten years. Could he have been stealing from me? All this time? Oh God." He ran his fingers through his hair, ruffling a hundred-dollar cut.

"That's a good question," Frank said. "You might want to get an auditor in here—an independent auditor, that is, to check your books."

"Shit, I can't believe it."

"Did you hear what I said?" Frank asked.

"Yes, yes, I will. Immediately. Yes."

"You might be interested to know the man you knew as Roger Steinberg was, at least, a physician."

"What?"

"The man who worked for you had at least some knowledge in helping your patients."

David's face crumpled. "Oh my God."

"Thought you'd want to know," Frank said and shot Will a disgusted glance.

"Is there anything else you can tell us about the deceased?" Will asked.

David looked up with a half-smile. "Yeah, he loved his work. Ironic, isn't it? He had no wife, no kids. We were his family, in a sense. Me and Maddie. But maybe all that was a lie too. Maybe he had a wife and kids somewhere."

Frank waited for more. David remained silent.

"Do you own a gun?" Will asked.

"What? No. Why would I need a gun?"

"Lots of folks own them that don't need them." Frank curled his lip. "What about your wife? Does she own a gun, say for protection?"

"Maddie? A gun? No, absolutely not." He paused as if thinking, then: "I'm sure I would know, Lieutenant, if my wife had a gun in the house."

That's exactly what Madelyn said about you.

"Are you insinuating that I had something to do with Roger's death?"

"Did you?" Frank asked.

"Good God, no. Why on earth would I? The man worked for me, we were friends, for Christ's sake." David stood, moved to the windows. "I had no idea. He completely duped me."

Frank kept the questions coming. "How much did Roger have to do with the business finances?"

"Everything."

"Didn't he deal mostly with the day to day operations?"

David leaned against the window frame. "Day to day, patient care, insurance claims, hiring and firing staff. He did...everything."

"Is that what you hired him to do?"

"Yes. To free me up."

"Free you up for what?" Will said. "Sailing, travel?"

"No, no, I work every day, for God's sake. I did sales."

"You solicited for patients?" Frank said.

"You make it sound like a prostitution ring or something." David grimaced. "I worked with the marketing director to get the word out about Aurora." His eyes turned steely. "Look, these are excellent facilities with excellent care—"

"For wealthy clients," Will added.

"Yes, true. But even rich people need care when they age."

"Fair enough," Frank said.

Will jumped in. "How did Missus Hunt get along with Roger?"

David swallowed hard. "What's that supposed to mean?"

"Were they friends? Did they like each other, you know?"

"They didn't have all that much contact, really. Just at an occasional function."

"Like a fundraiser?" Will said.

"Exactly. Maddie's role was to help with those types of charity events."

"Any idea who might want to hurt him?"

"No one. I mean everyone liked him." David winced. "Whoever he was."

Frank kept pushing. "What about the patients?"

"He was great with them."

"I assume there were times when there were treatment disputes or payment disputes?"

"Of course. But to murder him over demanding a late payment? Come on."

"Now that you mention payments, how were the payments handled? Did the patients pay out of pocket or was Medicare billed?"

"Both. That's why Roger was so important to the company. He kept track of which patients were with which insurance companies, who paid from their own personal accounts, and he made sure Medicare was billed promptly and properly, as well."

"So he had plenty of opportunity for embezzlement and fraud, I suspect," Will said.

Silence while David absorbed this information, then: "I hope to God not."

"What about his personal life?" Frank asked.

David choked on a laugh and returned to his chair behind the desk. "What personal life? Roger was all about work. He had no life."

"No women," Will asked, "or men in his life?"

"No."

"Did he go to parties, drink, travel, what?"

"If you knew Roger, you'd understand. He was all about work."

"Work and money," Frank said. "What else do people work for?"

"Roger did have some toys. A Mercedes sports car, a Hinckley yacht, a big house in Scarsdale. So, maybe that's what he did with his spare time. He bought toys."

"Well, what of it?" David shot back. "No law against toys."

"What was the falling out about?"

"What falling out?"

"The falling out between you and Roger?"

David worked his jaw. "What are you talking about?"

"I must have misunderstood your wife, then, sorry," Frank lied.

"Wait a minute. What did Maddie say? We had no falling out. She wouldn't have known if we did." David stood and stormed around his desk, face damp and flushed. "She couldn't have said anything like that."

Frank rose. "As I said, it's probably my mistake. She might not have meant a falling out at all." He turned to the door. "That's it for now. But we may have some more questions for you over the course of the investigation."

Will joined him. "We'll show ourselves out."

David stood there, glaring at them. The bad news had hit its mark dead center.

Out on the street, Will said, "Hard to believe that he knew nothing about the good doctor's nefarious past."

"Don't bet on it."

"I would sure like to know what he was doing at the office a day after the chief administrator is murdered," Will said. "He must have given everyone else the day off, you know, all those empty desks. Maybe he was purging files."

"I'd like to be Spiderman outside the window at the Hunt's house tonight to eavesdrop on the conversation between David and Madelyn." Frank shot Will a sly grin.

The next morning, Frank stopped by the old tenement to visit Lizzie. By the time he'd caught her up on the case, he was on his third cup of coffee.

"So, Ma, how did you know Sophie had a gun?"

"What do you mean?"

"I mean, how did you know that Sophie had a gun? It's not a trick question."

She tightened her lips. "You're not gonna like it."

"Tell me anyway."

"I got it for her."

Frank squeezed his eyes closed for a second. "You got Sophie, a woman in her seventies, a gun?" He shook his head, at a loss for words.

"I'm in my seventies and I've got a gun."

Frank stared at her, open-mouthed. "You've got a gun? Here?"

"You're catching flies." Lizzie rose and went to her bedroom, returned with a gun in her hand. She held it out to Frank.

He looked at a .22 Ruger.

"You know, Ma." He tried to keep his voice level. "This is the same type of gun that killed your best friend."

"She had exactly the same one."

Frank rubbed his forehead. "Can you please explain why you and Sophie had guns?"

"For protection. What else?" She set the weapon on the table and sat down. "It's not loaded, by the way."

"You know how to use it?"

"What do you think?"

He looked at her through slitted eyes.

"Yes, I do. So did Sophie. We took classes."

"Thank God for that."

She huffed, swallowed some coffee.

"You really think you need protection?"

"This is New York, Frank. There have been break-ins, some violent, and look at what happened to Sophie, for Chrissakes." Tears filled her eyes.

"She very well might be alive if she didn't have the gun in her apartment." He waved a hand.

"You're right, Frank. Maybe I made a mistake, shouldn't have helped Soph get a gun. Now, she--"

"Look, Ma, the only one responsible for Sophie's death is the guy who killed her. Not you, not Sophie."

She wiped her eyes.

Frank put his hand on hers. "Where did you get the guns?"

A full minute went by before she answered. "Vito."

"Vito Guardino? The guy who owns the Italian place up the street?"

"Yeah, Vito's. That Vito."

"Jesus."

"Why not? He has connections."

They sat in silence for a few moments.

"Can this Vito get any type of gun?" Frank's mind flashed to the gun that killed Steinberg. Most likely a Glock.

"He offered me the Glock G19, but I wanted the Ruger. Small, lightweight."

He nodded thinking what the hell is this world coming to when my seventy-five-year-old mother packs a gun?

"You know what I think happened?" she said.

He waited.

"She was surprised by an intruder. Someone who came looking for that damn suitcase. Sophie heard him, got out her gun, he wrestled it away from her and bang, she's dead."

"You may very well be right. But it might not have had anything to do with that suitcase."

"You can't possibly believe that."

Frank didn't answer.

"I think the question you should be asking is who the devil wanted that suitcase so badly...and why?"

"Good thing you don't have that suitcase here any more, Ma."

"Hmm. Maybe I'll sleep with the gun under my pillow...just in case."

New York City
1902

Chapter 30

March 7, 1902

The rain poured down like Niagara Falls in spring and Liam was soaked to the skin despite his hooded rain slicker. On the journey uptown, he mulled over the facts of the case. He had made copious notes the previous night in his murder book and drew up scenario after scenario in the Ruby Hunt case to give him the ammunition he needed. Things were not going well with Ruby and he needed a major break in the investigation.

On the trolley ride, his mind drifted, as it had so often, to Ruby. She had been through hell and back at the asylum, a place unfit for human habitation. She managed to survive so far, but her mind and body were deteriorating. Bridget worried that she would disappear into herself, never to return.

If this inquiry didn't resolve the case, even if it did eventually, he and Bridget had a plan to save Ruby. They would help her escape, keep her hidden, and get her started on a new life. Maybe one with Liam, somewhere in a new city.

Argh, don't go there.

But was Ruby strong enough, did she have the fortitude, the sheer will, to attempt such a dangerous feat? She looked so terribly beaten down the last time he saw her. He wasn't at all sure she could succeed.

So much rested on him and his next interview with the doorman. How should he handle it? Nice and easy or confrontational. One then the other? He'd like to beat a confession out of the man but knew that wouldn't accomplish his goals. *What goals?* Liam didn't expect Grady to confess to murder. He didn't believe Grady had committed the murders. He was too weak, a scared rabbit. No, Henry Grady was responsible for the distraction, the fire in the basement. That may be all he had done, but not all that he knew. After all, someone killed the Hunt family while he was setting fire in the basement. Grady knew who the killer was. How could Liam get him to expose him? Did the man have a conscience?

The trolley bell rang. Liam hopped off and sprinted across the street to Ruby's old apartment on Fifth Avenue.

Henry Grady, not recognizing the young police officer, opened the door for him.

"Good day for ducks, eh?" The doorman said.

Liam dropped his hood and wiped his face with his hands. "Aye, very good. Ducks and policemen."

Grady backed up a few steps, then turned and went back to his position at the lobby desk.

"I see you remember me, Henry," Liam said. "I need a word with you."

"Go on, then, have yer word."

"Not here, unless you want the residents to overhear." Liam tipped his head to an elderly couple who walked through the lobby and waved at him. "Get your pal, Flynn, to cover for a while."

Grady frowned and the creases in his forehead deepened. "Wait here." He stalked off to a door behind the elevator which stood empty at the moment. When he returned, Jeremiah Flynn followed. He sent a scathing look to Liam.

"This way." Grady led Liam to a small room behind the elevator. "Now what's this about?"

"Ruby Hunt."

"I thought the case was solved. Miss Ruby killed 'em and they locked her away."

Liam studied the man for a moment. *Never trust a man with no chin.* "Sit down, Henry." Liam pointed to a chair next to a small desk.

Henry sat.

"I've been visiting with Ruby. At the asylum."

Henry turned away. "So?"

"It's a terrible place. Especially for a young girl."

"A young girl who killed her family."

"I don't believe she did it. I think you don't either."

Henry's eyes bugged. "Course I believe it. She's locked up, ain't she? Cops proved it."

"Actually, I'm the cop in charge of the investigation and I haven't proved it. In fact, just the opposite. I think Ruby was railroaded."

Henry jumped up. "Yer crazy. She did it and ya can't prove otherwise."

"Sit down, Henry. Please." Liam half-sat on the corner of the desk. "There's something you should know." Liam stared down at Henry who fidgeted in his seat. "I've been examining insurance papers from the Hunt Liability & Assets Company, those policies covering the Hunt family, including Miss Ruby Hunt."

"So what?"

"Interestingly enough, there are at least three other patients at the Women's Lunatic Asylum at Hart Island who have similar insurance policies through Hunt Liability."

"What do I care?" Grady's face had paled and his eyes shone like gray marbles.

"Oh, I think you do care," Liam went on. "It seems the beneficiaries on these three policies are familiar to you."

"I don't know no bena-fishries."

"No? One of the names is Henry Flynn. The other is Jeremiah Grady. Isn't that odd? Both you and your pal's names scrambled?"

A bead of sweat dripped down Grady's forehead. "Don't mean nothin'. Them's common names."

"I'd say this was more than just a coincidence, Henry. It appears that you and Mister Hunt were trying to pull off a deliberate fraud here."

"Yer nuts. You don't know what the hell you're talking about. There ain't no fraud here."

Liam leaned into Grady to intimidate him. "It's not just the names on the policies that look suspicious, Henry. I've compared the writing on the documents."

Grady sat up in his chair.

"The signatures on all the policies look surprisingly similar."

"What the hell are you talkin' about?"

"Let me show you something." Liam pulled out a sheaf of papers from his inside jacket pocket. "See here. These are some of the policies I'm referring to." He flashed the papers at Grady. Then he unfolded one.

"The signature here, Henry Flynn, looks very similar to Thomas Hunt's signature. Look at the capital 'H' and you'll see what I mean."

Grady blinked and shook his head. "I don't know nothin' about that... and what difference does it make? So the 'H' is similar, so what?"

"If an expert was given these to compare, they might agree that both signatures were written by the same man."

"Not me," Grady yelled.

"Probably not, unless you're an expert forger. My guess is Mister Hunt signed those names."

Grady worked his jaw. "So, it's not my problem."

"Unless he decides to pin the blame on you."

Grady opened his mouth and closed it without speaking.

"Henry. Look, I'm trying to help you here."

"Shite."

"If Thomas Hunt murdered his brother's family, he's the one who should be in jail. Not Ruby. And not you."

"Got that right." Grady sat. "But you can't prove he did it, can you?" Grady smiled for the first time.

Liam decided to change tack. "Let me ask you something else."

Grady ran his hands over his face, wiping some beads of sweat from his upper lip.

"How much did Mister Hunt pay you?"

"Whadaya' mean?"

"Simple question. How much did he pay you?"

"For what?"

"For setting the fire and keeping your mouth shut?"

"He didn't pay me nothin'. I told ya I didn't start the fire in the basement. That's all I'm saying."

"What I don't understand is this: you took all the risk. You set the fire, you might have even signed the policies for which you could go to jail." Liam moved closer to Grady, whose eyes were big around with fright. "And you got a pittance."

"You're friggin' nuts, making all this up, man."

"All right, Henry. I want you to think about this. If a handwriting expert can prove the name on the documents was signed by you, I'll see to it you're hanged by the neck until dead."

Grady leaped out of his chair. "I didn't sign nothin' so you're barking up the wrong tree."

"Okay then, if the same expert finds that the bogus signature was written by Thomas Hunt, you have to ask yourself if Hunt paid you enough to take the fall for him?"

"He's got nothin' on me."

"Insurance fraud will get you twenty years…unless you turn state's evidence and help me nail the bastard. That'll get you immunity."

"I'm gettin' the hell outa here. We're done."

"Ask yourself, did Thomas Hunt play me for a fool? Am I the patsy that will go to jail for his crimes?"

Grady stormed out the office door.

"Think about it, Henry," Liam called to Grady's back. "It's your life."

※

Liam pulled up his hood and raced down the block to the corner. The rain would help keep him hidden under the awning at the corner apartment building. He would be able to keep an eye on Grady and follow him when he left. Liam felt sure he knew what his destination would be, but he needed to confirm it.

Barely twenty minutes went by and Grady dashed out of the building. He hurried to the corner and stood waiting in the pouring rain for the streetcar. When it arrived, he jumped on and Liam followed. He watched the man from under his hood, happily noting the nervous expression on his face.

Sure enough, Grady alighted at the New York World building. Liam followed. He wanted to be sure his suspect was going to visit Thomas Hunt. When Grady stepped into the elevator and the doors closed, Liam watched the dial stop at the seventh floor. Thomas Hunt's offices were the sole tenants on seven.

✑✒

At eight that evening, Liam hurried into Schrafft's. She was waiting for him at the counter like the last time.

"Hello," Nellie said.

"Sorry I'm late." He shrugged off his coat and hung it on a hook by the door.

"I hope the reason you're late is a positive one. About the case, I mean."

"I am making progress."

He picked up his menu and ordered the blue plate special: meatloaf and mashed potatoes.

"Me too."

"Man, I am starving."

"Did you confront the doorman?"

"I did. I have to admit Henry Grady is rather a dull light bulb."

"Don't keep me in suspense."

"I gave him the opportunity to come clean, about the fire, about the murders, and about the insurance policy signatures. Grady was nervous as a cat in a playroom of two-year-olds."

"But he didn't come clean?"

"Of course not, but the final insult pushed him over the edge."

"Oh?" Nellie said.

"I asked him how much he was paid to do Hunt's dirty work. He didn't take kindly to that." Liam smiled. "Twenty minutes after I spoke with him, he bolted, and I followed him, unbeknownst to him, of course."

"And where did he go?"

"The New York World building, seventh floor."

"I bet Hunt got an earful."

"I'm counting on it."

She grinned. "Well, that should amp up his anxiety."

"Amp up. I like that expression."

"We writers must create our own language, you know."

Their food arrived and they turned to their plates and dug in.

"So now what?" Nellie asked, after a few bites.

"Now, we wait a bit. See how Thomas Hunt calms his minions. Under pressure, he may make a mistake."

Nellie frowned. "Not likely."

"I know. He's too smooth for that but not Grady. I'm betting he'll crack then turn state's evidence against Hunt to save his own skin."

"I hope you're right."

Liam touched her arm. "I need your help with something else."

She set her fork down and turned to look directly at him.

"I'm considering a way to get Ruby out of that horrid place before it's too late. If I can get the evidence on Hunt and his followers, so much the better. But Ruby cannot wait."

"I understand."

"I don't yet have the details of an escape plan, but I'm working on it. Bridget, Ruby's caretaker will help me at the asylum. But there is a problem."

"Let me guess. What happens to Ruby after she's out?"

"The authorities will hunt her down, at least until I get her name cleared."

Nellie said, "I may have a solution. There's a place for women in trouble in upstate New York. They help women who are pregnant and not married, or who are running from men who abuse them, that sort of thing."

Liam nodded.

"I know the director there, and I'm sure she would be willing to take Ruby in and take care of her until her situation changes," Nellie said. "You know, of course, Ruby won't be able to return to the City."

"Not until I prove her innocence. Which I intend to do. For now, I just want her safe. To have a life."

"You're a good man, Liam."

"Let's save that judgment until we see how effective I am at freeing Ruby from her tormenters."

Chapter 31

March 8, 1902

The next day, Liam received a note from Bridget, urging him to come as soon as possible. Now he waited for the ferry with a wire in his blood. Every nerve in his body sizzled and popped, and he could barely keep himself still. He knew what Bridget had in mind and he felt confident he could pull it off. Especially with Nellie's help.

Bridget met him at the dock and they walked together, heads down against the stiff, chilly breeze to a sheltered area near the asylum.

"At least the wind won't get us here." Bridget lowered the hood on her jacket.

Liam noticed her hair had grayed noticeably since he'd first met her.

"Thank you for coming." She touched his arm with gloved hands. "You are the only chance she has, Liam."

"I'm close to solving this case. Soon, the real culprit will be behind bars."

"Aye, I know, pet. But Ruby does not have the time to wait. I don't think she'll last another month."

"Has something happened to her?"

"She's sick."

"How bad is it?"

"She can barely eat or drink, and anything she does manage to get down, she vomits back up. The poor child has no energy to get up in the morning."

"What is the doctor doing about it?"

"Doctor? Don't be daft, love. The doctors don't even see her." Bridget's eyes filled. "I've brought her myself to the infirmary. They keep her for a day, say there's naught wrong with her, just a minor stomach upset, and send her back to her room." She paused, looked down. "I'm worried that... she doesn't have time, Liam. She will die if she remains here. We must get her out."

"Or she'll follow in the path of those other three women patients."

"Aye."

"Escape for Ruby has been in the back of our minds, correct?"

"Yes, of course, it has."

"You've given thought to the details," Liam said. "Tell me."

Bridget inhaled a shaky breath. "There's an old sewage tunnel beneath the asylum. It begins under the kitchen and meanders a long way to an egress."

"How long?"

"Mile, maybe mile and a half."

"Which exits where?"

"Right by the Sound. That's the good news."

"And the bad news?"

The tunnel is dark, freezing cold, and filled with mold, filth, and rats. There are forks, and if she follows the wrong one..."

"She could get lost and die down there." Liam blew out a breath. "How can she possibly attempt this in her state?"

"We've been talking about it. Ruby understands the risks completely. She wants to try. She's pleaded with me every day, even in the state she's in."

"That's encouraging." He took her hand. "How will we proceed?"

"Can you get a boat to meet her at the end of the tunnel?"

"I can, of course. Show me where."

Liam followed Bridget as she hurried back toward the dock then veered south about two hundred yards. She pointed to a copse of winter-bare trees. "There, behind those trees. There is where the tunnel ends."

Liam could barely see a dilapidated concrete opening about fifty feet from the rocky shore, the remains of an old sewage tunnel still draining water. An awful stench wafted on the breeze, and a sign warned: *Prison*

– *Keep Out*. He started for the location, but she stopped him. "There's no time now to explore. They'll be missing me. I've got to get back."

"All right. I get the boat and wait for her there. How will she get to the tunnel? How long will it take her? What happens if—?"

"I know, love, a million questions. I haven't worked out the final details yet. I must see the week's schedule so I can work around that."

"This is very risky for you as well as Ruby," Liam said.

"I don't give a damn. I could never live with meself if something happens to that girl. She is…she is special." She looked at Liam. "But you know that, don't ye, lad?"

"Aye, Bridget, I do."

"All right. I will work out the details and send word before the week is out."

"I'll be ready."

The two stared at each other, co-conspirators on a dangerous path to ruin should Ruby fail to arrive at the tunnel's end.

Liam had his work cut out for him. During the next three days, he snuck out of work for hours at a time. George Twombley covered when anyone came looking for him. Thanks be to George. Liam trusted him and told him about his plan to rescue Ruby. George seemed thrilled to help and offered his services.

"It would be bad enough if I lost my job. It would be devastating if you lost yours as well," Liam had told him with an appreciative smile.

Liam found a fisherman on a wharf on City Island, right across from Hart, who agreed to rent him a boat for a period of one week, not knowing which day would turn out to be the escape day. He researched the Long Island Sound waterway between Hart Island and New York City: the currents, traffic patterns, channel markers, and underwater hazards, all to make the journey as safe as possible. With Nellie's help, he collected items of clothing for Ruby: wool coat, hat, boots, scarf, and gloves. March's in-like-a-lion had not transformed into a lamb yet. Temperatures were still in the forties, and the rain drove on without end.

Liam also shopped for food items that he hoped Ruby could digest without vomiting. Bridget gave him a few ideas, but he wondered what he would do if she couldn't eat. He checked local hospitals but decided that would be too dangerous. Most would ask questions. How would he explain her dire condition?

George came through once again. His cousin was a doctor in the Bronx who would be happy to examine Ruby and give her whatever first-aid medications she needed.

Bridget had the hardest job. She had to investigate the escape route to make sure it had not been blocked off, and she had to prepare Ruby for her solo trek. In two days, Liam would visit with Ruby and gauge her physical and mental condition to assess her ability for this challenge. He worried that she'd been so worn down over the last grueling weeks that she didn't have the strength to carry out the plan. A failed escape attempt would bring dire consequences on the heads of all involved.

On the fourth day following his preparations, Liam rode the ferry to Hart Island. The sun shone for the first time in a week and he felt cheered and optimistic. He hoped Bridget had arranged for Ruby to leave the building and walk the grounds.

When he stepped onto the pier, a uniformed guard from the Department of Corrections approached.

"You'll need to show a pass, sir," the man said, his hands resting on his belt.

"A pass? What pass?"

"New regulations. All visitors to the asylum must have prior permission to see the inmates, er, I mean patients."

Liam pulled out his badge and identification. "I'm a police officer investigating a case. I need no pass." He started walking past the guard.

The guard blocked the path. "Just a minute, sir. I don't have any orders giving exceptions here." He looked over his shoulder as if someone might be watching.

"I don't care what orders you have. I told you I'm with the NYPD. In fact, as a corrections guard, you work for me. So, step out of my way." Liam used his height to advantage as he looked down on the man.

The man stuttered, but let him by.

Liam worried that the man would contact a higher authority who would stop his visit. He strode quickly toward the red brick building where Bridget hurried down the steps with Ruby, their arms interlinked. Liam noticed Ruby had navigated the steps without stumbling. Thank heavens.

Ruby wore only a thin robe over her nightdress and Bridget had wrapped a blanket around her shoulders.

"Oh, Liam, you made it." Bridget's face was creased with worry. "There are new regulations—"

"It's all right, Bridget. I have some authority here, still, we may not have much time. Let's sit over there." He steered them to a wooden bench near a copse of trees. A ship's horn echoed off the water and reached them from across the Sound.

Ruby smiled. "That sound...it reminds me of freedom."

He gave her a faint smile but when he studied her close up, he all but gasped. She was a walking ghost. Her skin was translucent; he could actually see blue veins in her neck. Her lips were a ghastly shade of gray and there were dark bruises around her eyes.

"Ruby, has someone hit you?"

"No," Bridget answered. "She is but weak and unwell."

"Please, Liam," Ruby said. "Help me get out of here."

Liam swallowed hard. She looked so frail. He wished he could help her carry out her part of the escape plan.

"I know what you're thinking," Bridget said. "But Ruby and I have talked and she is ready. Give her a chance, please."

"Ruby?"

She looked at him, eyes directly on his. "I am ready, Liam."

He felt buoyed by the sound of her voice. Strong, confident. Still... "But you are so weak."

"I can do it. I don't care how difficult or dangerous it is. I must get out of here." She licked her cracked lips, looked up at him with fire in her eyes. "I will do it."

His heart burned for her pain. If only he could pack her under his arm and carry her away right now.

Bridget watched him. "I've checked the schedule and the best date is March 15. Several doctors and nurses will be away for a meeting in the city. Thursdays are usually quiet around here and the weather promises to remain dry."

Liam asked Ruby, "Do you know which way to go?"

She pulled the blanket tight around her. "Bridget showed me the entrance to the tunnel. I will follow it to the end, at which point I will be only a few yards from the shore."

"What about the lefts and rights at the various tunnels?"

"I will find the exit."

"Yes you will, dove. And then, once you get out, what next?" Bridget asked.

Ruby turned to Liam. "You'll meet me with a boat, right?"

"It's all arranged." *How trusting she is. She hardly knows me.* He took her hand and felt exhilarated.

"What happens when I escape?" Ruby asked, looking from Bridget to Liam. "Where will I go? Who will help me? I have no family I can trust... no one."

For that, Liam counted on Nellie Bly's connections. "One thing at a time, Ruby. You'll be okay." He hoped.

Chapter 32

March 13, 1902

The date of Ruby's escape drew near. Liam was as anxious as a puppy locked in a closet of cats. He had not heard from Bridget in two days but that didn't surprise him. She tried to make herself invisible so she could conspire behind the scenes.

But what if someone caught on to their plan? What if someone overheard Bridget and Ruby talking? What if Ruby had taken seriously ill? What if, what if? *Stop worrying,* Liam berated himself.

With Tallulah and Budgie hopping around the kitchen table, he made notes in his journal. He'd kept track of every detail, every interview, every piece of evidence that turned up, every theory that popped into his head, proven or not.

The interviews with Ruby's best friend, Juliet, and Patrick's friend, Terence, disappointed him. The two teenagers were devastated but had no inkling who might want to destroy the Hunt family. Neither of them personally had had any contact with Thomas Hunt, although both talked of *sour* Uncle Thomas, in a joking manner.

Liam mulled over his last interview with Thomas Hunt, this time at a café in midtown. The man was insufferable. He added no new information to what Liam already knew; he laid blame on his niece for the loss of his brother's family. And all was recited with a smug smile and a twinkle in his eye. The lying bastard. He knew that Liam didn't believe him but also that he had no proof to act.

He wondered what effect Grady had on Hunt when he ran to him whining that they were being harassed by the police. Maybe Grady even threatened Hunt with exposure if he didn't pay them more for the risks they took. Ha. That would be rich. Threatening a man like Thomas Hunt.

Liam intended to confront Grady again. He would break the man if it was the last thing he would do.

Tallulah hopped up to him and he stroked her belly. "Sweet birdie. You don't know how lucky you are that you can fly."

Liam continued writing until midnight, adding details of the escape plan, the strategy to get Ruby to a doctor. He suddenly threw the pencil down and dropped his head into his hands.

"So many flaws, so many gaps," he muttered. At least Nellie would help settle her in a place where she could be safe." She'd be running from the law, for God's sake." He waved his upraised arms.

Budgie screeched and flew across the room.

Once Ruby was free, he still had to track down the real killer. He knew it was Thomas but how could he prove it? And what about the clowns, Flynn and Grady? Would they give evidence against Thomas Hunt? Not likely. Hunt would pay them off and they'd leave town.

What about Thomas Hunt? What would he do once he realized Ruby had escaped? She couldn't testify against him because she hadn't actually seen the killer.

Bridget would help but all her information was based on speculation that would never hold up in a court of law.

Wait a minute, wait a minute. The only piece of evidence he had was that fingerprint with the scar on it. Could he match it to Thomas Hunt's print? He knew in his gut it would match. But how to get Hunt to offer up his fingerprints. Not bloody likely. The glass he had taken from Delmonico's that day proved to have only smeared prints.

Liam stretched his arms over his head and yawned mightily. He was bone weary, and thinking about this case gave him a headache.

The other possibility was the handwriting. Was there some way to prove that Hunt forged Grady and Flynn's signatures on the insurance policies? Damn, how many women died in the asylum because of his greed?

He went back to the kitchen table and added those notes. He closed his murder book and slipped it in a large envelope. He addressed it to his brother, Collin, who lived in the Bronx, with a note asking him to keep it safe if anything happened to him. Liam offered no options as to who Collin could give the murder book to. He couldn't trust anyone, well, maybe George, but that would only get poor George in hot water. No, Collin was best off keeping the journal hidden for now.

He didn't seal it, however, because he wanted to add several more notes: one about Thomas Hunt's fingerprint, if, as he hoped, Nellie would help him get it. And two, the handwriting analysis. He'd check with George on that one. But even if they found an expert, would it hold up in court? It really was just someone's opinion, not real science.

By the next evening, Liam had his answers. True to her word, Nellie had set up an appointment with Thomas Hunt the next day to interview him about the murders of his brother's family. She'd convinced Joseph Pulitzer, her boss, that the New York World would be the first to get the sensational story.

Despite her pointed questions, her digging into the family relationships, her probing into Ruby's committal to the asylum, she felt flummoxed by Hunt. He was charming, intelligent, and infinitely clever in his answers, so much so that he almost had her convinced he was innocent.

Worse yet, she could not get his fingerprints. He left the room at no time, had nothing to drink, picked up nothing from his desk. By the time she left Hunt's office, she felt frustrated and embarrassed that she had failed Liam and Ruby, whom she'd never even met.

George had fared no better that day with handwriting analysis. From his colleagues he learned that experts were often laughed out of court and could actually make things worse for the defense.

The second door slammed in Liam's face.

That night, he logged all the new information into his book. He knew that the legal pathway to Ruby's freedom had hit a stone wall, one that would be difficult to remove. His only hope to exonerate Ruby was a confession by Henry Grady or Jeremiah Flynn. That thought left him deflated.

Before a blue mood took hold of him, Liam tucked his murder book in the large envelope and this time he sealed it. He had already put postage on it, so he only needed to drop it in a mailbox. His brother would receive it in a day or two. For now, he would follow through on the plans to help Ruby escape.

Early the next evening, Liam headed to the dock on City Island, picked up his small skiff, and practiced his rowing technique for an hour near the dock. The boat smelled of fish since that's what it was used for, but he didn't think Ruby would mind. He smiled at the thought of her scrunching her nose up when she got in.

He left the boat tied up, ready to be picked up in the early morning hours. Bridget had sent him details of the plan. Ruby would head to the tunnel at one in the morning when the asylum was in deep sleep mode. If all went well, Ruby would exit the tunnel between three-thirty and four a.m. depending on how quickly she walked and, God forbid, if she took a wrong turn or two.

Liam wished he could be there with her, but he dared not leave the boat untended. His thoughts jumped from believing she could make it to knowing in his heart she could not. He sweated under his jacket even though it was forty-five degrees. He checked his pocket watch. Time for some supper, and then more waiting. But he would not leave the dock. He looked around for a pub, spotted one and ambled over.

After a hearty stew and two beers, Liam headed back to the boat. He hovered near for an hour, then at two in the morning, jumped in and began rowing to Hart Island. This would be the longest night of his life.

In an hour he reached the beach at Hart Island, just like planned. Now he waited, watching for movement from the distant tunnel. By five o'clock, Ruby had not shown up and he knew something was wrong. Dawn would be brightening the sky soon and he couldn't remain there without getting caught.

He hopped out of the skiff, pulled it onto the shore beneath a large overhanging maple, and took off at a run toward the tunnel exit. When he got there, he walked inside, keeping his back to the wall and listened. Nothing. A few more steps and a few more. He heard something. Footsteps? Ruby? Oh, God. He moved forward. Voices. He stopped to listen. First, a woman's voice, then a man's.

"Hello Ruby, we were worried about you."

His heart dropped like a stone.

Feeling glum and at a loss with what to do next, Liam dropped off the boat at six a.m. and headed to the train station. He would visit his brother in the Bronx and tell him everything. The murder book had already been mailed, but Liam would make sure in person that Collin understood the truth about Ruby Hunt. He had no idea what his next steps would be.

At this time of day, Grand Central Station was bustling with commuters rushing to get to work. He purchased a ticket, then went into the men's room to wash his face. He knew he looked like a dead man walking. The mirror confirmed his suspicions. His face was gaunt with deep hollows in his cheeks, his eyes were red and felt scratchy, and his hair had grown into a long fringe over his eyes.

As he stood on the platform, waiting for the train to Scarsdale, with several stops in New York City and the Bronx, he felt like his life was over. He'd lost Ruby for good. He probably would lose his job. He felt like a failure on all counts.

Quit feeling sorry for yourself, man. You'll think of a way to save her... and your job. Ruby's face floated before him and he stepped toward the platform's edge.

A whistle sounded down the tracks and he spotted the beam of light from the oncoming train rumbling into the station. The crowd pushed forward to the edge of the platform. He felt hands gripping his shoulders from behind. A hot breath touched his ear. In one horrifying millisecond he realized he'd been wrong about the killer. Deadly wrong.

"Careful, Detective, you could fall to your death," Dr. Franz Uber whispered.

New York City
2016

Chapter 33

May 24, 2016

It felt like he'd barely closed his eyes when the phone rang. Lizzie. He sat up, turned on the lamp by his bed and grabbed his cell. The clock read: *11:30*. The caller ID name read: Amanda. His heart beat quickened. "Hey, everything okay?"

"Don't freak, Dad." Everything's all right with Grandma. Not to worry."

He sank back into the bed. "Do you know what time it is?"

"You're usually up. Sorry."

He laughed. "I'm up now. What's going on?"

"Can I come over?"

"Now?"

"I think you'll want to see what I found."

"Come on over. Drive, though, no subways at this time of night. Call me from downstairs and I'll come down and put a permit in your windshield."

"Cool. Later."

Frank rolled out of bed, threw on sweat pants and a tee shirt and staggered into the kitchen to start some coffee. He took the pillowcase off Dexter's cage.

"Dexter, your girlfriend is coming over, so wake up and look alert."

The parrot gave a soft squawk.

"Yeah, I know, I know. It's late." Frank ambled into the bathroom and washed his face with cold water. This case had taken a toll on him. He felt exhausted.

The bell rang and he opened the door to his daughter. She carried a large carryall and a greasy bag. "Kaplan's." She smiled.

He kissed her cheek and took the bag of doughnuts, set them on a plate and brought coffee to the kitchen table.

"Hang on, let me go put my placard in your car."

He ran downstairs and was out of breath when he returned. *Man, I am out of shape.*

"So, what have you got that can't wait until morning?"

"You'll be thanking me for this, trust me." Amanda bit into a doughnut and reached down into her carryall to fish out a large file folder. "Guess what this is?"

"Ugh, a guessing game at midnight?"

"Okay, I'll tell you. It's a notebook that Nellie Bly kept."

"No shit. How on earth did you get that?"

Amanda's eyes glittered. "I started wondering about Nellie Bly and the whole asylum thing. Was she around during Ruby's time? Doing stories and all?"

Frank's blood sped up in his veins.

"Not only was she around, but she was in touch with all the main characters."

"What are the chances of that?"

She flipped through her notes. "She still worked for Joseph Pulitzer at the New York World and did a story on the Hunt family murders about two months after the event."

Frank said nothing.

"She interviewed Thomas Hunt and other friends and distant relatives of the Hunts. Here's the rub, though. Her story was rather benign, no accusations were made, and Uncle Thomas came out smelling like a rose."

"Hmph, not surprising."

"But wait, don't blame Nellie. She was forced to write the story like that...by her boss."

"Pulitzer?"

"Yes. Would you believe he was a dear friend of Thomas Hunt's? They palled around together, played golf, went to the men's club, all that guy stuff."

"Did Nellie—?"

"Yes, indeedy. Nellie told all in her own personal diary, which was stored in the World files from 1902. She actually left there not long after and worked at other papers, plus wrote books and such. But she was required to leave her investigative notes behind."

"Like her own murder book?"

"I thought it was odd, too. But remember, Ruby was now dead, so what more could she do?"

"She could have still exposed the goings on at the asylum."

"Only if she wanted to ruin her career. My guess is that Pulitzer wouldn't have wanted another asylum exposé. Certainly not one with his two good pals as the focus of the story."

"Thomas Hunt and Franz Uber?" Frank got up and poured them another mug of coffee. "What happened to her diary?"

Amanda pulled a black leather-bound book from her carryall. "Voilà."

"Jesus, Amanda, you actually have Nellie Bly's diary?" He sat at the table.

"From one investigative reporter to another."

"Did you read it?"

"What do you think?"

He grinned. "Tell me what it says."

"Okay, here's a summary of Nellie's story." She settled back into her seat. Dexter nodded off on the perch in his cage.

"In a sense, the detective in 1902, Liam McCarty, recruited Nellie. He had read her book, *Ten Days in a Madhouse*, and wanted to meet her. When she learned about the Ruby Hunt case, she offered to help in any way possible. She managed to get McCarty into the office of Hunt Assets to go through the files and dig up anything related to the asylum."

"They find anything?"

"Insurance policies that clearly pointed to Thomas and his co-conspirators, Grady and Flynn."

"I knew it," Frank said.

"Unfortunately, they couldn't prove he had anything to do with the murders."

"The killer didn't leave a trace?"

"Not exactly. Nellie tried to get Thomas Hunt's fingerprints. McCarty believed the killer had a scar on his finger. They'd found such a print on the murder weapon...a straight razor, by the way." Amanda sipped coffee. "In an attempt to get Hunt's fingerprints, Nellie claimed to be writing a story on the sensational murder case. Her boss went along, but dumbed down the final article. In the end, she was never able to obtain a fingerprint. Hunt was too shrewd."

"A scar on the fingerprint on the blade, huh?"

"Say, do you think that blade would still be around You know...in some evidence box from the 1902 murders?"

Frank stared at her. "Make a note to check that."

Amanda jotted it down. "And finally, listen to this. McCarty, along with Ruby's caretaker, Bridget, and Nellie planned to help Ruby escape the asylum."

"Was escape even possible?"

"There was an old sewage tunnel Ruby would have to navigate. McCarty supplied the boat. Nellie's role was to find a safe house for Ruby to stay after her escape."

"When was this escape?"

Amanda flipped through pages. "The date was set for March 15."

"March 15?" Frank stood and walked to the window, gazed into the dark street below. "That's the date McCarty fell, or was pushed in front of a train at Grand Central Station."

Amanda's eyes widened. "Of course. Wait, is that why the escape never took place?"

"No. I think the escape would have been much earlier, probably in early hours of the morning."

"Naturally, it had to be when no one in the asylum was up."

"I think the escape went bust, and Liam, probably mucho despondent, headed out of town by rail, where he was killed and had no time to talk to Nellie about the failed escape."

Amanda sighed. "Where would he have been going?"

"Probably to his brother, Collin, in the Bronx."

"You're right. According to Nellie, Liam had written all his notes in his murder book and sent it off to Collin."

"Maybe he needed someone to talk to at that point."

"Yeah, I'd be feeling pretty depressed," Amanda said.

"What else?"

"Nellie tried to investigate McCarty's death but Pulitzer put a stop to it. Said it was an accident and not worthy of news coverage. He gave her an assignment in upstate New York, where she remained for three or four weeks. By the time she returned to the City, Bridget was gone and Ruby was already dead and buried."

Frank exhaled deeply. "Poor Liam."

Amanda looked at her father. "Poor Ruby. Jeez, what a rotten deal. Say, did the DNA ever prove it was Ruby buried in that trench?"

"Yup. It was a definitive match to David Hunt's family tree. Sorry, I thought I'd mentioned it."

Amanda stood and stretched. Dexter hopped from his cage to her outstretched arm and gave her a kiss.

Frank smiled at his two kids.

"What now, Dad?"

"Here's where I tell you what a fantastic job you did and how much help this will be in the investigation."

"In the old case, maybe, but what about the present case…Sophie and the doctor, Steinberg?"

"I've got a few ideas."

"But you can't talk about an ongoing investigation."

"It's not that I don't trust you, but being a reporter—"

"I know, I know." Amanda gathered her keys and carryall and moved to the door. "I'm going to leave Nellie's diary and notebook with you. I know you enjoy reading historic murder mysteries."

Chapter 34

May 25, 2016

The day was uncomfortably warm. When Frank left his apartment and reached the heat of the street, he took off his jacket. High temperature, high humidity, no breeze, and the concrete sidewalks radiated the heat back up into the air. Ahh, summer in the city.

Before he had time to start his car and turn on the air, his cell rang.

"Mead."

"Hey, Frank, this is Connor McCarty."

"Yeah, Connor, hey, what's up?"

"Remember I told you my wife and I were moving? Even though we hadn't bought a house yet, my wife started goin' through stuff. That's when I came across Liam's diary, you remember?"

"Sure. His murder book."

"We bought a house right after that conversation and are moving *tout suite,* so now my wife is *really* going through everything. It's called downsizing, I guess. Anyway, to make a long story endless, she recruited me for this effort. So we're cleaning out the attic and you'll never guess what I found."

Why does everyone like to play guessing games?

"I give up."

"Evidence from the murders in 1902."

"What kind of evidence?"

"A box of physical evidence from the Hunt murders."

A buzzing began in Frank's ears. "Why the hell—?"

"Why wasn't it turned in to Evidence? Good question. Two reasons, I think. First, Liam was still going over all the evidence to try and prove his case."

"And second, he was killed by a train," Frank said.

"He was murdered . . . didn't have time to get it there and file the stuff into evidence."

"How did you get it?"

"Collin must've collected all Liam's stuff after he died. Cleaned out his apartment. Probably didn't know what the box contained. I doubt he even opened it. Just took it and packed it away with the rest of Liam's belongings."

"Pretty sad statement. Did Liam have a lot of stuff?"

"From what Collin implied in some letters he wrote, Liam did have a lot of stuff. He was a collector of sorts."

"Yeah?"

"Seems he had some coins, nothing valuable, unfortunately, and books. Lots of old mysteries, and those old mystery magazines, would ya' believe?"

"I would." Frank laughed.

"He also had two birds."

Frank flashed to Dexter.

"Yeah, uh, parakeets, you know. Guess he was an animal lover but couldn't have a dog in the apartment, so he got two keets."

"Hmph."

"Collin took care of them, course."

"Right, birds." Frank and Liam had a lot in common.

"Sorry, getting off track here. Kinda makes me sad, ya know, about Liam, dying so young and all. I think he was a good cop."

Silence.

"I think you're right, Connor. Liam was a good cop and he would've solved the case had he lived."

"Yeah. Anyways, the box of evidence is sitting in front of me on my desk. I really should be logging it in as evidence. After all it was an official NYPD case. But I thought you'd want to check it out first."

"You bet I do. On my way."

Frank called Will and told him he would pick him up asap. He got into his car and slid into a furnace of a front seat. He opened all the windows, started up the Beemer and turned the A/C on high. Jesus, what will the summer bring if May is like this? *Fuckin' global warming.*

Twenty minutes later, he picked up Will outside the station. He explained on the way.

"This is incredible, you realize?" Will said. "A find like this?"

"Almost too incredible."

They didn't speak on the ride, which took only ten minutes.

In Connor's office, they didn't take the time to sit.

"Hey, guys, coffee?"

"No," Frank said.

"Yes," Will said.

All three chuckled.

Connor poured a mug for Will. "Here's the evidence box. I looked through it, but didn't open any of the packages. Or touch anything, of course." He pointed to a beat-up corrugated carton.

Frank opened the flaps. It seemed like a religious moment and he couldn't quell the blood thudding in his ears.

First, he lifted out four paper bags. One was marked Laura Hunt, one Patrick Hunt, one Jonas Hunt, and finally, one marked Ruby Hunt. Each one contained an item of clothing stained with blood. A blouse from Laura, a shirt from Jonas, a shirt from Patrick, and a blouse from Ruby. Frank removed each item gently and laid them on the table near Connor's desk.

When he got to Ruby's blouse, he said, "These bloodstains are different from the other family members, smears, not spatters."

"Proves she obtained those by hugging her family members, not slicing their throats." Will looked at the rest of the items. "These other stains are clearly blood spurting from a cut artery."

"How could they not know that?" Connor said. "It was 1902, but couldn't they have known the difference between contact blood and arterial bursts? Or were bloodstains just bloodstains back then?"

"I think Liam recognized the difference," Frank said. "That may be another reason why he didn't turn the clothing into evidence."

"He may have thought the evidence would disappear," Will said. "Especially if Uncle Thomas had a good friend in the NYPD."

"Right, like the Commissioner," Connor said.

Frank returned to the box. "Four teacups and saucers, one cracked." He rested them on the table next to the clothes."

"Think there could be prints?" Connor asked.

"Even if there were, who would we match them to?" Will said.

"Ruby had her prints taken at the asylum. They should be in the system. But I'm more interested in Thomas' prints."

"Are they in the system, such that it was back then?" Connor said. "Doubtful, unless he'd been arrested for something."

"There may be a way to identify Thomas' prints," Frank said.

"Oh yeah," Connor said. "Liam mentioned something about a scar on one of his fingers, right?"

Frank nodded.

"Well, we'll check the china for that," Will said.

"Hold on." Frank reached in the box and pulled out something small, wrapped in a bloodied cloth.

"They sure didn't know how to preserve evidence." He unwrapped the cloth and was elated at the find a Sheffield straight razor blade tinged with blood.

"Gentlemen, here is the murder weapon."

"Fingerprints on the blade would be proof positive," Will said.

"Not necessarily," Frank said. "Remember, Ruby may have picked it up at the scene. Or, if she was framed, her prints may have been pressed onto the handle while she was in shock."

"In that case, the killer would have wiped it clean before," Will said.

"What kind of man would kill his own family and then pin it on his niece, a nineteen-year-old girl?" Connor said. "And condemn her to hell in a lunatic asylum?"

"A cold-hearted man." Frank packed the evidence into the box. "We'll get onto this right away. And we'll log it into Evidence. Thanks, Connor. This may well resolve a very cold case."

"My pleasure. Let me know, will you? Like I said before, I want to know who killed my great uncle."

Frank exited, box in hand. Will followed. When they reached his car, Frank's cell went off. Maggie. Will took the box and set it in the back seat.

"Hey, Maggie."

"Frank. I know you're eager to hear my news so I won't make small talk. The official incarceration photos of the three women definitely match the three women patients in the group shot."

"No doubt?"

"I'd put my name to it."

"That's good enough for me."

"Glad to help."

"You're not exactly done," he said.

"Oh?"

"Remember when you were working on the Salem witch trial documents? You were able to use your digital skills in analyzing handwriting, right?"

"With the help of an FBI *questioned documents* expert, yeah. Why?"

"I've got a handwriting dilemma I need to resolve. It has to do with insurance policies. I'm sure that one man forged the signatures of two others on several insurance policies."

"In 1902?"

"Yes. Any way you can check for me?"

She sighed. "Sure. Send me the docs with the signatures you want checked plainly marked. Don't tell me whose is whose. I'll figure it out."

"Thanks, Maggie, again. I will get those sent over today. I really appreciate this."

"You owe me. Big time."

"I hear you." He clicked off.

With these latest findings, he might actually be able to close Liam McCarty's case. Now, if only he could close Sophie's and Steinberg's.

Chapter 35

That evening, Frank met Rachel at Bryant Park where they ordered summery-salad dinners. He watched her as she ate and felt an unexpected pang in his chest, a poignant longing. He'd been thinking of his wife Jeannie of late, not surprising, since the anniversary of her suicide fast approached.

Looking at Rachel, her similarity in looks to Jeannie brought back memories. The color and fall of her hair, the sparkle in her eyes, the sharp wit and intellect, all reminded him of his dead wife.

Funny how it's not Amanda who makes me think of her, but Rachel.

"Something wrong, Frank?" Rachel asked.

"No, why do you say that?"

"You just sighed the sigh of the ages."

He smiled. "Just this case, I guess. Can't stop the wheels, you know?"

"Why don't you fill me in? Then I'll share what I found out in my research."

"Deal." Frank gave her an overview of the latest info.

"That's incredible," Rachel said. "Nellie Bly? Amanda actually found her diary? Wow. Two great women reporters."

"Amanda is definitely following in her footsteps."

"And to think Nellie helped Liam McCarty break into Hunt's insurance company. Wow."

"Yeah, you said it."

She laughed. "Sorry. When I get blown away like that, I have trouble finding words. 'Wow' kinda' fills in."

"You were right, by the way. My expert in D.C. confirmed that the women in Bridget's photo matched the three inmate photos you dug up. Now this same expert is working on the handwriting. I'd bet my Beemer the handwriting on all those insurance documents is Thomas Hunt's."

"You're probably right. And if Thomas did kill his own brother's family, murder Liam McCarty, and lock up his own niece in an asylum, it doesn't surprise me that he was responsible for the strange deaths of Henry Grady and Jeremiah Flynn."

"What's this?" Frank leaned forward, fork in hand. "Grady and Flynn?"

With a sly curl to her lips, Rachel reached in her purse for her notes. "It seems the elevator man at the Hunt apartment building somehow managed to fall out of the tenth story window of said building."

"What? An accident, I'll bet."

"Yup. Papers say he was moving some furniture for one of the tenants, tripped and, whoops, out he went." She handed him the article.

"Holy cow." Frank searched for the date. "June, 1902. A few months after Liam and Ruby died."

"Now Henry Grady's death, the doorman, is even more bizarre."

"I can't wait to hear."

"A month after Flynn died, Grady just happened to plunge down the elevator shaft of the Hunt apartment building...from the same tenth floor. Terrible accident, just terrible." She grinned as she handed him the article. "Deadly year, 1902."

"It's too bad that Liam didn't realize how dangerous Hunt was. He might have been on guard and stayed alive."

"And he might have been able to get enough evidence against Hunt to lock him away for a few lifetimes." Rachel pushed her empty plate away. "It seems like you're closer to closing this cold case than the current one. That true?"

"Afraid so." He leaned back in his chair. "Except my job is not to solve the *Ruby* Hunt case, but to solve the *Sophie* Hunt case."

"I'm rather glad you solved the Ruby Hunt case, actually. And the Liam McCarty case."

He didn't say anything.

"Something still bothers you, doesn't it?"

"Money's a powerful motive but I keep wondering why Thomas Hunt would kill his whole family for it. Was he that greedy or needy? I mean, this is his own brother."

"Do you think he hired someone to do the actual killings?"

"I'd feel a little better about that, I suppose. To slit the throat of your family, a young nephew and a woman? I don't get it."

"Ruby was poisoned in the asylum," Rachel said. "So Thomas had someone else handle that murder. One of the doctors or caretakers, I presume. Maybe even Franz Uber."

"And what about Liam McCarty? Was he getting too close? Uncovering the insurance fraud?"

"Makes sense. Kill the detective, tie up loose ends."

Frank nodded. "And if we extend this reason to today's case, maybe David Hunt was operating a similar scheme and had to silence anyone who caught onto it."

"Sophie and Steinberg?" she said. "I hate to use the cliché but an apple doesn't fall far from the tree does it?"

"The ancestral tree?" Frank smiled.

"What now?" Rachel asked.

"Now is when I take another hard, fresh look at the case, lay out everything I have and, honestly, start over."

"How about we talk about it now? Bounce a few ideas off me."

"You know what I think?"

"What?"

"I think you're a frustrated detective," Frank said.

Rachel's face reddened. "Actually, maybe a frustrated mystery novelist."

"Ha. That could be remedied."

"I'm working on it."

"You seriously want me to bounce ideas off you?"

"I do. Go for it."

"All right. Let's start with Sophie. She had a gun, a .22 Ruger, one many women select if they want a gun for protection. My mother, would you believe, helped her get it."

"I like Lizzie even more."

"Hmph. Anyway, the way the scene looked, it's my theory that there was an intruder, someone looking for the suitcase, perhaps. Sophie managed to get her gun out, there was a struggle and she gets shot with her own gun."

"An accident, then?"

"Not premeditated, at least."

"But the suitcase was not at her apartment, so the intruder was unsuccessful."

The waitress came by and they both ordered coffees and desserts, blueberry pies with lots of extra whipped cream.

"Okay," Rachel said. "Who was after the suitcase?"

"David would be the only one threatened by anything in it. Maybe he worried that there was some connection to his insurance company."

"Wait. Hunt Liability? That was Thomas Hunt's company. Did that company morph into the one that exists today?"

Frank shook his head. "I don't believe so. Aurora care facilities are a spinoff of Hunt Liability. The Hunt family of today continued the insurance business of their ancestors, just a different model."

"Yeah, a much richer one. Care facilities are gold mines."

Pies and coffee arrived.

Frank dug into his pie.

"What about Madelyn? Could she have killed Sophie?"

"Doubtful. She gave the suitcase to Sophie in the first place."

"Right." She sipped coffee, her pie untouched. "Assuming the suitcase is the reason for Sophie's death."

Frank snapped his head up. "Why would you say that?"

"We're, excuse the 'we,' as if I'm on the case… You're assuming the suitcase is the reason for the murder. What if it has nothing to do with the suitcase?"

Frank rubbed his stubbled chin as he mulled this over. His mother insisted that it was the reason for Sophie's death. But what was in it that was so threatening? The idea stuck like a thorn in his side. Had he been wrong about motive all this time?

Rachel interrupted his thoughts. "Just saying, maybe a plain vanilla intruder broke in and accidently killed her because she had a gun?"

"Nothing was stolen."

Rachel stared at him, thinking. "Right. Makes no sense, does it? Okay, let's assume the suitcase is the reason. And Madelyn gave the suitcase to Sophie. That would leave her out. What about Doctor Steinberg? Did he know about the suitcase and why would he care?"

"To the second question, he might care if, like David, he believed there was something in the suitcase, a past connection to the company, something that could damage their business or their reputation."

She nodded, sipped coffee.

"As to the first question, did he even know about the suitcase?" Frank shrugged. "How would he? Who would tell him? David? Madelyn? If so, why?"

"In any event, Steinberg winds up dead, so, is it safe to say, he's not Sophie's killer?"

"I don't think he would have any reason to even know who Sophie was." Frank scooped up a forkful of pie.

"Do you think the same person killed both Sophie and Steinberg?"

He chewed, swallowed, then: "They are connected, but the answer to that is, 'I don't know.' The murder weapon was different in each crime."

"Is that unusual? Would a killer always use the same weapon?"

"Not necessarily the exact same one, but they tend to favor a certain type. That is, he may use a .22 or a 9mm, but not the same .22 or 9mm. But then there's opportunistic murders where the perp uses whatever he can get his hands on." Frank paused. "Besides, if the .22 in this case was Sophie's, it would behoove the perp to get rid of it asap."

They lapsed into silence. Frank finished his coffee and the waitress refilled it. Rachel attacked her pie like it might be her last meal.

"Let's take another tack," Frank began. "Steinberg and David have a ten-year relationship: David hires him to administer the Aurora facilities, leaving Steinberg access to all the finances."

"Back up," Rachel said. "Did David really *not* know that Steinberg isn't Steinberg?"

"I don't believe he knew. When we told him, he seemed genuinely shocked, and angry that he was duped all those years. Unless he's an award-winning actor."

"Maybe we're making this too complicated," she said. "Maybe it could be all about the money. Steinberg wanted more money to keep the finances in order, keep any misappropriations of funds hidden. Perhaps there was some Medicare fraud going on, and the two were raking in the dough. Maybe something tripped them up and their scam was about to be exposed. Or maybe Steinberg just wanted a bigger piece of the action."

"It's possible."

"Then David could be the killer."

"He could be...right. Then why do I think he isn't? At least not Steinberg's killer. Sophie's yes, because that was an accident. And he had reason to wonder what was in the infamous suitcase."

"You don't think David is ruthless enough to just murder someone in cold blood for the almighty dollar?"

"I don't. And I'm never wrong." Frank grinned and chucked another bite of pie.

"Who else could have killed him, then?"

"There is another possibility. Remember Steinberg was hiding his true identity for years. Maybe someone who knew him in a previous life may have found him, crept out of the woodwork and...bang."

"Jeez, I didn't even think of that." Rachel frowned. "What does your instinct tell you, Frank?"

"That I'm missing something. It's just out of reach." He held his hand up in the air ready to catch it.

She nodded.

"This has helped, though, Rachel. Thanks. Gives me a sharper perspective, looking back on the whole case with a new set of eyes. Pretty eyes, too."

She smiled at his compliment. "You'll figure it out, Frank. I have faith in you."

I wish I had as much faith in myself. He took out his frustration on his last bite of pie.

Chapter 36

May 26, 2016

By six-thirty a.m., Frank had jotted notes in his case file—the Ruby Hunt case file—and drank his second cup of coffee. If only he had as much to add to his Sophie Hunt slash Roger Steinberg case file.

A door closed in the outer office and Will sauntered in.

"What are you doing here so early?" Frank asked.

"Is it early?" Will yawned.

"For you? I'd say so." A smile curved one side of his mouth. "What's up?"

"I wanted to be the first to give you the news."

"Good news, I hope. I've had more than my share of bad."

"The fingerprints on the teacups at Ruby Hunt's house. There was, indeed, an 'artifact' found on one of the prints. Lab surmises it's a scar on the finger. Probably a thumb print by the way the print was laid down."

"Which means," Will went on, "dear old Uncle Thomas was the one who slipped the chloral hydrate into the cups."

"Or, at the very least, he was there." Frank threw his pen down. "Easier to kill them when they're groggy."

"Looks that way. Bad news is that his print was not found on the razor blade. Only print is Ruby's."

"Not surprising. Thomas wiped his own prints off then left the blade on Patrick's body."

"For Ruby to pick up." Will squinted at him. "You know this for a fact?"

"It's exactly what I would do if I were in his place."

"Works for me." Will rose and poured himself a cup of coffee. "Any news from Maggie?"

"She bets her reputation that the handwriting on the insurance documents were all done by none other than—"

"Uncle Thomas. So, he bamboozled those clowns, Grady and Flynn. Those bozos didn't even sign those policies. Didn't even know about them. Christ, Thomas must have had a good laugh when Grady bitched at him for trying to cheat him."

Frank frowned.

"You should be happy. A century-old murder case...sol-ved."

Frank chuckled at Will's two-syllable pronunciation of solved, a take-off on Inspector *Clousseau*. His cell rang out *Despacito*. "Crime lab," he mouthed to Will.

"Uh oh," Will said. "Pretty early for good news."

Frank held the phone, listened. First one eyebrow shot up, then the second. Frank clicked off. "What the fuck?"

"You gonna tell me?"

"The hairs they found at Sophie's crime scene? They're not a DNA match to David Hunt."

"Shit, there goes our prime suspect."

Frank stood, grabbed his jacket.

"Where are we going?" Will followed him out the door.

"The crime lab. They got a match on another guy."

Twenty minutes later, Frank and Will burst into the crime lab at headquarters.

"Hey, guys, knew you'd be down here asap. Didn't think you could make it this fast, though." Spoken by Roberto Fanta, DNA tech.

"I need some answers here," Frank said. "Who have you got at my crime scene?"

Roberto reached for a folder on his desk. "Those hairs matched a guy named Adolfo Cruz, twenty-five-year-old handyman turned small-time-criminal in Queens. Jackson Heights."

"A petty thief?"

"Here's the screwy thing," Roberto went on. "Four days ago, Cruz was banged up pretty bad in a car wreck on the Belt Parkway. Drunk driving doesn't pay. Paramedics found no identification on him. Registration in the car was in the name of one..." Roberto sorted through his notes, "...one Javier Santos."

"And you're sure the guy in the hospital is not Javier because..?" Will asked.

"Javier is sixty-eight. Anyways, we called Javier and to make a long story longer, found out Adolfo is his nephew. He's wanted for a few burglaries, purse-snatches, and whatnot. No felony convictions. Javier claims Adolfo stole the car. No stolen car report, though." Roberto winked.

Frank's head was spinning. "With no felonies, how did his DNA get into the database?"

"Not the database, but in an unrelated case, an old lady identified him from a mug shot as the guy who had grabbed her bag a week ago and wonked her on the head with it."

"Okay, she recognized him," Will said. "But DNA?"

"Let me finish, will ya?"

Will held up two hands.

"So here's this old gal lying on the sidewalk with a head wound, and she has the balls to grab the son-of-a-bitch by the ankle. Her nails tore the skin. Ha. We got his DNA as further proof to back up her identification of him."

"Good thing since eye witnesses are often unreliable," Will said. "Especially under the duress of a mugging."

"Cruz's DNA report was still sitting on my desk when your report came in. Talk about déjà vu. I recognized it right away. And turns out the old gal he mugged lives in the same building as Sophie Hunt. Wasn't hard to figure out that Cruz was preying on little old ladies in the neighborhood."

"A genius," Will said.

Roberto smiled. "The shithead demolishes his uncle's car and lands in the hospital, so I personally stayed late a couple nights ago to prove his DNA matched what we found under the old lady's fingernails."

"And it matched?" Will said.

"Bada-bing. Perfectly, just like it matched the hairs in Sophie Hunt's place. Give the old lady a medal. Without her, we wouldn't have had a suspect to match to your DNA report."

"Nice work, Roberto," Will said.

"Shit." Frank's voice came out thick. "A run of the mill burglar?" His theory about David Hunt just went down the tubes.

Will ran his palms over his head. "All this time we've been thinking the suitcase was at the heart of this case. Now, it's just an ordinary B and E gone bad. What the hell?"

"I'm not convinced." Frank turned to Will. "We need to talk to this guy, Cruz. Hospital or no hospital. Now."

Will raced after Frank who blew out the door like a Santa Ana wind.

※

Frank had despised hospitals ever since he was eight years old and broke his arm falling out of an elm tree in Strauss Square Park, an old playground in the Lower East Side. He'd been horsing around with his friend, Vinny Ruffolo, chasing each other up and down the slides, swinging on the monkey bars, when Vinny tackled him and he pitched and rolled, landing on his left elbow.

That was all well and good and stuff of kids' play, except the doctors screwed up the surgery and he had to have a second surgery to fix it. Hospitals. Hell.

Then, there was his mom's chemo treatments. Another gruesome story.

Frank strode through the entrance of New York Presbyterian, Will close at his heels. He spoke to the woman at the information desk clerk. "Looking for Adolfo Cruz."

She immediately scrolled through lines on her monitor. "Room 202, one floor up to the left. There's an officer outside his room."

Will asked, "How is he?"

"You'll have to ask the doctor."

Will showed her his badge. "I'm asking you."

She clicked to a new screen. "He's mostly unconscious. Woke up once or twice but then went under again."

"See. That wasn't so hard, was it?"

"Come on." Frank led Will to the elevator. "Let's hope the perp is awake."

"We might be wasting our time," Will said.

Frank gave him an odd frown. "More than we've wasted on David Hunt?"

"Touché." He followed Frank to 202.

Frank flashed his badge to the officer on guard duty. "He awake?"

Guard shrugged. "Nah, just sleeps."

Frank opened the door and approached the bed. Monitors beeped; wires ran every which way from patient to machines, complete with a tube to an IV bag. No blood. No bandages. No casts. Nothing but a bruise on his forehead.

Frank leaned in. "Hey, Adolfo, can you hear me?"

"Frank." Will tapped Frank's shoulder. "Looks like he's sedated. Can't hear for shit."

"Nah." He pointed to the IV bag. "Saline solution. I bet he's just sleeping off a hangover." Frank took a small vial out of his pocket. "Smelling salts." He held it under Cruz's nose.

The man cried out and woke up. "Hey, man, whaa? Where am I? Who the hell are you?"

Will's mouth fell open.

"Hey, Mister Cruz, nice to have you back with us."

"Fuck you." Cruz blinked and then started to close his eyes.

"No, no, hang in there a bit." Frank brought the inhalant closer. Cruz coughed and his eyes watered.

"I'm a homicide detective and I just want to ask you a few questions. Then you can go back to sleep. I promise."

"I got nothin' to say to no cops."

Frank pulled a chair over to the bed. "Now listen. You hearing me?"

Cruz stared at him.

"You're a small-time crook, and I don't give a damn what you did or got away with in the past. This is more serious. This is murder."

Cruz's head swung from left to right as if he were looking for an escape route.

Frank held onto his shoulder with an iron grip. "I just want to know what happened to an old lady on Essex Street."

Sweat seeped out of his pores until his whole face was damp. "No man, no man." He started to sit.

This time Will put a hand on his chest and pushed him down on the bed. "You better talk to the man."

"I'll do what I can to help you, but you've got to tell me the truth. *Comprende*?"

Cruz blinked and whimpered, "I don't feel good, man."

"I hear you had a tough night."

"Maybe I need a lawyer."

Frank glanced at Will. "He wants a lawyer."

Will shook his head. "I didn't hear that."

Frank noticed a defibrillator on a nearby cart. "What he really needs is some encouragement." He wheeled the cart to the bed. "Let's see." He turned a switch.

"Charging," an electronic female voice said, followed by a high-pitched whine.

"How about that. It works." Frank picked up the paddles.

Adolfo's black eyes were ringed in white. "Whatcha doin', man?"

Will stood back, hands up.

The whine stopped. *"Charged,"* the voice announced.

Frank stepped up and hovered the paddles over Adolfo's chest. "I think I'm supposed to yell 'clear', right?"

"Wait, wait, no," Adolfo shouted. "I didn't mean it, man. She, I mean, she came at me with a gun. I just wanted some bucks, man, you know, jewelry, something to sell for drugs. I no meana' hurt anybody. It was an accident, a mistake, you know?" He started crying.

"All right, all right, Adolfo, I believe you. But now you have to help me here. I have an important question for you."

Cruz sniffed.

"Are you listening?"

Cruz gave a barely perceptible nod.

"Who sent you to get the suitcase?"

Cruz scrunched up his face. "Whaa? What suitcase, man?"

"You know the suitcase that was in the old lady's apartment. That's really why you went there, right?"

"No, man, you crazy."

Frank waved the paddles in Adolfo's face. "You don't want me to yell 'clear' do you?"

"I don't know nothin' 'bout no suitcase, man. What I need with a suitcase for? Ya think I go to Riviera or somethin'? I ain't gone nowhere."

Got that right.

"Fuck." Frank pitched the paddles onto the cart and turned off the defibrillator. "You're right, Will."

Will shook his head. "It wasn't about the suitcase, after all." Will said. "If that don't beat all."

Frank scoffed. "I still think David Hunt is up to no good."

Chapter 37

Windshield wipers clacked a steady rhythm as Frank drove through blinding rain to the apartment of Doctor Roger Steinberg a.k.a. Theodore Jessup. There had to be something Frank missed. Adolfo Cruz had not killed Steinberg. Was he back to David Hunt? Or someone else entirely? Someone from Steinberg's past.

When he arrived, he parked in front of the building and rushed through the rain to the front door. A doorman let him in.

"Nice day for ducks," the doorman said.

Frank stared at him, wondering if it was a clichéd line for all doormen. Maybe Henry Grady used it on Liam McCarty a hundred years ago. He held out his badge. "I'll be upstairs a while."

"Do you need me to let you in?"

"Got a key, thanks."

Frank pressed four in the elevator and wiped raindrops off his shoulders. The door pinged and he stepped out, turned right and unlocked apartment 4C. Then he lifted the yellow crime scene tape and walked inside for the second time.

The apartment was warm and sticky. The air conditioning had been turned off. A musty smell of emptiness and disuse wafted over him. Dust particles danced in the rays of light beaming in between the blind slats.

He stood a moment in the dim light, hoping for inspiration but the only thing that came to him was frustration. He flicked on the lights.

Steinberg had rented the apartment eight years ago, around the time he began working for David Hunt. His taste in furnishings ran from art deco to cubist modern. Black and white with a few shades of gray. Stainless steel coffee table with glass top. Black leather couches and chairs, white plush carpeting, black ice walls. Not Frank's taste at all.

He browsed the art. Angles, cubes, stark and cold. Looked like a display at MoMA. Probably not authentic. But how would he know? Exhaling a deep breath, he headed to the bedroom where a bit of red was added to the black and white color scheme. In addition to some bloodstains on the bed, there were burgundy drapes and a rose-colored lampshade.

Frank checked the bed clothes then looked underneath. He opened the closet and pulled out shoe boxes and hat boxes. He knew they'd already been searched, but still he dumped them on the bed and shook out the contents. Shoes, hats, what did he expect? Something.

He rifled through the clothes on hangers in the closet and searched through suit and shirt pockets. Checked the closet for a secret panel. Was he kidding? Had he watched too many movies? He stood, looked around. What was wrong with this picture? Pictures, that's it. There were none. Where were Steinberg's photos? Sure, he was hiding his past as Jessup, but he had eight years as Steinberg with no relationships to show for it. No parents, no kids, no wives, girlfriends, guy friends, dogs, birds? No travel photos? Wouldn't someone notice?

Frank went to a small cherry desk opposite the bed and pulled open drawers. A few scraps of paper, a television guide, a remote for the big screen. Not even a Christmas card. He paced around the bedroom, checked the headboard and nightstand. He made his way back to the closet, this time with a small stepstool that leaned up against the wall.

He switched on the closet light, stepped up on the stool and looked up. He began tapping on the walls in the closet. Nothing. Besides, the lab guys already looked. He stepped down. A thought struck him. What about the ceiling. He'd really have to look and feel around for a seam. Shit, he wished he had a flashlight. He stepped down and hustled into the kitchen, jerked open drawers until he found a torch.

He set up the stool again and checked the closet ceiling. He searched with the flashlight and felt around with his fingers. Damn, nothing.

As he made to step off the stool, his foot caught on a pair of slacks hanging on the clothes rod. He couldn't pull it free and felt himself falling into the hanging clothes. The rod came loose and the clothes tumbled to the floor. But Frank fell inward to the back wall.

The wall gave way into a second hidden closet.

"Holy shit." He kicked the stool and clothes aside and pushed through into the space. Empty shelves lined an inner wall. Frank beamed the flashlight around and spied an access panel above the top shelf. He pushed on it, and it slid open. He shined the light around inside. At the far end of the opening sat a lonely shoebox.

Frank felt electric energy buzz through him. This has got to be important. He pulled the box out and carried it to the bed. Inside was Steinberg's life. Photos and letters that told a story of a man incognito, in hiding from his real self. Frank sat down and began going through the photos.

He traced the man back to his younger days, maybe forty years ago. But Frank wanted to know why someone would kill him today. He flipped through the photos until one grabbed him. It was a color snap, maybe twenty-five years old. The photo depicted Steinberg with a woman. Clearly they were romantically involved, from the way his arm was around her and they were smiling. Her hair was long, dark auburn and...*shit, shit*. It was Madelyn. A younger, prettier Madelyn Hunt.

What the hell did it mean? She knew him as Jessup, years ago. Before she was married...or not? And had David known about him?

Frank flipped over to the back. St. Paul, MN, 1980. Madelyn would be what? In her thirties? He grabbed his cell, speed-dialed Will. "When did David and Madelyn Hunt get married?" He waited.

"1988," Will told him.

Holy crap. She and Jessup knew each other for at least eight years before she married David Hunt. Did David know about him and Madelyn? Frank was dizzy with possibilities.

He set the photos down, picked up a stack of yellowed and torn letters. After ten minutes, he knew he'd struck gold. Love letters from Madelyn to Jessup, and ones in return. Madelyn knew Steinberg was Jessup. Why didn't she tell the police after he was murdered? *She's obviously hiding something.* What about David? Did he have any knowledge of their tryst?

Frank felt a moment of sorrow for David. Were you a cuckold, David? Or were you part of a more sinister plot to scam the insurance world with Madelyn and Jessup?

Frank didn't know the answers yet. But he would damn well find out.

※

Madelyn Hunt didn't answer the door when he and Will rang the bell, so they went around to the back of the brownstone and tried the kitchen door. No response. Frank leaned over to look through a window and saw Madelyn on her hands and knees, scrubbing the floor. They'd caught her at her obsessive pastime, cleaning.

He turned to Will. "She's going to be freaked. Let me do the talking."

Will nodded.

Frank pounded on the door. "Missus Hunt, open up, please."

"I'm busy."

"So are we, Missus Hunt," Frank said. "I need to talk to you. Please open the door." He waited, wondering what they would do if she didn't open the door.

She did.

His jaw dropped at the sight of her. The well-put together woman he had met on several occasions looked like an old washer-woman. Her hair was tied back with a yellow bandana, her eyes had deep indigo rims under them, and her face, damp with exertion, was pasty-white. She held a scrub brush in one hand and wiped her forehead with the other rubber-gloved hand.

"What is it? I have to finish the floor."

Frank stepped inside, not waiting for an invitation. Will followed. "It won't take long. Shall we sit down?"

She harrumphed and spun about, pulling out chairs near the kitchen table. Madelyn fell into one of them and snapped the rubber gloves off her hands. Frank sat across from her, Will next to him.

He reached into his pocket and pulled out the photograph of Madelyn and Jessup. "Look familiar?"

She sprang to her feet. "Wh-where did you get that?"

"You recognize it, then?"

"He was supposed to get rid of all our pictures."

"Sit and let's talk about it." Frank waited.

She collapsed into the chair and slumped down, elbows on the table, hands on her forehead.

"This proves you knew Roger Steinberg as Theodore Jessup. Funny how you failed to tell us that little fact."

She chewed her lower lip.

"Come on, Madelyn. Jessup is dead. It's time to own up to the truth."

Will took out his notepad and pen as surreptitiously as possible so as not to distract her.

She glared at Frank as if he were the bad guy. "Isn't it obvious? I had a relationship with Teddy, but it was years ago, years before I met David. That's it. It was over long ago."

"Did David know?"

"No."

"You expect me to believe that when David hired Steinberg to run Aurora facilities, you never mentioned you knew him as Jessup?"

"I didn't know he had hired him. The name Steinberg meant nothing to me."

"When did you find out?"

"At a fund-raiser party. David introduced us."

Frank looked at her. "At that point, you knew Jessup was pretending to be someone he wasn't. Why didn't you tell David then?"

She turned away, gazing down at the unfinished floor. "I'd like my lawyer present."

"You have every right, Madelyn, to have a lawyer. But if you have nothing to hide, why don't you just tell us now, and save us all a lot of trouble?"

She chewed a thumbnail.

"Madelyn?" Frank softened his voice. "Off the record."

"All right. Teddy and I had an affair, but it ended before I met David. I didn't even know who Steinberg was until I met him at that party."

"You must have been surprised."

"I was. Yes, I was."

"You hadn't seen him or been in touch in how long?"

"Oh, years. Yes, years."

"So, when you realized Jessup had taken on a new name, you didn't want to know why?"

She sniffed. "I knew why. I thought I did, anyway. He was a con-artist in those days. I just assumed he had to change his name, take on a new identity to start a new life."

"Why didn't you tell David once you knew it was him?"

Madelyn stood up. "I have nothing more to say. Please leave."

"How about if I tell you my theory?"

"I don't want to hear your God damned theory. Get out."

Will stood to leave but Frank plowed on. "I think Jessup came back into your life and a new affair sparked. You two picked up where you left off years ago."

Madelyn turned her back to him.

"If David found out, he'd divorce you, cut you off from your comfortable income stream."

She glowered at him. "I worked hard for this comfort."

"Worse, he might expose Jessup for who he was." He paused to interpret the expression on Madelyn's face. Terrified. "You didn't want him to go to jail, did you?"

"Get out."

"That's why you couldn't tell David. You wanted to protect Jessup because you still loved him."

Tears ran down her cheeks. "Please don't tell David."

"We're leaving now." Frank stood and looked down at her. "Madelyn. This is not going to go away. The truth will emerge, one way or another, and you will pay a stiff price for keeping it from him."

Frank signaled Will and the two left.

On the way to the car, Frank said, "You know, I actually feel sorry for her. Jessup might have been the only man to show her love."

That night, Frank met Rachel at McSorley's Old Ale House for a late-night drink. Seeing her was like a gentle warm breeze in the middle of a blizzard. In this crazy case, he couldn't see the truth for the lies, and Rachel often brought a new perspective. Plus, she was good on the eyes, intelligent, and well, damn sexy.

They talked for an hour during which he told her about his conversation with Madelyn.

"Are you going to tell David? she asked him.

"Not my place. She didn't break any laws by having an affair and risking a divorce."

"Maybe there's another reason she didn't tell him. Maybe it wasn't about divorce."

"Oh?" he said.

"Maybe she was afraid of him."

Chapter 38

Frank, Will, Lizzie and Amanda sat around the table in his mom's kitchen, chomping down two large pizzas.

"I have to tell you I was flabbergasted that Ruby's suitcase wasn't behind Sophie's murder," Lizzie said. "I still don't really believe it. I mean, are you sure this creep, Cortez—?"

"Cruz," Frank said after swallowing a string of mozzarella.

"Whatever, Cruz. You're sure he wasn't paid to burgle the place to get the suitcase?"

"Nah," Will said. "He was clueless about the suitcase. I don't think he could've faked that dumb-ass look."

"Anyone with half a brain would never hire a guy like that to get a job done," Frank added.

"Ha," Amanda said. "It's kind of disappointing to think Sophie was murdered for…for nothing, really."

Frank looked at his mother. "You know, Ma, if Sophie didn't have a gun she would still be alive."

"So now you blame the victim? What? You think this Cruz wouldn't have brought his own gun, or used a knife, even?"

"He had neither, Ma."

"What about this Doctor Steinberg or Jessup?" Amanda changed the subject. "Who do you think killed him? Surely not another intruder?"

"No, this was more personal," Frank said.

"Did he own a gun?" Amanda asked. "Steinberg?"

Will jumped in. "Not that was registered, either to a Roger Steinberg or a Theodore Jessup."

"What kind of gun killed him?" Lizzie asked.

"9mm Glock."

Lizzie stared down at her uneaten slice.

"You feel okay, Ma?"

"Fine."

Everyone fell silent.

Lizzie held her breath as if she was about to make a pronouncement. Then: "Maddie, uh, Madelyn Hunt, she has a Glock."

Frank felt his heartbeat spike. "Let me guess." His voice was low. "She got it from Vito?"

"See, you are a good detective." Lizzie smirked.

"There's more, right?"

"Remember I told you Sophie and I took classes at the shooting range?"

"I remember."

Will and Amanda stopped eating.

"Maddie took them with us. The classes."

Will asked, "Any reason she didn't get a .22 like you and Sophie?"

Lizzie cleared her throat. "Maddie said, and I quote: 'If I have to stop someone to protect myself, I want him stopped dead.'"

Frank dropped his head in his hands. "Ma..."

"Mama Mia," Amanda said. "You think it was Madelyn who killed Jessup?"

Frank scoffed. "She was in love with him."

"Maybe David found out, got hold of her gun, you think?" Lizzie shook her head. "I'm sorry, Frank, that I didn't tell you sooner. It just didn't seem important."

Amanda put her hand on Frank's arm to keep him from blowing up.

Will stepped in. "We need to find that gun."

"I think she got rid of it," Amanda said.

"Maybe," Will said, "but she's been feeling pretty confident until today, at least until we confronted her on her affair with Jessup."

Frank lifted his head. "Maybe it's not too late."

"Yeah, she still may have it," Will said.

Amanda frowned. "But she would have ditched it after you were there, wouldn't she?"

"If she wanted to get rid of it," Will put in, "she'd probably wait until after dark."

They all turned to the window. Dusk was setting in.

Frank and Will jumped up and sprinted for the door.

"Wait," Lizzie said. "I'm going with you."

"No way, Ma. You stay here."

"I can handle her. If she tries something foolish, I can talk to her, keep her from doing something crazy."

"Something crazy? We're talking about ditching a gun."

"I'm talking about her killing herself," Lizzie said.

☙❧

Frank would not let Lizzie or Amanda accompany them but swore to keep them apprised of events. He and Will drove to the 56th Street brownstone under a full moon that lit their way.

"You know, of course, we'll get there and nothing will have happened. We'll just wake them up and they'll be pissed, threaten to sue the department and—"

"Yeah, yeah, I know." Frank gripped the wheel. "Still, something in what Lizzie said makes me wonder. Madelyn's desperate. She may do something stupid."

"She's also rich and entitled. She may simply call her lawyer and clam up."

"Right. We don't have enough evidence to prove a damn thing," Frank said. "Still, Madelyn strikes me as weak. She'll be scared now. After all, she doesn't know what we have."

Frank turned onto 56th Street and screeched to a stop. Lights were flashing at the end of the block. Two NYPD cars and an ambulance were parked in front of the Hunt's brownstone.

"Shit," Frank said.

He and Will hopped out and ran down the street.

Frank flashed his badge to a patrol officer standing guard.

"Glad you're here, Lieutenant. Just called it in. Woman inside, dead from a bullet wound to the head. Neighbor called 9-11." He tipped his head to a woman in a robe near the police car. "She heard screaming, an argument maybe, then a gunshot. When we got here, we found the vic, no gun, and no one else in the house."

"No gun rules out suicide," Frank said.

The officer agreed. "Killer must've taken it with him."

Frank turned and hurried up the front steps, Will at his heels.

In the living room, lights blazed.

"Jesus," Will said. "Is every light in the house on?" He turned to another officer. "Did you turn the lights on?"

"Everything is exactly how we found it."

Frank walked over to the body on the floor in front of the cold fireplace. *Madelyn.* "God damn it."

"David," Will said.

"We need to find him," Frank said.

Will got on the phone to put out an APB on David Hunt then: "Why the hell didn't he leave the gun, at least to try to make it look like suicide?"

Frank looked startled. "It is suicide."

Will turned back to survey the scene.

"Blood everywhere except on her hand, gunshot residue plainly visible there instead."

Will leaned over Madelyn to examine her hand. "Damn."

"Come on." Frank raced down the steps and out to the street. The crime scene lab was pulling up. Serena Oliver had already parked the Medical Examiner vehicle and was walking toward them.

"Another Hunt?" she said.

Frank nodded. "Do your thing, I'm off to find the husband before there's one more death."

She raised an eyebrow, but he was running to his car.

Frank backed his car up the street, turned on the sirens and raced down one block then another until he weaved his way to the East River.

"You think he's going to ditch the gun?" Will said.

"I'm afraid he's going to do more than that."

"What? Kill himself?"

"Keep your eyes open."

"Lucky there's a full moon. Where would he go?"

"I'm thinking Bobby Wagner Walk, you know the walkway along the river?"

"Yeah, yeah. An easy place to jump off," Will said. "Pretty low railing."

"And David Hunt strikes me as a man who takes the easy route whenever he can."

Frank drove to 67th Street. That's where he saw him. A lone figure walking along the promenade. He pulled over and got out. "Let me talk to him. Stand by."

Frank ran until he was within twenty yards before David Hunt saw him. They faced each other.

"David?"

"It's too late."

"No, it's not. There's still time to end this."

"No. They're dead, you know. Steinberg and Maddie."

"Yes, I know. You killed them."

"No and yes. In a way, I did kill Maddie." David leaned heavily on the rail. He pulled his hand out of his pocket and dangled a gun.

The Glock, Frank saw. "What do you mean no and yes?"

"It's my fault that Maddie is dead. I wasn't a good husband, never had time, never gave her the attention she needed."

"But Steinberg did." Frank said.

"What a joke. Jessup, that was his real name, right? Lying bastard. They were having an affair. You knew all that, didn't you? Did she tell you?"

"Put the gun down, David. It won't fix anything." Frank stepped closer.

David waved the gun. "Stay back."

Frank stopped. "What happened, David? When you found out?"

"What the hell do you think? I confronted her." He dropped his head. "I wanted to know, you see, if she had any feelings for me at all. And guess what?"

"What?"

"She told me Steinberg was cheating on her. Ha. Imagine that? He was cheating on her. She loved the son-of-a-bitch." David half-cried and laughed as his words cut into the quiet night.

"So, you killed him?"

"No. Madelyn killed him. Ain't that one for the books? She killed her lover."

"And you killed Madelyn?"

David laughed. "No."

Frank's face morphed into disbelief. "What are you saying?"

"I'm saying Maddie killed herself." He was crying now.

"Why did you take the gun?"

"I didn't want anyone to know. Didn't want a major scandal. Bad enough she cheated on me and Steinberg blackmailed me."

"How would your covering her suicide prevent a scandal?"

"Just another intruder-slash-killing in the big city."

"Ahh," Frank said.

"Ironic that she loved him so much she didn't want to live without him. He clearly didn't give a damn about her. All his other women." He turned to Frank. "What about me? Didn't she love me at all?"

"You really loved her, David, didn't you?"

"I did." David wiped his eyes with his sleeve. "But it meant nothing. Nothing."

"Madelyn shot herself and you took the gun?"

"I was going to throw it in the river."

"And what about you?"

"My life is worth shit now."

"David."

"This is all your fault." He pointed the gun at Frank. "If you hadn't been asking all those questions about Ruby Hunt, none of this would've happened. No one would know about my crazy fucking family and their dirty dealings." David sobbed and Frank thought he would sink to the ground.

Instead, before Frank could react, David climbed the railing. Frank rushed him, grabbed him by the arm and they both fell to the ground. The gun bounced out of his hand. Will raced in and helped Frank subdue the man, who was now screaming and crying and flailing at them. It took several minutes to cuff him, and he finally collapsed into a heap on the walkway.

Will had called for backup and a police car and ambulance came screaming down the street. They escorted David to the ambulance.

Frank picked up the gun with a pen he had in his pocket and dropped it into a bag that an officer held out. "Take very good care of that. It's the key to this case."

The officer nodded. "Yes, sir."

Frank pulled out his cell and called Serena. "What's your best take on Madelyn Hunt? Suicide or murder?"

"I'd say suicide, but it would be nice to have the gun for confirmation."

"We've got the gun." Frank clicked off.

Will spun on his heels, went back to the officer and took the evidence bag with the gun away from him. "Change of plans. We'll take care of this."

Frank nodded. "I'll give it to Serena myself."

Chapter 39

Frank felt Rachel's eyes on him as he licked his double-fudge-vanilla-swirl ice cream cone. Instead of returning her gaze he focused on the snow monkey in the enclosure in front of him.

"The zoo has come a long way since monkeys were in cages," he said.

"He's beautiful, isn't he?" Rachel crunched on her sugar cone. "Snow monkeys. Kind of like chimps, but with red faces."

"Their eyes are so human. Kind of freaks me out."

"Yeah, like he knows what you're thinking."

"I wonder if Ruby ever came here." Frank turned to Rachel. "You know, maybe she stood right here looking at the primates."

"She lived across the street. I would guess she did."

"She wouldn't see this great habitat, though, with the rocks and waterfall."

"No, they would have been locked in tiny cages."

They fell silent, thinking of Ruby's plight in a lunatic asylum.

"From everything you've told me and the letters, photos, I'd bet anything that Liam was a little bit in love with Ruby."

"I believe that, too," Frank said. "Seems to me he already had his mind made up she was innocent the minute he saw her in that painting."

"Let's walk to the pond." She linked her arm in his.

A few minutes later they sat on a bench by a pond filled with geese, ducks, and swans. Central Park was filling with pedestrians now, both tourists and locals. The day, warm, sunny, and dry, beckoned everyone who had a few moments to spare for nature and beauty.

"What happens now to David Hunt?" Rachel asked.

"Nothing. We're not pressing charges for obstructing an investigation or anything. Guy's been punished enough, I think."

"You're a softie, aren't you?"

"Hmph."

"Sad, really. What people do to each other," Rachel said. "This guy Steinberg, was one nasty piece of work."

"Yup. I'm sorry about Madelyn."

"The M-E is sure it's suicide?"

"Yup. Gunshot residue on her hand, angle of the shot, blood spatter... all conclusive."

"I can't imagine shooting myself over a man. Over anyone, for that matter."

He looked at her with a small smile. "No? Never loved anyone that much?"

"To death, you mean? Maybe a dog I had once as a kid. When Ginger died, I was beside myself with grief. So, maybe, yeah." She looked at him. "What about you?"

"My wife committed suicide fifteen years ago."

Rachel's mouth fell open.

"She was having an affair, this guy was cheating on her...same kind of ending as Madelyn, really and, well, doesn't matter in the end. I felt guilt, sorrow, devastated for Amanda. I missed her for a long time. Blamed myself, you know. Why wasn't I enough? But in the end, I accepted it."

"Wow." Rachel shook her head. "My comment for everything these days. Wow."

He took her hand and stood up. "Enough of this morbid talk. Let's go."

"Where?"

"I have someone I want you to meet."

"Oh?"

"He's my best friend, roommate, actually."

"I didn't know you had a roommate."

"He takes up very little space, is a bit messy, quite noisy, but always a gentleman."

She stopped walking. "Who is this?"

He took her arm in his and they meandered up the stone path. "His name is Dexter."

Afterword

This is a work of fiction. Most of the characters exist only in my imagination but a few: Nellie Bly, Joseph Pulitzer, exist in history. A number of places are also authentic for the historic time period: Schrafft's Restaurant, McSorley's Old Ale House and, of course, Hart Island.

New York City in 1902 was a tumultuous and thriving city. The underground subway would open in October of 1904. Electricity was still new and rare. Both of these innovations would soon change the city forever.

Hart Island was a little-known slice of land off the coast of the Bronx, reachable only by boat. In 1869, the city fathers began purchasing parcels of land on the Island to be set aside as a burial ground. Space within the city itself was becoming increasingly limited.

By the end of the first year, close to 2,000 burials had taken place there. Initially indigent and unnamed adults and children were buried in mass-grave trenches, in some cases three coffins high and two across. Each plot or trench was marked by a single white post. The trenches contain upward of 1,000 bodies each.

In addition to the potter's field, Hart Island became home to a number of facilities: A Civil War prison camp, a tuberculosis sanatorium, a boys' reformatory, and a women's lunatic asylum. Women were brought from Blackwell's Island Asylum when it shut down--thanks to a feisty investigative journalist, Nellie Bly, who documented her stay there in the book *Ten Days in a Madhouse*.

Today, no one lives on Hart Island and the buildings are in a sad state of deterioration. Inmates of Rikers Island continue to bury paupers in the potter's field and there is said to be about one million lost souls now interred there. For a fascinating, interactive view of the island, check out this link: https://www.nytimes.com/interactive/2016/05/15/nyregion/new-york-mass-graves-hart-island.html?_r=0

The Department of Corrections gained control of the land in 1968, and it has been closed to the public ever since.

That's all changing, though, thanks to artist Melinda Hunt, who created the Hart Island Project, an interactive online memorial that provides access to information about the burials on Hart Island and tools for storytelling so that no one is omitted from history. Now, persons who believe they have a loved one buried on Hart Island, can apply for permission to visit.

Sadly, as this book goes to press, articles have emerged about human bones washing up on Orchard Beach and City Island due to the lack of upkeep on Hart Island, particularly after Hurricane Sandy hit in 2012, exposing bodies and damaging the sea wall.

The idea of a potter's field of this magnitude located in the largest city in this country, and where, in past centuries, was also housed a women's lunatic asylum. . . Well, I couldn't have dreamed for a more sinister place to set a mystery.

About the Author

With a Masters' Degree in Science and more than 28 years as a science museum director, Lynne Kennedy has had the opportunity to study history and forensic science, both of which play significant roles in her novels. She has written award-winning historical mysteries, each solved by modern technology.

Time Exposure: Civil War photography meets digital photography to solve a series of murders in two centuries. It was awarded the B.R.A.G. Medallion Honoree Award for independent books of high standards.

The Triangle Murders was the winner of the Rocky Mountain Fiction Writers Mystery Category, 2011, and was awarded the B.R.A.G. Medallion Honoree Award.

Deadly Provenance was also awarded a B.R.A.G. Medallion and was a finalist for the San Diego Book Awards. With the release of Deadly Provenance, Lynne has launched a "hunt for a missing Van Gogh," the painting which features prominently in the book. "Still Life: Vase with Oleanders" has, in actuality, been missing since WWII.

Her fourth book, Pure Lies, won the 2014 "Best Published Mystery, Sisters in Crime" award by the San Diego Book Awards, and was a finalist in Amazon's Breakthrough Novel Award.

Time Lapse, her fifth mystery, premiered at the end of 2016 to all 5-star reviews.

She blogs regularly and has many loyal readers and fans. Visit her website at lynnekennedymysteries.com.

Made in the USA
Middletown, DE
10 July 2021